Morning's Refrain

SONG OF ALASKA — *Two*

Morning's Refrain

TRACIE PETERSON

BETHANY HOUSE PUBLISHERS
Minneapolis, Minnesota

Morning's Refrain
Copyright © 2010
Tracie Peterson

Cover design by Jennifer Parker
Cover photography by Mike Habermann Photography, LLC

Scripture quotations are from the King James Version of the Bible.

Published by Bethany House Publishers
11400 Hampshire Avenue South
Bloomington, Minnesota 55438

Bethany House Publishers is a division of
Baker Publishing Group, Grand Rapids, Michigan.

Printed in the United States of America

Library of Congress Cataloging-in-Publication Data

Peterson, Tracie.
    Morning's refrain / Tracie Peterson.
        p.   cm. — (Song of Alaska ; 2)
    ISBN 978-0-7642-0745-7 (hardcover : alk. paper) — ISBN 978-0-7642-0152-3 (pbk.) — ISBN 978-0-7642-0744-0 (large-print pbk.)
    1. Widows—Fiction. 2. Family secrets—Fiction. 3. Alaska—Fiction. 4. Triangles (Interpersonal relations)—Fiction. I. Title.
    PS3566.E7717M67   20010
    813'.54—dc22
                                                                    2009040891

To

Steve, Debra, Noelle, and Carra

Thanks for all you do to help this ministry.
You are each so special to me,
and I'm blessed by your gifts and your love of God.

Books by Tracie Peterson

www.traciepeterson.com

A Slender Thread • *What She Left For Me* • *Where My Heart Belongs*

SONG OF ALASKA
Dawn's Prelude • *Morning's Refrain*

ALASKAN QUEST
Summer of the Midnight Sun
Under the Northern Lights • *Whispers of Winter*
Alaskan Quest (3 in 1)

BRIDES OF GALLATIN COUNTY
A Promise to Believe In • *A Love to Last Forever*
A Dream to Call My Own

THE BROADMOOR LEGACY*
A Daughter's Inheritance • *An Unexpected Love*
A Surrendered Heart

BELLS OF LOWELL*
Daughter of the Loom • *A Fragile Design* • *These Tangled Threads*
Bells of Lowell (3 in 1)

LIGHTS OF LOWELL*
A Tapestry of Hope • *A Love Woven True* • *The Pattern of Her Heart*

DESERT ROSES
Shadows of the Canyon • *Across the Years* • *Beneath a Harvest Sky*

HEIRS OF MONTANA
Land of My Heart • *The Coming Storm*
To Dream Anew • *The Hope Within*

LADIES OF LIBERTY
A Lady of High Regard • *A Lady of Hidden Intent*
A Lady of Secret Devotion

RIBBONS OF STEEL**
Distant Dreams • *A Hope Beyond* • *A Promise for Tomorrow*

WESTWARD CHRONICLES
A Shelter of Hope • *Hidden in a Whisper* • *A Veiled Reflection*

YUKON QUEST
Treasures of the North • *Ashes and Ice* • *Rivers of Gold*

*with Judith Miller   **with Judith Pella

TRACIE PETERSON is the author of over eighty novels, both historical and contemporary. Her avid research resonates in her stories, as seen in her bestselling HEIRS OF MONTANA and ALASKAN QUEST series. Tracie and her family make their home in Montana.

Visit Tracie's Web site at *www.traciepeterson.com*.
Visit Tracie's blog at *www.writespasssage.blogspot.com*.

Chapter 1

June 1889

*I*f a person needed to know what was happening in Sitka, the general store was the center of all news—whether true or gossip. Even so, this time Dalton Lindquist didn't anticipate his family being a part of the tale spewing from Mrs. Putshukoff's mouth.

And yet, to be honest, all of his life there had been a measure of secrecy about his past, mainly because no one was willing to talk about it. Some sort of trouble surrounded his birth or shortly thereafter—that much Dalton knew. His questions made his mother uncomfortable, and his father would admonish him to wait until he was older. Father had once admitted that someone had attempted to take Dalton and his mother had been wounded in the process, but he wouldn't say anything more. It was Mother's story to tell.

"Then it's time she told me," he muttered, stalking down the street. "I deserve to know the truth."

It was a good two-mile walk back home, but Dalton didn't mind. He used the time to clear his head and reconsider what he'd heard Mrs. Putshukoff say to Arnie, the storekeeper. She had come into the store all excited. Apparently there had been some untimely deaths in the Tlingit village; a fight of some sort had seen two men killed and a woman gravely injured. Mrs. Putshukoff declared there hadn't been so much trouble since the mess that year Lydia Gray had come to live on the island.

Dalton had been standing near the back of the store, looking over a supply of paint, when the conversation had begun. He'd tried to edge closer without looking obvious, but Arnie knew he was there and hurried to hush Mrs. Putshukoff. In a town where gossip ruled, Dalton found people particularly closemouthed about his past. Perhaps it was out of respect to his mother. She was quite beloved and a pillar of the community. Maybe folks felt they owed her their silence. Then again, so many of the folks who'd lived in Sitka the year Dalton had been born were long gone.

The sun remained positioned high in the sky even though it was half past five. Summer days were long in Sitka, and there would still be a good four or five more hours of light. Today was even better, because they were blessed with no rain. The clear skies would give everyone a reason to celebrate with outdoor activities well into the evening.

Dalton's father always said this was his favorite time of the year, and Dalton felt much the same. It really was a pity that such a perfect day had to be ruined by the weight of the secrets concealed from him. The long walk home had done nothing to calm his spirit; if anything, Dalton felt his need for answers only heightened. He longed to know about his birth—about his real father. All he knew for certain was this: His mother had been a widow when she'd come to Sitka, and she had come because her aunt lived on the island. Zerelda Rockford had established herself in this isolated place years before Dalton's mother arrived, and she welcomed her pregnant niece with open arms. Kjell Lindquist fell in love with Lydia, and they married shortly before Dalton's birth.

The next year, his older half sister Evie had joined them from Kansas City. When as a child he asked about Evie's husband and why she lived in Alaska instead of wherever her husband resided, Dalton was quickly dismissed with the assurance that it was not necessary for him to know and painful for Evie to discuss. It wasn't until just a few years ago that he'd learned Evie had left her husband because he held her no love and truly hadn't wanted a wife. Still, there were secrets about her life in Kansas City that she refused to speak about, and Dalton was again left on the outside looking in.

"Dalton!" His ten-year-old sister, Kjerstin, came bounding down the hill toward the road. "Look what I made." She held up a piece of cloth. "It's a napkin, and I've put a Z on it. I made it for Aunt Zerelda. Mama says I should put an *R* on it, too, so that comes next."

Pushing aside his thoughts, Dalton inspected the material. "It's quite good. You've really mastered embroidery."

"Mama says I'm a natural." She took back the napkin and fairly danced around Dalton. Her brown pigtails swung in the air. "Britta isn't a natural. She always gets knots in her thread."

"Britta's only seven. Give her some time," Dalton countered. "And don't be so prideful. When someone says you're good at something, you're supposed to say thank you."

Kjerstin stopped and looked up at him most woefully. "I'm sorry. Thank you."

Dalton laughed. "You needn't mourn the matter." He rubbed the top of her head. After so many years of being an only child, Dalton had been thrilled when his mother announced she was going to have a baby. He had wanted a brother, but Kjerstin had proved to be an interesting alternative.

"Where's Mother?"

"She's in the garden. You want me to get her for you?"

Dalton shook his head. "No, I'll find her. You go back to your sewing."

"I can come with you."

"No. I want to talk to her alone."

Kjerstin put her hands on her hips. "Why can't I come along?"

He didn't want to alarm her, but neither would he lie. "I just have some private questions to ask her. Nothing that needs to concern your pretty head."

"Are you going to ask her about kissing a girl?"

Dalton looked at his sister oddly. "What in the world gave you that idea?"

"Well, I heard Papa and Mama talking about how it wouldn't be long before you noticed girls and found one to marry."

Laughing, Dalton whirled her in a circle, then set her back down on the ground. "I've already noticed girls," he told her conspiratorially, "and I think I can figure out the kissing part by myself." He swatted her backside playfully. "Now go on."

She giggled and hurried up the porch stairs. "If you get married," she called back to him, "I want to be in the wedding and wear a beautiful dress."

"I'll do what I can to accommodate you, but first I need to find a bride."

Walking around the side of the house and toward the back, where his mother was bent over a row of plants, Dalton couldn't help but wonder what had prompted his mother and father's discussion about him getting married. Since finishing his education, Dalton's only focus had been on boat building—something he'd worked at since turning thirteen. He was apprenticing with Mr.

Belikov, the father of his best friend, Yuri. Building boats was all he wanted to do for the rest of his life. He loved the work, as well as the finished product. In fact, there wasn't a part of the process that he didn't love.

His mother straightened and caught sight of him. Dalton put aside his sister's prattle and thoughts of boats. Remembering why he'd wanted to seek her out in the first place, Dalton frowned.

"You look like a man with a purpose," his mother declared.

"I am," he said in a serious tone. "Can we sit and talk?"

Lydia Lindquist's face paled just a bit as she squared her shoulders. "Is something wrong?"

"Nothing that a few answers won't help." He led her to an arrangement of wooden chairs his father had made for enjoying the outdoors. "I need to know the truth about my father—about my birth. I'm eighteen. I think I'm old enough to know what everyone else does."

His mother took a seat and nodded. "I suppose I owe you that much."

He wanted to snap back a reply that she owed him that and so much more. Instead, Dalton pulled one of the chairs very close and sat directly in front of her. "I know the past was bad. I can figure that out without you saying anything about it. So if you're worried about hurting me, stop."

She gave him a weak smile. "I'm ashamed to say my silence has been more about my own discomfort than yours. It's painful to remember. I always hoped it wouldn't have to come up."

"I don't want to see you in pain, Mother, but other people always seem to know more about my past than I do. Today, I overheard a comment down at the general store about the trouble that happened when you came to live here—the year I was born. I want to know what it was all about, and I don't want to learn it from strangers."

His mother drew a deep breath. "Well, it actually happened

two months after you were born. I'll try to explain it, but you may be sorry you asked. Where do you want me to start?"

"Who was my father?" Dalton asked rather than reply to her comment.

"Floyd Gray. I was very young when I was wed to him in an arranged marriage. He had been married before and his wife had recently died," she began. "He and my father made a business contract that included me."

"So you were forced to marry him?"

"Yes," she answered. "I'm sorry to say that I never loved him. He was a cruel man, and he never showed me the least amount of affection."

"But what of me—the fact that you were expecting me when he died?"

"You will find this difficult to understand. . . ." She turned her gaze to her lap. "I'm sorry, but you were not conceived in love. You weren't my only pregnancy, but you were the only one that I carried to birth. The others I lost when your father became angry and took it out on me."

Indignant at the thought that any man would hurt his mother, Dalton stiffened. "How did he die?"

"In a carriage accident with my father. My father outlived him by two days, and this in turn started a series of problems that involved the money they'd made and Floyd's other children."

"You mean Evie?"

His mother looked up. He could recognize fear in her brown eyes. "No. I mean the others. Your brothers and another sister."

"What?" He shook his head. "I have brothers? Another sister? What are you talking about?"

"It's a very long story. Floyd and his first wife had twin sons who are considerably older than you, as well as another daughter besides Eve. They all lived in Kansas City, and they all hated me, except Eve. When I married their father, they saw me as an intruder. Eve was just a little girl at the time. I suppose that's why she didn't share their hatred. They were cruel to her, however, anytime she showed me the slightest affection."

"I can't believe this. Why didn't you ever tell me?" His anger rose. "Did it not occur to you that I might want to know my other siblings?"

"That's exactly why I didn't tell you," she admitted. "I hoped you would never need to know them. Dalton, they are not good people."

"Shouldn't that have been my choice to decide? You had no right to keep that information from me." He felt a huge sense of betrayal. "What else have you kept from me?" He thought back to the conversation at the store. "What happened the year I was born? Who was killed?"

Her expression tightened. "What have you already heard?"

"Not enough to understand," he replied. "I want to know the truth."

To his surprise, tears formed in her eyes. "I always intended to tell you the truth, but . . ." She choked up and buried her face in her hands.

Dalton felt bad for having upset her, but now, more than ever, he wanted to know the reason for her tears. "Please, Mother, you must tell me."

He could see that his mother was working hard to regain control of her emotions, and so he said nothing more for a moment. When she finally spoke, Dalton found her words alarming.

"You will have to give me time. It's hard for me even now. . . . So much happened the night they came to take you, and some of it I still can't remember."

"Who? Who came to take me? What are you talking about?"

Her gaze seemed to look right through him, as if she'd gone

15

back in time to that moment. "There were two of them. They were men who held your father a grudge."

"My real father?"

She shook her head. "No. Kjell. But they didn't take you for that reason. They were hired."

"Hired?"

"They came that night and Zerelda tried to fight them off. They hit her in the head and knocked her unconscious." His mother got to her feet, her state trancelike. "I had gone upstairs to tend to you, and I heard the commotion. Zerelda fired her gun. One of the men was saying something about finding the baby."

Dalton got to his feet and took hold of her shoulders. "Mother, are you all right?"

She looked at him but didn't seem to see him. "When he came for you, I didn't know what to do. Kjell was working late. There was no one else to help." She shuddered. "I tried to keep him from taking you."

"Who? Who was it, Mother?"

"Anatolli Sidorov." Her voice was barely audible. She drew a deep breath and seemed to refocus on Dalton. "It was Anatolli and his brother."

"Who are they? I've never heard of them before."

Tears began to stream down his mother's face. "They were the ones who took you. I tried to fight him. I tried to keep him from taking you, but he wouldn't listen. Instead he . . . he . . ."

"He what? Tell me. Please."

"Lydia!"

It was Evie. She was coming down the path toward them. "Kjell is looking for you. He needs your help in the house."

"Mother, please finish what you were saying."

She wiped her eyes with the edge of her apron. "He shot me."

The words were so matter-of-fact that for a moment they didn't register in Dalton's mind. "He what?"

"I can't," his mother said, shaking her head.

Evie had nearly reached them. Lydia turned to look at her. "You tell him. You tell him what happened after Anatolli shot me. You tell Dalton who was responsible for them coming to take him."

The woman's eyes widened in surprise. Dalton said nothing as his mother walked away. He felt torn between a desperate need for her to return and sorrow that he'd caused her such distress. It was clear that she was shaken to the very soul of her being.

He looked at Evie. "I want to know what this is all about. All I understand is that those who've lived in this town long enough know more about my life than I do. It isn't right, and I want answers."

"Even at the price you've cost her?"

"It's my right!" Dalton pounded his fist against the chair. "I'm tired of the lies and the secrets. I want answers."

"Stop throwing a fit and maybe I'll give them to you. You're a grown man now, Dalton. Act like one—instead of a demanding child."

"I've lived with this shadow over me all of my life, Evie. I have brothers and another sister I was never told about. Why did you never say anything?"

She shrugged. "Because your mother preferred for me to say nothing."

"But it doesn't make sense. So what if my real father—our father—was a difficult man? Why should she not tell me about him, about my family? Now Mother says someone came to take me from her—someone who shot her? What is that all about? What is going on?"

"Our brother Marston hired two men to steal you from Lydia. Our brothers are just as corrupt and evil as our father. Our sister Jeannette is just as selfish and heartless."

"Jeannette? The same one you get letters from? She is our sister?" Dalton asked.

Evie nodded. "Yes, we occasionally correspond, though we've never been close. Jeannette is not a very good sister to anyone, and I often forget about her altogether. But that aside, Marston is the one who caused most of the trouble."

"But I don't understand. Why would he want to take me from my mother?"

"Money," Evie said frankly. "Your mother had inherited our father's fortune. Our brothers and sister were livid. They wanted it returned. Your mother graciously gave them back a portion, but because you were also a Gray child, she felt you deserved to inherit, as well."

"I know nothing about an inheritance. This doesn't make sense."

Evie put her hand to her temple for a moment. To Dalton, it looked as if she was struggling to determine how much she could really say and how much needed to remain a secret. Finally she spoke in a soft, deliberate manner.

"Perhaps . . . in time it will. For now you have to understand that our brother was responsible for nearly killing your mother. He ordered it done—he planned for her to die so that he could lay claim as your next of kin. That way the money would come back to the family through you."

Dalton sat down hard. The wind was nearly knocked from his lungs. "What happened after the man shot Mother?"

Evie's tone softened as she sat down in the seat Lydia had occupied only moments earlier. "The men who attacked her that night took you to Marston. In turn, Marston killed Anatolli, but his brother, Ioann, got away. Marston took you to Kansas City, but everyone here thought you were dead. That was what Marston wanted people to believe. Kjell fought to save your mother's life—getting her and Zerelda to the hospital as quickly as he could. Lydia was unconscious for a long time—they didn't think she would make it."

"What happened to Marston?"

"When he arrived in Kansas City several weeks later, he put you in my care, telling me your mother had died in childbirth. I was miserable in my marriage and desperately needed to focus on something else. You were the answer. I was content to raise you and forget about my other problems. I felt it was something I could do to honor your mother. But the truth came out. Your mother hadn't died. She very nearly did, and even when she recovered she had no memory for a long while. She didn't know Kjell or Zerelda, and she didn't remember having a son."

"How could she not know?" he asked.

Evie shook her head. "She had lost a lot of blood, and the doctor said that, along with the shock of what had happened, had caused her to temporarily forget."

"How did you learn that she was still alive?"

"I overheard a conversation between our brothers and my husband one afternoon. It was then that I realized that Marston had tried to end Lydia's life in order to have control of you and the inheritance. The entire matter sickened me. I felt a fool for not having figured it out sooner."

"What happened then?"

"I set plans into motion to get you back to Lydia. I told my husband I wanted to take you to England and show you off to friends. My brothers thought this a great plan. See, I knew they would want to get you out of sight so that if Lydia sent the police, they wouldn't find you."

"So you pretended to go to England but came here instead?"

"Yes. It wasn't until I showed up with you that Lydia regained her memory in full. She had been getting bits and pieces of it back over her long recovery. But when I showed up with you, she passed out from the shock. It was as if everything came back to her at once and was simply too much to bear."

Dalton rubbed his eyes, nearly overwhelmed by all that Evie had just shared. "Please go on. What happened after that?"

"With my testimony and that of Ioann Sidorov, we saw Marston tried for kidnapping. He wasn't charged with murder or even attempted murder. He denied having anything to do with Anatolli's death and suggested that Ioann had done it.

"He did admit to arranging the kidnapping, but he said that he had never wanted any harm to come to anyone in the process. He lied and said that he was simply worried for your well-being in the wilds of Alaska. He said your mother was ill-equipped to care for you, and that her mind had never been strong. The judge didn't know her, of course, and chose to believe Marston. At least he believed in the money Marston paid him behind the scenes. Marston was sentenced to five years in prison but served none of it. Instead, he was given probation. While the verdict removed him from his place in polite society, it seemed to garner him an even more powerful position among those in the world of crime. From what I've heard from our sister, he's made a nice sum of money for himself once again and has a great many dangerous friends."

"So he got away with killing that Anatolli man and trying to kill my mother."

"And injuring Aunt Zee. Not only that, but there were other things that happened, and Marston seemed to be tied to those, as well. But he's so crafty. He always manages to buy or talk his way out of any guilt. Can you see now why your mother kept this from you?" Evie took hold of his hand. "Dalton, you mustn't hate her for the secrets she kept. The truth was so hideous, so distasteful, that she couldn't bear to let it affect your upbringing. She thought it would protect you in the long run."

He shook his head. "Protect me from what?"

Evie straightened. "From Marston, of course. He won't let the matter rest forever. We fear he will someday find you—try to persuade you to join him—to be your father's son."

Chapter 2

Dalton thought long and hard on the facts his sister had delivered. They sat in silence, staring out at the lush forest and snow-capped mountains. Dalton's mother had once told him there was a symphony of music that seemed to come from Alaska itself, but right now all he could hear was the drumming of his heart. The accusations and angry replies were hurled back and forth.

They lied to me.

They didn't really lie; they simply concealed the truth.

But the truth was important—it was the truth about my life, about who I am.

They were protecting you. The man your sister described would have killed you if you crossed him. Your mother didn't betray you; she only tried to keep you from harm.

She should have told me.

"She should have told me," Dalton murmured in echo to his thoughts.

"What?"

He looked at Evie. "Mother should have told me the truth. I deserved to know. I needed to know."

"No matter the cost to herself? My, this really is all about your selfish needs." Evie got to her feet and stared down at him. "I thought you were mature enough to handle this, but maybe I was wrong. You're acting like a spoiled child who suddenly learns the last of the pudding was secreted away to another member of the family."

Dalton jumped to his feet. "That's not fair! I haven't pushed for this until now. If it were your life, you'd want to know."

"Yes. I'd want to know. But I fail to see how it would be productive to assign blame and point fingers. Dalton, at this point it doesn't matter who should have told you and how much detail they should have shared. Choices were made with your welfare in mind. What can it possibly matter now?"

He thought about this for a moment. "All of my life I've felt that there was something more to me—some important part that was missing. I suppose that's because I knew there was another part of my life that no one wanted to talk about." Dalton looked at his sister. "I just need to know who I am."

She shrugged. "You're Dalton Gray Lindquist. You are what you make of yourself."

"But there's more to it than that. You talk about a father I never knew. Mother called him cruel. You tell me he was an evil man—but I don't know that for myself."

"Thank God!" she declared. Her face contorted in disgust as she gave a shudder. "You have no idea what God has saved you from."

"But he was our father."

Evie shook her head. "Forgive my crudity, but he was only the man who impregnated our mothers. Dalton, he cared only for himself. Children were nothing more to him than pawns. He cared more for making money than for seeing to the needs of anyone in his family."

"But that doesn't make him evil."

"He killed my mother!" Evie declared without warning. She put her hand to her mouth as if to smother the truth, then just as quickly drew it away. "I saw him."

"I'm so sorry, Evie. I had no . . . idea."

A gentle breeze blew across them and Evie shivered. Dalton didn't know if it was from the chill in the air or her memories, but he put his arm around her shoulder. Evie looked up at him.

"Dalton, I was just four years old when I saw my father throw my mother to her death. He had no idea I'd seen him. For years I lived in fear he would discover I knew the truth, and so I said nothing. He is a person best forgotten. You are nothing like him— take comfort in that."

But he didn't take comfort. So far he'd heard that his father and brother were killers—that they were ruthless and took what they wanted no matter the price. This was his heritage. What comfort could he possibly take in such knowledge?

"It just seems there's always been something missing . . . and it certainly has nothing to do with whether or not Kjell was a good father. He was. He is. But there is this shadow that hangs over me." Dalton shook his head. "And now with all that you've told me, it feels almost overwhelming. I can't explain it, but it's as if parts of the past are fighting to find their place in my life."

"For your sake, and that of your family, I hope you'll find a way to kill them before they have a chance to take hold of you," Evie replied.

Dalton was silent a moment before responding. It wasn't like Evie to suggest such a violent measure. "I can't very well put an end to something that I don't even know or recognize."

Evie looked at him intently. "The Bible says to flee the devil, Dalton. Our father . . . Marston . . . Mitchell . . . even Jeannette . . . they have always done the devil's bidding. I have no evidence to suggest they are any different today than they were the year you were born. They are best forgotten."

"I just don't know that I can do that. They are a part of who I am. It's like you're suggesting I cut off my hand."

"If your hand were harming you as Marston has and may still try to do in the future," Evie countered, "I'd cut it off myself . . . just to save you."

———

Joshua Broadstreet looked up to find Kjell Lindquist brushing rain from his jacket as he made his way through the door. The sawmill had once belonged to Kjell, but years ago he'd made Josh his partner and then eventually sold his interests in order to pursue building houses and businesses in the area.

"I knew yesterday's sunshine wouldn't last," Kjell said with a smile.

"I have some coffee on. Wanna cup?"

"Sounds good." He followed Joshua into the office. "Will you have any trouble getting me that order of lumber by the first?"

Josh poured the coffee and brought it to Kjell. "I don't think so. We haven't produced as much, what with my Tlingit workers gone. I have logs coming in steady, and most of your order is cut or nearly so. My other guys have been better about showing up sober since I started withholding pay when they come in drunk or suffering from the day after. The Creole boys I hired aren't giving me the quality of work I prefer, but I'll just have to take what I can get. If they just stop drinking, we should get by all right. Somehow, even with the Tlingits out of the village, the Creoles still seem to get a hold of that hooch the natives make. I swear that stuff is strong enough to strip rust off of metal."

"For a district that isn't allowed to import liquor, we certainly have our fair share. I suppose import laws don't apply to making the stuff here." Kjell sipped the hot liquid and took a seat. "That pot never fails to make good coffee."

Joshua joined Kjell and took a seat. "It serves me well."

"You've done a good job with the business. I'm glad it's worked out. I'm a lot happier with what I'm doing. I just finished up some repair work on the governor's house, in fact."

Josh nodded. "I heard that the new governor is due here any day. It'll be interesting to see what changes occur around here."

"No doubt he has his own agenda." Kjell smiled. "Still, political newcomers never quite seem to know what to expect in coming here. It's always rather amusing."

"Especially when they come from one of those big eastern cities. When they're used to being able to snap their fingers and get whatever they want, it's always a shock to come to Sitka."

"Some folks aren't cut out for life here." Kjell took a sip of his coffee. "I remember how hard it was on a lot of the enlisted men who served with the army. They never did seem to adapt to being stationed up here. Men were always deserting and trying to stow aboard whatever ship they could."

"When the army moved out of here, I had my concerns, but the navy seems to have adapted well to protecting and bringing order to the area. Now that Sitka is an organized district and we're getting judges and governors, I would expect things to go even better."

"It should prove interesting to see what changes come next. Lydia and Evie are worried the region will grow too fast and too big. They prefer the small, intimate feel of living here."

At the sound of Evie's name, Josh turned away. He tried hard not to think of the beautiful blond-haired woman. She was married. He reminded himself of that fact countless times a day. It didn't matter that she hadn't seen her husband in eighteen years. It didn't matter that Josh had loved her since he'd first laid eyes on her. She was still married.

"For two women who grew up in a luxurious big city, they've done quite well. Lydia tells me she prefers the quiet of life here. She said there was constant noise in the city."

"I remember it, too. You forget I'm not a native to the area, either," Josh said, trying to put aside his discomfort. "Although after all these years, I feel like it. I can hardly remember my life before coming here." *Before Evie came here. Why can't I purge my thoughts of her?*

He knew nothing could ever come of his adoration for the woman. He was already forty-four, and it seemed the hope of a wife and family had passed him by. But truthfully, he wanted no other woman. Evie had complete control of his heart. He had loved her in silence for all these years, and he would go on loving her. The one thing he would never do was dishonor her with a declaration. He loved her too much for that.

As if thoughts of her had willed her to him, Evie Gadston peered into the office. "I've come bearing gifts," she announced. "Zee and Lydia sent these." She deposited a plate of cinnamon rolls on Joshua's desk and flashed him a smile. "They're still warm."

The years had been most kind to Genevieve Gadston. At thirty-six, she could have passed for ten years younger. She comported herself in grace and refinement as if she still walked among society's finest.

The scent of the rolls drew his attention from her face momentarily. "They're the perfect thing to go with our coffee," he said. He met her deep blue eyes again. *Oh, Evie.*

"So are you two getting any work done today?" she asked. "It was beginning to drizzle at home, but by the time I made it to town, it was pouring. I thought I might actually see you on the road headed home, Kjell. Didn't Lydia say you were supposed to be putting a roof on a house today? Surely it's much too slippery for that in this rain."

"I saw I wasn't going to get much done and came to jaw with Josh," Kjell admitted. "What about you? How come you came out in this? Surely there was more to it than just delivering food to Josh here."

She laughed. "I've lived here long enough now to know that if you don't go out in the rain, you don't get anything done. Besides, Lydia wanted me to pick up some things for her at Arnie's."

"I'm glad you stopped by," Josh said, trying not to sound overly eager. "It's always nice to have an excuse to take a break. With you and Kjell here, I don't feel the least bit guilty in sitting around. In fact, I think I'll just treat myself." He popped the remaining bite of roll into his mouth and reached for another.

"So have you two managed to solve all the issues of the world?" Evie asked.

"Haven't gotten much further than discussing the new governor. Seems everyone is fairly excited about it. They say he's bringing his wife and children. At least three of his four children. I guess a fourth is off on his own or otherwise occupied."

Evie pushed back an errant wisp of hair. "I hope his wife isn't too uppity. She'll be in for a real shock if she is. Folks coming here always seem so surprised that such places really do exist."

"We were just discussing that," Kjell said. "I was telling Josh that it always impressed me how well you and Lydia adapted. I've seen many army wives come here only to leave before their husband's time was up. They usually went to live with family back down in the States. They couldn't bear the long waits between letters from home."

"I know. I've been at many a gathering of ladies where such matters were the sole topic of discussion," Evie said. "Frankly, I'm glad to get mail just once a month. That way, if Jeannette has written to complain in more than one letter, I can get it all out of the way in one sitting."

Kjell laughed. "And she seems quite content to complain, doesn't she?"

Evie nodded. "More than most. You'd think she'd find some satisfaction in her life, but she never does. She has the house we grew up in, because, as she told Mitchell and Marston, she couldn't be happy anywhere else. Her children are grown and gone, or very nearly so, and her husband allows her the freedom to do pretty much whatever she wants—so long as she keeps to her budget. I suppose that is the most grievous thing in her life, however."

The men exchanged a knowing smile. Josh had heard most of the women in Sitka complain about having to keep tight budgets. Things up here cost a whole lot more than elsewhere. Many of the women had family members from the States ship them supplies at outrageous freighting costs, and still managed to save money. It wasn't that Arnie and the other shopkeepers were unfair in their pricing, but things were precious here. It was harder to get even common items.

"So are they planning a big party for the governor?" Joshua asked no one in particular.

"Lydia says there will be a big reception to greet him and the family on the day they arrive. Then sometime next month there's to be a party and dance. She's getting her musicians ready for the occasion."

"Our own little Sitka orchestra," Josh said with a grin. "That Lydia can sure play the violin. I've never heard anything sweeter."

"I marvel at her abilities," Evie admitted. "I never had a talent like that."

"You sing like a lark," Kjell countered. "Your instrument is your voice."

"I agree," Josh said, meeting her gaze. The moment their eyes met, he felt his heart skip a beat. Why couldn't she be free? He didn't want to dishonor her or God by having selfish thoughts about her. He drew a deep breath and looked away. *God, forgive me for loving her.* "I guess I should get back to work. I need to finish cutting boards."

"Want some help?" Kjell asked.

Josh put aside his uneaten pastry. "No. I'll be just fine. The boys will be back soon, and I'll have more than enough help."

"In that case," Kjell said, getting to his feet and extending his arm to Evie, "may I escort you somewhere?"

"I'm going to Arnie's. You're welcome to help me make my way through the mud."

"I'd be honored. Perhaps we can find Mrs. Murphy's lost rain barrel. I heard it said that the poor woman believed it blew off her porch during a windstorm. She thinks it rolled all the way out to sea, but I'm more of a mind to believe it sank in the mud and is still stuck somewhere."

Evie laughed. "I'm sure if we dug around in the mud of Lincoln Street, we'd find entire regiments of soldiers and their gear still mucking about. I saw a man sink up to his thigh a couple of weeks ago. Traversing the area is not for the weak."

The men laughed. "Perhaps," Kjell said with a wink at Josh, "we should work on creating some mud shoes. Something along the lines of snowshoes, only for the streets of Sitka."

"Mother, can I talk to you?" Dalton asked. He hesitated. "I don't want to upset you again."

Lydia looked up and smiled. "I'm not upset. Come sit beside me." She patted the sofa cushion.

"I just want to apologize for getting so riled up yesterday." He sat down and rubbed his hands rather nervously on his trousers. "I feel kind of lost."

She put her hand over his. "I'm so sorry. I never meant to make this harder on you."

He could see the sadness in her expression. "I wanted to say the same thing. It's just that I need to understand. I need to know. It's so hard to realize there's a whole part of my life that remains a mystery."

"I know how that feels," his mother told him. "When I lost my memory after the attack, I was so frustrated and angry. I knew there was so much I should understand, and yet I didn't. I didn't know the people around me, and that hurt most of all. Now you feel that you don't know us—that we've betrayed you."

He nodded. "I know you didn't intend to, but that is how it feels. Evie told me I should just forget about our father and siblings. She said I should flee them as if they were the devil himself, but I can't do that. I know everyone wants what's best for me—that you've always wanted that."

"You're right. I only meant to protect you," she said softly. "I don't know what Marston and Mitchell might do—even now. If they thought you could benefit them, they would stop at nothing."

"But, Mother, I'm a grown man now. I can take care of myself."

She smiled sadly. "I know, Dalton. But in my mind you're still a little boy. You'll always be my little boy."

He hugged her. "I have so many questions. Evie said she'd talk to me about anything I wanted to know, but some of it only you can answer."

"Yesterday came as a bit of a shock, but I'm prepared now. I knew the day would come when we would need to relive the past. I never intended that you be kept from the truth forever."

"Thank you," he said, pulling back to look at her once more.

Reaching up, she gently touched his jaw. "You've grown up so fast. When I think of how I nearly lost you . . . well, I can't even imagine a life without you. I wanted children so very much. I feared you would be an only child, and then God finally blessed us with the girls. I'm so afraid . . ." Her words faded as she dropped her hold.

"Afraid of what, Mother?"

She lowered her gaze to the fire. "I suppose I'm afraid of losing you again."

"How? How could you possibly lose me?"

"Your brothers are very persuasive. Life in the States is much different from here. I'm afraid you'll be enticed to stay once you go there."

"Who said anything about me going there?"

She looked up at him and smiled knowingly. "You will. Maybe not tomorrow or the next day, but you will go to better understand what it was that brought me here. You'll go to meet your siblings face to face so that you can ask your brothers what possessed them to do the things they did." Mother turned back to the fire. "You'll go, but I pray you'll return. That's my only hope."

Chapter 3

The tenth of June dawned, overcast with a blanket of mist that hung heavy over the mountains. Within a few hours, however, the weather had cleared and the sun came out to welcome the new governor and his family.

Lyman Knapp had been installed as the third governor of the District of Alaska. Appointed by President Harrison earlier in the year, Governor Knapp and his family were about to arrive at the docks in Sitka, along with three of their four children. Nearly the entire populace of Sitka had turned out to welcome the newcomers. Russians, Creoles, Tlingits, and Americans stood side by side to cheer the event. Everyone wanted to know what news he would bring of the States and of the future for Alaska.

Dalton stood to the far side of the wharf watching with the others. He caught a glimpse of the bearded man as his launch approached the docks. The harbor was too shallow for the larger ships to enter close to shore, but it was only a minor inconvenience. The approach of the launch allowed the people ashore to watch and assess the passengers. It also allowed the governor and his family to consider their new home.

"They ain't gonna like it here," Briney Roberts announced. The man was an old salt who'd long been a friend of the family. "I can tell you, the president makes a big mistake every time he appoints a governor who don't know nothing about this place."

"I agree with you there, Briney." Dalton shrugged. "I suppose they mean to put politicians in place who know how the game is played back in Washington. I guess they feel it doesn't matter whether they know how to live here or not."

Briney scratched his graying beard. "Your pa would make a better governor than that fellow."

"Well, give the guy a chance. Pa says he's a war hero. He served in the Union Army and was wounded several times during the War Between the States. He's been a lawyer and judge, as well as a congressman."

Briney spit out into the water. "Bah. Ain't none of those things gonna give him the wherewithal to live here. A lawyer. Bah! A waste of time, if you ask me."

Dalton shrugged. Briney made a good point, but he didn't want to encourage dissension. "Only time will tell if it's given him the knowledge he needs for running the district. A governor will need a good understanding of the law. Maybe we can teach him the rest."

A loud round of applause went up as Governor Knapp appeared safely on the dock. The man bowed and presented his wife. More applause. Knapp motioned for the noise to cease, and the crowd fell silent.

"Citizens of Sitka, I want to thank you for such a warm welcome.

I am Governor Lyman Knapp, and I have come to serve this district to the best of my ability. Though this is an isolated land, I am persuaded to believe that there is a great wealth of resources and advantages to this place."

The clapping began again, and Briney nudged Dalton. "Got 'em eating out of his hand."

Knapp was now speaking with the city officials. There seemed to be some confusion as to what was to happen next. Dalton suppressed a yawn and glanced out to see a second, smaller boat making its way to the wharf. Perhaps these people were part of the governor's family or staff. Dalton noted several women, as well as children, huddled together. They seemed to consider the town with some interest. Once in a while, someone would point and others would nod. Deciding he'd seen enough, Dalton was just about to move away when he saw a woman near the front of the boat jump to her feet. Fashionably dressed and groomed, she seemed oblivious to the danger.

Dalton frowned. They were still a good ways from docking—it really was foolish of her to stand. The woman waved her hands as if swatting at some unseen attacker. The people in the boat were admonishing her to sit, but she seemed not to hear them. Instead she turned rather quickly and entangled herself in her dark green traveling suit.

Dalton watched in a kind of strange fascination as the woman tipped backward almost in slow motion. The people around her reached out to take hold of her and keep her from falling off the boat, but it was to no avail. Another of the passengers screamed, calling out a name that Dalton couldn't quite make out, as the woman disappeared under the water.

The pilot of the boat didn't seem to realize what had happened. He didn't even attempt to slow his approach to the docks. People in the boat were calling out and trying to move to help the victim, but it was only serving to make the launch unstable.

Slapping at the water as she resurfaced, the woman fought to keep her head above the waves. She clearly could not swim. She struggled in such a panicked manner, it left little doubt in Dalton's mind that she was fighting for her life.

Without another thought, Dalton pulled off his boots and jacket and, before Briney could even attempt to stop him, headed into the water.

The shock of the cold momentarily stunned Dalton. He would have to move fast before the water lowered his body temperature to a dangerous level. Swimming with long, steady strokes, Dalton tried to look up long enough to get a fix on the woman. When he didn't spy her immediately, he began to fear it was too late. He prayed he wouldn't have to dive to locate her. Just then he caught sight of her odd little hat as she bobbed up for air. With a few strong thrusts, he reached her side just as she sank once again.

Dalton knew she would probably fight him, but to his surprise she all but collapsed against him as he pulled her backward by the collar. She had either the good sense to let him rescue her or she'd passed out. Either way, he didn't care, so long as she didn't resist his efforts. With a strong single-armed stroke, Dalton began the journey back to shore. He heard cheers from the people but ignored them to focus on the job at hand. Neither one of them was out of danger just yet.

When he got close enough to touch the ground, Dalton stopped and stood. Panting and exhausted, he reached around and lifted the water-logged woman in his arms. Blond hair spilled down from what had once been a carefully pinned bun. Somewhere in her struggle she'd lost the little hat.

"You're . . . hur-hurting . . . me," she protested, her teeth chattering.

"Excuse me?" He looked down to meet her frowning expression.

"I said . . . you're hurting m-me. You're . . . holding me . . . too tight. In fact . . . I d-d- . . . don't know why you're o carrying me . . . at all."

He could see she was younger than he'd originally thought. Instead of a more matronly woman, he found himself eye to eye with a girl surely no more than his own eighteen years.

"I'm trying to save your life and get you to shore." Sharp rocks cut into his feet, but Dalton pressed on.

She seemed to gain control of her teeth. "But you're pulling my hair," she declared.

Dalton stopped at this and looked at her in disbelief. "You have a strange way of being grateful for someone saving your life."

She reddened and shook her head. "My hair is caught. Put me down at once."

Seeing that the water was no more than a foot deep, Dalton nodded. "As you wish." He released her and watched as she fell back into the water. The look on her face was one of complete disbelief.

Dalton watched as she hit the bottom and bounced back up. Sputtering and shrieking, she fought the water and tried to reposition herself. He smiled as she managed to regain some control. With her skirts molded to her slim body, she struggled to steady herself.

"How dare you!"

He chuckled. "You told me to put you down. I just did what you said."

"How accommodating," she said, taking her skirt in hand.

Dalton shrugged. "You're welcome."

She fixed him with a glare. "You are no doubt one of those uneducated ruffians I was warned about."

This only served to amuse Dalton even more. "I certainly hope so."

He laughed heartily as he moved toward shore. Other would-be rescuers were approaching, so he pushed through them to retrieve his coat and boots from Briney.

"You gotta get out of them wet clothes. Come on over to my boat."

Just then Joshua Broadstreet approached. He held out a blanket to Dalton. "I have another blanket for the young lady."

"I'd be careful in giving it to her. She's the testy sort."

Josh laughed. "Well, she just very nearly drowned."

"Because of her own stupidity," Dalton countered. He stripped off his shirt and wrapped the blanket around his shivering body.

"Maybe she'd be grateful to you if you brought her this bit of warmth," Josh teased.

Dalton looked at the blanket for a moment and shook his head. "She wasn't grateful for having her life saved, so I doubt a blanket will change her position."

"Come on, Dalton." Briney pulled him away from the approaching young woman and her crowd of helpers. "No sense worrying after her now."

"Believe me, I do not intend to give her a second thought."

———

"I was terrified when I saw you go into the water," Lydia told her son as the family ate supper that evening. "Are you certain that you're doing all right? You aren't chilled, are you?" She reached out and felt his head.

"Honestly, Mother, I'm fine. The water was cold, but Briney saw that I dried out quickly. I'm far more interested in the food on my plate and the pie you promised."

"Let him eat, Liddie. He's just fine," Kjell said, taking hold of his wife's hand. "Relax."

"Illiyana said you're the fastest swimmer in Sitka," Britta announced.

Dalton reached over and gave a gentle pull on his sister's earlobe. "I'll bet her brothers would have something to say about that. I know for a fact Yuri considers himself a great swimmer."

"Well, you were really fast," Kjerstin declared. "I think if you had a race, you would win."

"I'd rather not give it another shot just now," Dalton replied. "That water was much too cold."

"How come the Tlingit children go in the water all the time?" she asked, looking to her great-aunt for answers.

Zerelda exchanged a look with Lydia. "Well, the Tlingit have their ways and we have ours. They take their children into the water at an early age to toughen their skin and strengthen their constitution. The law has forbidden it, but some still bathe their infants quite early in the icy water. I don't suggest it, however."

"But why?" Kjerstin asked. "Why do they do that?"

"Well, the native people do a lot of things that would probably be harmful to whites. For instance, they eat a variety of things that often make us sick."

"But you said we were all made the same in God's eyes."

Zerelda nodded. "That we are. Even so, we needn't all do the same things."

"But the missionaries say that the Tlingits should be like the whites," Kjerstin pressed.

Her comment was clearly unexpected. Lydia looked at Kjell and then to Zerelda. "People say a great many things. It doesn't mean it's wise or sensible."

The ten-year-old was visibly concerned. "But they're doing

God's work. You said that when people are doing God's work, they are often misunderstood."

Lydia smiled. "I'm glad to know you've been listening. It's true that missionaries are often misunderstood."

"And they often misunderstand. Sometimes they simply make mistakes in how they handle things," Zerelda interjected.

Lydia frowned. This had long been a bone of contention for her aunt. When Sheldon Jackson and his missionaries moved into the area, Zerelda Rockford had voiced a mix of praise and frustration. Her agitation over the way the Tlingits were treated was a frequent topic at the Lindquist table.

Evie gave Lydia a smile. "I think we all make mistakes. We say and do things we wish we could take back."

"So the missionaries are wrong?" Kjerstin asked.

Zerelda put down her fork. "I believe sometimes they are. They have good hearts and long to do God's work, but I think some go about it all wrong. They haven't really bothered to understand the people and their culture because they believe the old ways should be put aside. That leads to resentment and confusion among the native people, and I can't say that I don't feel the same way."

"Now, now, Zee. We hardly need to get all up in arms at supper," Kjell said in a good-natured manner. He gave his daughters a wink. "You girls owe me a game of checkers tonight. What say we have our pie by the fire and get started?"

"Yes!" Britta declared, getting to her feet. She looked to her mother. "May we please?"

Lydia was surprised that Kjell had suggested such a thing, but it was clear he didn't want his daughters drawn up in an argument about the politics of serving God. She nodded. "I think that would be just fine. You three go ahead, and I will bring your dessert." Kjell smiled and pushed back from the table.

Once they were gone, Lydia turned to her aunt. "Zee, you

know Kjell doesn't like to see the girls in the middle of this. It's bad enough that folks discuss it at church."

"Well, it should be discussed. It's a problem that has been with us for a long while." Then Zerelda's hard expression softened, and she pushed away from the table. "Still, I want to keep the peace. I'm sorry. I simply feel passionate about this matter. I feel so many of the Tlingits are suffering at the hands of the whites, rather than being benefited as so many like to believe. It's like the Russian church and the Presbyterians are playing a game of tug-of-war with the hearts and minds of the children. Goodness, but it seems almost criminal the way they go at it."

Dalton reached out and patted his great-aunt's hand. "Your love of the Tlingit people is amazing, Aunt Zee. You've worked to better understand the people and their culture. You've shown them that the love of Jesus transcends everything else."

"Speaking of which, I have some more material for quilt squares," Lydia announced. "Mrs. Vargas brought us what had been collected at church."

"That's wonderful. We'll have plenty of time to cut squares. The Tlingit girls won't be returning until fall," Zerelda replied. "I know they are needed at home for the salmon run and such, but I hate for them to put aside their lessons."

"Perhaps they'll find a way to continue studying at home." Lydia got to her feet and looked at Dalton. "Would you like more fish?"

"No, but I'm ready for that pie. I've still got plenty of room for that."

She laughed as he patted his stomach. "I've no doubt."

"Well, saving a life is hard work. Gives you a big appetite," he said in a teasing tone.

"You were quite the hero," Lydia told her son. "I think it helps when the person you have to rescue is so pretty."

Dalton laughed. "She was also full of spit and vinegar."

"I'm sure she was embarrassed by what had happened. Goodness, but the whole town had turned out to greet the new governor, and there she was, making a scene."

"I hadn't really thought of it that way. Just figured she didn't like me."

"And would that matter to you?" Lydia asked.

His expression grew thoughtful, and then he simply said, "I think it would."

Chapter 4

Phoebe Robbins finished pinning her long blond hair into a neat roll at the back of her head. She stared at her reflection in the mirror for a moment and sighed. She had not wanted to come to Sitka, Alaska. Had it not been for her mother's pleading, Phoebe would have taken up her grandmother's offer to remain in Vermont. Her brothers, Theodore and Grady, seemed more than happy to make the trek to the wilds of the frontier. But at fifteen and thirteen, all of life was an adventure to them.

"If you continue to frown that way," her mother said, sweeping into the room with fresh linens, "you'll have permanent lines on your face."

Phoebe rose from the dressing table and offered her mother a weak smile. "I'm sorry."

"If you're still fretting over that incident last week when we arrived, why not do something positive instead?"

"What are you talking about?"

Mother placed the linens at the end of Phoebe's bed. "That nice young man who saved your life. You told me you regretted how you acted. I have arranged to go meet his mother this afternoon and personally thank him for what he did. Perhaps you could make him a gift of apology—maybe some cookies."

She considered this for a moment. "I do owe him an apology. I hardly know what got into me." She followed her mother out of the room. "But he owes me one, as well. He threw me down in the water. I could have been injured."

"Oh, Phoebe. Your embarrassment got the best of you. If you'd not lashed out, he would never have reacted in such a way. Make him a batch of cookies, and he will quickly forget your caustic tongue."

Phoebe tied on her apron and moved among the collection of unpacked crates. "Why did Father have to agree to take this job?"

"You know he's good friends with Mr. Knapp—Governor Knapp. It was always supposed that if he was appointed to be governor over the district, we would accompany his family and your father would work for him. Personally, I'm glad to have a good friend in his wife. Martha is the kindest of women, and I shan't grow too lonely with her near."

Frowning again, Phoebe wanted to comment that this was all well and fine for her mother, but Phoebe had no real friendship with either the governor's wife or their children. Who was she to befriend in this vast and desolate country?

"Besides, we have each other—you and me. We must simply make the best of our situation," her mother continued. "I believe we shall have a great need for our candles. If our supplies were undamaged on the move here, we shall have to get to work right away."

The women in their family had been chandlers for five generations. Her mother had taught Phoebe the various secrets to making candles, along with recipes for a variety of types. It was both fascinating and enjoyable work.

"I know the people up here use a great deal of oil—whale, seal, and even a type of fish, although the name escapes me. We might be able to utilize some of these things in our candle making."

"Yes, but as Father said, getting any kind of supply brought to us from the States will be quite expensive. We may well find it a futile effort."

Her mother shrugged. "Perhaps, but I will not disappoint my ancestors and put it aside. I will do whatever I can to continue. Now, why don't you make the cookies while I continue unpacking the crates. We'll go to the Lindquists after our noontime meal."

"Lindquist? That's his name?"

"That's the family name. Kjell and Lydia Lindquist are the parents of the young man who saved you. His name is Dalton."

Phoebe smiled. "Dalton." She let the name slip over her tongue. She could still see his blue eyes staring hard at her. "Very well. I will make cookies for Dalton."

———

They were nearly to the Lindquist house when Phoebe got a case of the jitters. "Maybe this wasn't such a good idea," she told her mother. There was something about Dalton Lindquist and the memory of his arms around her that greatly unnerved her.

The older woman laughed and brought the wagon to a stop. "Well, it's a little late to decide that now. We're already here. See there, the women have come to greet us."

Phoebe looked up to see a dark-haired woman, dressed simply

in a white muslin shirtwaist and a dark blue cotton skirt. Beside her stood a much-older-looking woman who wore her hair in a short bob rather than pinned atop her head.

"Good afternoon, ladies. We are so pleased to have you visit," the younger of the two women announced. "I'm Lydia Lindquist, and this is my aunt, Miss Zerelda Rockford."

"But folks around here call me Zee," the older woman threw in.

Phoebe helped her mother down, then turned to smile. Her mother made quick introductions. "I'm Bethel Robbins, and this is my daughter, Phoebe. She's the one your son, Dalton, saved from drowning."

Phoebe bowed her head quickly. Her mother needn't have reminded everyone of the incident now several days past. How humiliating to have one's mistakes thrown out for everyone to comment upon.

"We are very happy to make your acquaintance. We thought it might be nice to have tea out here on the porch since the day is so pleasant. Would that be to your liking?" Mrs. Lindquist asked.

Phoebe's mother nodded. "Oh, that would be ideal." Forgetting about her offering of cookies and the man she'd come to honor, Phoebe instead studied the two-story log house. It was quite lovely. Someone had taken great care in the details.

Lydia Lindquist directed them to take seats at the small tea table. Lovely hand-carved wooden chairs graced the arrangement. The backs were ornate with a lovely design of hearts and flowers. In Vermont, she had known a family of Swedes who had furnished their home entirely with furniture from the old country. Their dining room chairs were similar to the ones Phoebe now studied.

"Please be seated," Lydia instructed. "I shall bring out the refreshments."

She and the older woman made their way back into the house

while Phoebe took the opportunity to lean closer to her mother. "They seem very nice."

"I was thinking much the same. Apparently, they harbor no ill feelings toward you."

"And you are certain these are the right people—that their son is the one who saved me?"

Her mother laughed. "Of course. You know that your father leaves nothing to chance. He knew their names before you had even managed to change into dry clothing." Mother glanced around. "Such a lovely setting, and so peaceful. I like that it's well away from the bustle of the docks. Seems we are always inundated with noise in our new home."

"It is nice," Phoebe admitted. "Still, I miss Vermont. I used to think our town so tiny, but compared to Sitka, Montpelier seems huge."

"Here we are," Lydia announced as she came out the door with a large silver tea service. She placed the tray on the table, and Zerelda followed suit by arranging a platter on either side. Phoebe could see that the one held bite-size pieces of dessert, while the other had tiny sandwiches.

The woman called Zee offered a prayer of thanks, then began pouring tea. "We were happy to meet the new governor. Are you well acquainted with him?" Zee asked.

Phoebe's mother nodded. "We have been friends for some time now. I know his wife, Martha, quite well."

"And what are his intentions for Alaska?"

"Zee, they've only just arrived. Must we wax political right away?"

The older woman handed Phoebe a cup and saucer. "You must forgive me. I'm one who always tends to get right to the heart of a matter."

"It's quite all right," Mother answered in her best diplomatic tone. "I really cannot say what the governor has planned. He is a fair man and very intelligent. I believe he has a good heart, as well."

"Has he any experience that would give him knowledge of such a situation?" Zee pressed.

"In what way?"

Phoebe could see that Mrs. Lindquist was rather uncomfortable with this line of questioning. Thinking she might change the subject, Phoebe held up her cup. "Might I trouble you for some sugar?"

"Certainly," Lydia said. She reached for the sugar service and opened the lid. "You are such a lovely young woman." Her genuine smile immediately put Phoebe at ease. "May I ask your age?"

"Phoebe is eighteen," her mother interjected. "Just this last March. She is my oldest. We have two sons, Theodore and Grady, as well."

"We have two young daughters besides our son, Dalton," Lydia offered. "Kjerstin is ten, and Britta is seven. They should return soon from school. Dalton will bring them, and then you'll have a chance to thank him in person, Miss Robbins."

Phoebe felt her face grow hot. "I'm afraid I wasn't very congenial at our first meeting. I'm sure he probably told you."

Mrs. Lindquist and her aunt exchanged a look that suggested they had no idea what Phoebe was talking about. *Great*, she thought. He hadn't said anything, and now she would have to explain—all because she had to open her big mouth in defense.

"Dalton said very little, actually. He's a man of few words," his mother offered. "I'm sure the shock of your accident left him little concern as to your reaction. I can say that if I had fallen into the harbor, I might have lacked congeniality, too." She smiled warmly, again putting Phoebe at ease.

Her mother picked up one of the offered sweets. "Phoebe made him some cookies to show her gratitude."

"Then all will be perfectly well," Zee announced. "There are few things that boy likes more."

"I find that true of most men," Phoebe's mother replied. "Might I ask how long you've made your home here in Sitka, Miss Rockford?"

Zerelda smiled and eased back in the chair. "I've been here since before the purchase. When Russia sold Alaska to America, I was already a citizen. I came here to work as a nurse for a German family. The wife took ill quite often and needed constant care. Later, my niece moved here, as well, and we've managed to stay on ever since."

"My husband, Kjell, was born and raised here," Lydia added.

"So you certainly know all there is to know about the place."

Phoebe knew her mother had a million unanswered questions. Not the least of which was concerns about the Indians. As if reading her daughter's mind, she pressed on.

"What do you know of the Indians here?"

Zerelda raised a brow. "Enough to know they don't like to be called Indians. They are Tlingits. The Russians call them the Kolash."

"I haven't seen very many of them. Are they . . . well . . . are there many here?"

"Quite a few, but this is summer and they are out gathering food. They live in the village for most of the winter, then head out around April, when the herring spawn. They'll be gone for most of the summer and early fall, hunting and even visiting other *kwaans.* Those are tribal units of other Tlingits. The group here is called the *Sheet'ká kwaan,* or 'inhabitants of Sitka.'"

Phoebe sensed her mother's discomfort at this comeuppance. "And what are these people like, Miss Rockford? We have seen only a few of them around the town. They are rather frightening with their faces painted black and red. Is this normal, or are they dressed that way for a specific purpose?"

"It serves various purposes, not the least of which is protection against the sun and insects," Zerelda replied. "The flies and mosquitoes can be vicious up here, if you haven't already encountered them. This remedy has served them well."

Mother gave a shiver. "Well, they are rather frightening to me."

"They are good people," Mrs. Lindquist said. "Their skill in fishing and herbal remedies is not to be underestimated. I have learned so much since coming here, and a great bit of that knowledge has come from the native people. They have problems, just as anyone would, but I find most Tlingits to be highly industrious. You will learn this for yourself come fall. When they return for the winter, you will find the town quite populated with them."

"Are they violent? I heard they've had uprisings here. Someone mentioned it on the ship."

"There have been issues from time to time," Mrs. Lindquist conceded. "But all people—white or otherwise—disagree from time to time. We have no further to look than our own War Between the States. Which reminds me—I understand that your husband and our new governor are heroes of that war."

Phoebe admired how easily and quickly Mrs. Lindquist moved the conversation away from the controversy of the Tlingit people. She knew her mother was happy to share praise for her father's accomplishments. He and the governor had both been highly honored for their service.

The ladies continued to exchange pleasantries until the sound of an approaching wagon reached their ears. Phoebe couldn't help but feel a nervous anticipation when Mrs. Lindquist announced that her son and daughters had returned.

"I'd love to show you around the property," Mrs. Lindquist told Phoebe's mother. "Would you care to see my home?"

"Oh, please." She looked to Phoebe rather conspiratorially. "I was hoping for just such an invitation."

The ladies laughed at this. Mrs. Lindquist waved to her children. The little girls leaped from the wagon into their brother's strong arms before flying up the walk to greet their mother.

"Dalton promised to take us to see the jellyfish. Can we go today?" the smallest one asked.

"Where are your manners, Miss Britta?" Mrs. Lindquist asked.

The girl paused. Her eyes grew wide. Giving a brief curtsy toward Phoebe and her mother, the little girl offered her apology. "I am sorry, and I am perfectly happy to meet you."

Phoebe couldn't suppress a giggle. She dipped in return. "And I am perfectly happy to meet you."

"I'm Kjerstin," her sister announced. "She's Britta."

"And I am Phoebe, and this is my mother, Mrs. Robbins."

After a moment of silence, Britta turned back to her mother. "So can we go see the jellyfish?"

"Not just yet," their mother replied. "Why don't you run upstairs and change your clothes. I was just about to give Mrs. Robbins a tour of the house. I believe Miss Phoebe would like to speak to your brother."

Britta leaned close to Phoebe. "Don't let him kiss you. He's been eating lutefisk."

Phoebe had no idea what lutefisk was, but the fact that Dalton's little sister would tell a complete stranger not to kiss her brother was rather shocking. She didn't know what to say, and when she looked up to meet the equally surprised faces of the women around her, she was further humiliated to find Dalton had overheard the entire thing.

He only laughed. "Britta, you are such a ninny."

Everyone chuckled except Phoebe. She felt hopelessly embarrassed and quickly moved away from the group. "I'll be right back." She made her way to the wagon, where she'd left the cookies. Taking several deep breaths, she fought against the pounding of her heart.

My, but his eyes were even bluer than she'd remembered. He had a stubbly growth of whiskers that suggested he'd not shaved that day, and all Phoebe could think about was touching his face.

"You are the ninny," she chided herself in a mumble.

She reached over the side of the wagon for the plate of cookies and had just lifted them over the edge when Dalton spoke from directly behind her.

"Might I help you?"

Phoebe had such a start that she threw the plate high into the air. This was followed by a muffled cry and a frantic flailing to secure the lost treats.

Losing her balance, she stumbled back against Dalton. He tried to steady her, but they both realized too late that this was impossible. He fell backward, his hands still secured about her waist. Phoebe followed him down, landing on top of his stomach—and a loud groan broke the silence. The only problem was, it wasn't her loud groan.

"I'm so sorry." She tried to free herself, but her gown was caught beneath his hip. When she fought to pull it away, Dalton quickly raised up. When he did so, the dress released and Phoebe pitched face-first onto the ground.

Realizing that further action might only serve to cause more humiliation, Phoebe remained still for a moment. She didn't know exactly what to do. If she got up, she would have to face Dalton. But if she didn't get up, he might think her injured and make an even bigger fuss. Finally, she leaned up on her elbow and shot him a sheepish smile. "So much for kissing."

Dalton burst into a roar of laughter. "Like that would ever stop me."

Phoebe eased into a sitting position. "What about the lut . . . Whatever it was."

"Lutefisk." He sat up and dusted off his hands. "I doubt there's a man worth his salt that would let smelly fish keep him from kissing a beautiful girl."

She felt her cheeks grow even hotter. A million butterflies fought for position in her stomach. Phoebe looked at the cookies, now scattered about the ground. "I baked those for you," she offered. "It was my way of apologizing for being so rude when you rescued me."

To her surprise, Dalton reached over and picked a cookie up off the ground and popped it into his mouth. After a moment, he smiled. "Apology accepted."

Phoebe couldn't help but giggle. "I'm Phoebe Robbins."

"Yes, I know." Dalton flashed a smile that left her feeling as though she'd melted into the ground. "I'm glad to meet you. I'm Dalton Lindquist."

She nodded, finding it impossible to speak. Maybe life in Sitka wouldn't be so bad after all.

Chapter 5

Dalton studied the staircase for a moment. With most of the Tlingit workers off to hunt and trade, Dalton's father had asked for his help with his construction project, and this, in turn, presented an opportunity for them to talk. Still, as much as he wanted to know Father's thoughts on the past—on what had happened when his mother had been injured—Dalton was at a loss as to how to start the conversation.

"You seem to have a lot on your mind lately."

Dalton looked up and nodded. "I suppose I do."

Father smiled and gave his blond-brown beard a scratch. "The stairs will keep. Why don't we take a walk?"

They left the house his father had been building for one of the new government families. The day was overcast, but so far, the rain was holding off. His father seemed to be in no hurry to solicit conversation, so the two men simply walked for a time along the rocky shore. Kjell Lindquist had been a good father and mentor, teaching Dalton how to work with wood. Dalton had always felt at home in the sawmill and workshop where his father made furniture and other things for the family. Dalton's true love, however, was building boats. It wasn't so very different from making furniture.

The path wound away from the water and up the hill, leading them to a stand of spruce and alder. Salmonberry bushes were blooming with their purplish-pink blossoms, while other flowers colored the ground from place to place.

"I've always loved this island," Dalton said, not really meaning to speak the words aloud.

"For some, it's a hard place to even like," his father countered.

Dalton looked at the man and nodded. "Until lately, I always felt I belonged here."

"But not now?"

There was no condemnation in his tone, but Dalton felt guilty just the same. "Ever since Mother and Evie told me about the kidnapping—about my brothers and other sister—I've felt out of place." Dalton waited for his father to comment, but he said nothing as the path turned and took them higher.

"I've always known that Mother was expecting me when she came to Sitka. No one ever talked about my father, and for a lot of years, I figured it was because the sorrow was too great. I honestly never figured it was because he was such a heinous man. I mean, there were times when comments were made about trouble in the past, but I gave it no thought."

"There was no need for you to give it consideration. You were just a child." Father picked up a rock and gave it a toss to the water below. "Nothing in the past was your fault or yours to make up for. It hurt your mother to remember those days, so it was just as easy to forget about them."

"Until I had to force the issue," Dalton said, feeling terrible for the pain he'd caused. "I never wanted to hurt her. I still don't."

"But?"

Dalton looked at his father. "But I find myself vacillating from one feeling to the next. On one hand, I want revenge for her. I hate that anyone would cause her fear or pain, but that they would try to kill her . . . well, that just makes me want to return the favor."

"I felt the same way," his father admitted.

He shook his head. "On the other hand, I feel a strange need to know more, to know them—my brothers and sister. Even my father. Does that make any sense at all?"

Kjell considered the words for a moment. "I think there's a reason and purpose for everything, Dalton. I can see why you would want to meet them and know them better. I can vouch for the fact that, nineteen years ago, they were very dangerous people. Especially your brother Marston. He was the one who seemed to instigate everything. Mitchell is his twin and went along with the plan, but Marston seemed to always make the decisions."

"I just feel like I . . . that I . . ." Dalton shook his head again. "I don't know who I am. But that sounds crazy. I'm Dalton Lindquist. I live in Sitka, and I have a wonderful family who loves me. You've been an incredible father to me. I don't want you to think otherwise. I will always love you and be grateful that you chose to be my father. I should be happy with that . . . and I hate it that I feel so restless instead."

"It's not nearly so important to know who you are, as to know *whose* you are."

"I don't understand."

Kjell reached out and touched his shoulder. "Son, you might have been conceived a Gray and born a Lindquist, but there's something so much more important. You chose to belong to God—to accept that Jesus died for your sins and rose again to give you life eternal. You made those choices a long time ago. You belong to Him. That's where your identity should come from. That's where you can find peace when everything else goes wrong."

"But there's still a need to understand my earthly past. You know who your parents were—who your people are. You didn't have this horrible thing hanging over your head—this secret shame of what once happened."

"Everyone has something in their past that they'd just as soon forget, Dalton. But even so, you had nothing to do with the choices and decisions that others made before you were born—or even after. Your father's actions might have set certain courses in motion for you, but they needn't determine your future."

"Do you think my brothers could have changed? Do you think my other sister would want to know me like Evie does?"

Father shrugged. "It's hard to say. Folks can certainly change, if they allow the right influences. Of course, they can change for the worse, too."

"It doesn't sound as though my brothers could have become much worse." Dalton moved away from his father and walked to the edge of the trail. The water below looked as gray as the sky. Seals surfaced and dove as they played in the harbor, and Dalton wished he could be as carefree. Maybe it would have been better if he'd never known the truth. And if that were possible, then maybe knowing anything more would be a mistake.

"Dalton, no matter what you decide, talk it over with your mother. She deserves to know what your plans are in this matter." Kjell paused until Dalton turned to face him. "All of your life, she's only wanted to keep you safe. Her fear of what they might do to you kept her vigilant. I don't think she's ever really had a moment when she wasn't looking over her shoulder to make certain you weren't in danger."

"But—"

Kjell held up his hand. "Just hear me out, son. Your mother loves you—probably in a way that goes even deeper than the love she has for our girls. She almost lost you, and she knows she could lose you still."

"No one is going to steal me away. I'd feel sorry for the man who tried," Dalton said with a cocky grin.

"Maybe not physically, but emotionally or spiritually, it wouldn't be difficult to sway a man who wasn't on his guard. Your brothers are men who have spent their lives learning the art of manipulation. They are devious and conniving, and I have no reason to believe they have changed. I don't know them like your mother once did, but it would be wise to listen to her counsel. If you plan to go to them—to get to know them better—I ask only that you talk to your mother first. Heed her warnings and truly consider whether the changes you are making are going to be worth the price you'll pay."

———

Phoebe sat opposite her father at the dining table. Mother had hired a local Russian woman to cook and clean, and her father was not at all pleased.

"You should have consulted me," he told her.

"I thought the running of the household was to be my responsibility," her mother replied. "I have certain obligations and duties and cannot possibly hope to keep up with everything. The woman will not be living with us, so she needn't get in your way."

"Still, you know how I feel about strangers being amongst our things."

Phoebe had heard the argument with every move they'd made. Sooner or later, her mother would simply find a girl, despite her husband's protests.

"Her name is Darya Belikov. She comes highly recommended

by Mrs. Lindquist. Darya is the wife of a local boat builder and has four children of her own. They live just three blocks away. She will come around noon each day and clean the house, then prepare our dinner. I'll still be taking care of breakfast and the noon meal, so stop fretting."

"With two grown women in the house, hired help should be unnecessary."

Phoebe's mother smiled. "Yes, but I also have three men who care nothing for picking up after themselves and certainly have no talent at mending, laundry, or candle making."

Tired of the battle, Phoebe's father blew out a heavy breath and pushed away from the table. "I suppose if it must be." He got to his feet. "I won't be home until late. Lyman and I have a great many things to see to, not the least of which is a meeting we shall attend with a group of naval officials." He leaned over and kissed Phoebe's mother on the head. "I do hope you have a good day, my dear."

Once he'd gone, Phoebe picked up the breakfast plates and headed for the tiny kitchen. She had lived in much bigger houses in the past and found this small, run-down place to be adequate at best—that's all that could be said for it.

"I would think," she said as Mother joined her with the last of the breakfast things, "that Father would weary of this argument. You have the same conversation with each move."

Mother laughed. "I suppose we do. Still, it's his way. He knows we will have a cook and housekeeper, but he doesn't like it. He fears that someone might learn something about him that would cause scandal for his friend."

"But Father has an impeccable reputation," Phoebe said, shaking her head. "He's never been in trouble."

"Everyone has things in their past that they are ashamed to

admit to. Your father is no different. His family background does not always complement the man he's become today."

Phoebe knew about her grandfather's underhanded dealings and even the jail time he had served. He had owned a bank, and Phoebe's father had worked for him. When it came out that Grandfather had swindled a great many people, it was presumed that her father was also guilty. It seemed that society was only too happy to wrap future generations in the sins of their fathers.

"Well, I can't imagine that anyone in this isolated place would even care, much less try to use Father's family against him."

"Still, it grieves him. He had such high expectations for his future. If not for that bad fate, he might be the governor here or even president one day. At the very least, he might still own the bank his father started. Those who know the truth aren't about to let him forget, and those who want to know the secrets of his past will stop at nothing to learn them."

Phoebe knew her mother was right, but still it troubled her. Her father was a good man, and he deserved to stand on his own merits.

"I was wondering if you would mind making a trip out to the Lindquists for me," her mother said, suddenly changing the subject. "Mrs. Lindquist sent word that we could pick up some bear fat from their recent kill. I thought you might take the wagon and retrieve it. We'll see if we can work with it for the candles."

"We've never used bear before," Phoebe said skeptically. The worst part about making tallow candles was the smell of the fat. She could only imagine the odor of bear. Perhaps they could add extra frankincense to counteract the pungency of the wild animal. Then again, maybe it wouldn't be that bad. Perhaps bear fat was mild compared to that of ox or sheep, but she doubted it.

"We must experiment with what we have at hand," her mother

replied. "Mrs. Lindquist said candles would sell well here. Oh, and she told me she might very well be able to get us some beeswax."

"That would be wonderful." Candles made from the wax of bees were by far and away superior to any other, as far as Phoebe was concerned. "Do we have plenty of cream of tartar and alum for bleaching?"

Her mother tied on an apron. "I believe so. We will order more if need be. Your father said that the governor has assured us we needn't fret over supplies. He will ensure that our orders are combined with his own."

A fine mist fell as Phoebe made her way to the Lindquist place. She tried to wrestle with an umbrella and the reins for a time, to no avail. Giving up on keeping dry, Phoebe pressed on. Did it always rain in this place?

When Phoebe arrived, Miss Rockford was sitting on the porch, bent over her sewing. She gave a little wave and went back to work even as Phoebe drew the horse to a stop.

"Hello, Miss Rockford," Phoebe called as she lifted her umbrella. Dismounting with the cumbersome thing in hand, however, only added to Phoebe's frustration.

The older woman smiled. "Good morning to you."

Phoebe tried to shake off as much of the rain as possible. Zerelda got to her feet and motioned to the door. "Come on inside and dry by the fire. You mustn't get a chill."

Grateful for the warmth of the house, Phoebe settled onto a small stool by the fire and Miss Rockford returned with a cup of hot tea. "This will warm you from the inside," she told Phoebe.

"Thank you so much. I'm afraid I've not learned the secret of driving a wagon and keeping my head dry."

The woman laughed. "Up here, we gave up on such things long

ago. Most folks don't even worry about it. You'll know you're one of us when you give it no thought at all."

"It seems like it's always threatening rain or actually raining," Phoebe replied. "I had no idea it would be so damp all the time."

"We have our dry spells, too," Zerelda said with a grin. "Why, last month there was a whole twenty-four-hour period when it didn't rain even once."

Phoebe couldn't help but giggle. "Was there a celebration?"

"Of course. Folks closed their businesses and enjoyed the day. Before long, you'll get used to it."

"I can't imagine ever getting used to it. The isolation alone must surely be maddening."

"I suppose it depends on what a person is looking for in life. Sitka has much to offer in the way of peace and simplicity. I've come to greatly enjoy it."

Phoebe hoped she hadn't spoken out of turn. She truly hadn't meant to suggest that Sitka was a bad place. She sipped her tea, then offered an apology. "I'm sorry if I offended you. I'm just not used to this yet."

Miss Rockford laughed. "I could hardly expect that you are, and I'm not at all offended. I hope in turn I didn't offend you. I tend to be rather prideful when it comes to this place. It's a fault of mine that I haven't worked hard enough to overcome. Do you come from a large city?"

"No. Well, large compared to this place," Phoebe admitted. "We lived in the capital of Vermont—Montpelier. It isn't anything like Boston or New York, certainly."

"I've not ever been to either of those, but I do know something about Seattle and Portland. Those were big enough places for me."

Phoebe felt herself relax. Miss Rockford was openly honest, and Phoebe found that refreshing. "Miss Rockford, I was interested in what you had to say about the Tlingit people. I'd very much like to know more."

"Please call me Zerelda. Or better yet, Zee." Zerelda shifted and picked up the sewing she'd earlier deposited on the table. "I'm making some flannels for the girls. Winter will come soon enough, and they've both grown a great deal since last year. But as for the Tlingits, I'm not sure what to tell you. They have a rich history that is quite different from ours. Their cultural practices stand as a barrier between us at times, but I've come to care a great deal about them."

"What are they like? Mother is afraid, you know. We had one woman approach us, trying to sell us something, and it sent Mother into a fit of nerves."

Zerelda nodded. "The Tlingit are an industrious people. They've been quick to learn various trades—first from the Russians, and now from the Americans. My most sincere concerns for them are related to education, medicine, and spiritual matters. Father Donskoi and Sheldon Jackson have become rivals for their attention."

"Who are they?"

"Father Donskoi heads up the Russian Orthodox Church here, while Mr. Jackson established the Presbyterian mission and is the general agent for education in Alaska. Both are good men who have benevolent regard for the natives. However, both have issues when it comes to how they perform their duties."

"I see. Are the Tlingit people interested in what our churches and schools have to offer them?" Phoebe asked.

"Yes, I have found them to be very interested. They are no different from anyone else in seeking a better life for their children. They have been receptive to Christianity, although some are hard-pressed to put aside their old traditions. This is one of the reasons Brother Jackson wants to contract the Tlingit children to live at the Industrial School for five years. He wants to get them away from the customs and cultural issues of their people. He believes they will be better suited to learn and accept our ways if their own aren't presented constantly in conflict."

"I see."

Zerelda shook her head. "Unfortunately, Jackson's method of ministering has turned many away. The Orthodox Church doesn't demand as many changes and tries to come alongside and serve the people as an addition to their own culture. At the same time, they are encouraged to put aside the more harmful or less beneficial traditions. The Tlingit find that Father Donskoi meets them where they are—spends time in their village. He shows them respect and honor. They do not feel the same way about Brother Jackson and his people—at least not most of them."

"That is sad. I suppose, too, that the Tlingit have had a longer understanding of the Russians. Perhaps that also helps them to trust them more."

Zerelda nodded. "I believe it can. Of course, the man in charge prior to Father Donskoi was not as well liked. Many of the Tlingits who were a part of the church left because they felt he held them in contempt. There was a time when they believed the Russians only cared about them for the furs they could provide. The fur trade here was substantial. Now it has diminished, but you still see quite a bit going on."

"Oh yes, I know something about that already. My father has his eye on some nice pieces and hopes to have a coat made for my mother."

"She'll find a fur coat to be too hot for this area. A nice cape would serve her better."

Phoebe nodded. "I'll let her know." The clock chimed the hour, and Phoebe put aside her tea. "Oh my. I suppose I should load the bear fat and return home. Mother will be expecting me."

Zerelda glanced up. "Have you warmed up sufficiently? I wouldn't want you catching a cold. Summer colds are so miserable."

"I'm fine. I really enjoyed our visit. Maybe I could come another time and hear more about the island and the Tlingit people?"

Zerelda smiled. "I'd like that very much. Please feel free to come by any time. You needn't wait for an invitation."

"I'll remember that." Phoebe thought briefly of Dalton and how nice it might be to run into him, as well. Her cheeks warmed at the memory of their last encounter. Stumbling over the edge of the rug, Phoebe barely caught herself before crashing headlong into the back of Zerelda.

Goodness, but I've become such a clumsy oaf since moving to Sitka. If I'm not careful people will think me teched in the head. She straightened and realized Zerelda hadn't even noticed. With a sigh, Phoebe continued on her way. It would be best to keep thoughts of Dalton at arm's length. At least until she could be seated and not hurt herself or anyone else.

Chapter 6

July 1889

*P*hoebe anticipated the upcoming dance to welcome the new governor as much as a visit to the dentist. She had never really cared for parties, and while most of her friends were overjoyed at the prospect of dancing the night away, Phoebe longed only for the quiet of her room.

"Ma says you'd better hurry," her brother Theodore called from outside her door. "She said she and Pa are supposed to arrive with the governor, and that means we need to, also."

"I'll be right there."

Phoebe worked at a stubborn curl, hoping to pin it securely. Her hair never wanted to cooperate when it really mattered. Studying the result in the mirror, Phoebe felt as satisfied as she could. Her long blond hair cascaded in ringlets from the top of her head and down her back. She'd learned how to create the popular style from the governor's wife.

The gown she'd chosen was one of her newer ones, made just before they'd come to Sitka. Cut from a lovely shade of pink silk, the underskirt stood out in sharp contrast to the plum- and pink-striped overskirt. The bodice was a combination of both colors, arranged with a gentle sweeping neckline.

Phoebe sighed and took up her gloves. Already, she'd had numerous men come courting. Her mother assured her that it wasn't unusual in a place where the men outnumbered the women ten to one. However, Phoebe was uncomfortable with all of the attention. Especially since the attention thus far hadn't included Dalton Lindquist.

"Well, here you are at last," her father declared. "Come along or we'll be late."

"You look like a pink circus tent," her little brother announced.

"Grady, that was unkind. Phoebe looks nothing of the sort," their mother admonished.

"Well, remember that circus we went to last year? The tent was all striped and—"

"Do be quiet," Mother demanded. "We are about to join the governor and his wife."

Grady giggled and poked Theodore in the side. Phoebe shook her head. It promised to be a long evening.

There was great pomp and ceremony—at least as much as the people of Sitka could arrange. Phoebe was impressed with the festivities, but even more so with the ensemble that played for the event. Having loved music all of her life, Phoebe had once performed with Montpelier's orchestra, playing her flute. In fact, her music was the one thing that had kept her sane on the long trip by ship to Alaska.

To Phoebe's surprise, Lydia Lindquist appeared to be the leader of the little orchestra. Dressed impeccably in a gown of dark gold, the woman was a striking figure as she spoke to her fellow musicians. Phoebe could see that along with Lydia and her violin, there was a cellist, a French horn player, and guitar player, as well as a pianist. She'd already heard some of the music they'd created. It was amazing they could get such a beautiful sound from so few instruments.

Perhaps they would let me join, she thought. What a joy that would be. She missed her music more than anything else.

Just then she saw Dalton make his way through the crowd. He spoke momentarily to his mother, then moved to the side. Phoebe suddenly got an idea. If Dalton wouldn't come to her, then perhaps she could approach him on the excuse of asking about the orchestra.

She started to make her way toward him. Just then the music began and the governor and his wife stepped forward to start the dance. Phoebe had barely taken two steps when a tall man dressed in black asked her for the dance. She had been unprepared for the question, even though she knew she was one of the few unattached young women. Nodding, she allowed herself to be led onto the dance floor.

Phoebe tried to keep track of where Dalton was. At the moment he was standing with another young man, deep in conversation. Where Dalton was dark haired, the other man was blond. They were about the same height and weight, and both looked quite capable of doing a hard day's work.

Another man approached Phoebe and her partner, not even waiting for the music to end. They quickly exchanged Phoebe as if by earlier agreement. As the new stranger danced her away, he introduced himself.

"Reginald Cavendish, at your service. I hope you don't mind

that I stepped in. We have so few women with whom to dance that we rarely wait for the break of a song."

Phoebe nodded. "I was surprised, I must say."

"You should get used to it. Most dances will find you with three or four partners before the music concludes. If I'm not mistaken, we are being approached even now."

She glanced over her shoulder to see an older man draw near. He smiled in greeting, revealing a missing tooth. Phoebe recognized him as one of the store owners, but for the life of her, she couldn't remember his name.

And so the evening went. Phoebe found herself passed from man to man, all in the name of good manners and fun. She hated to disappoint anyone, but after dancing for nearly an hour, Phoebe felt a desperate desire to leave the party. When the orchestra took a break, Phoebe decided it would be the perfect moment to excuse herself.

Making her way through a gathering of Sitka wives, she paused only long enough to allow her mother to introduce her to several women. Phoebe smiled and made all the appropriate replies to their questions.

"I hope you'll excuse me," she finally said, turning a hopeful gaze toward her mother's watchful eye. "I need a bit of air."

"Don't go too far," her mother warned. "Better yet, try to find one of your brothers to accompany you."

Phoebe nodded but had no intention of asking her brothers for help. She hurried from the room and bounded out the door.

Right into the arms of Dalton Lindquist.

"Running away?" he asked.

She looked up, mortified to have once again entangled herself with the handsome man. Phoebe tried to turn and free herself from his hold, but Dalton held her secure.

"You sure have a way of creating a scene."

Phoebe felt the heat rise in her cheeks. Why must she always be doing the wrong thing when in the presence of the only man she wanted to impress? She pulled her elbow free from his grasp. "Yes, first by falling out of the boat, and now this."

"Don't forget our mishap at the house," he interjected.

"How could I--especially with your lovely reminder."

She lowered her face and wished silently that the earth would swallow her up. Why did it have to be so light outside? He could, no doubt, see her embarrassment.

He laughed, making her all the more uncomfortable. Phoebe fought the urge to reprimand him as she might one of her brothers.

"You really shouldn't take yourself so seriously," he said.

Phoebe looked up at this. "I beg your pardon?"

"You worry too much. Folks around here hardly care that you fell into the harbor. They care more about the fact that you're all right and suffered no ill effects. Sure, it gives everyone something to talk about for a time, but so what? It's not like they can go to the opera for entertainment." His face held a mischievous grin, and his expression almost dared her to contradict his comment.

"Well, I don't like to make a spectacle of myself." She frowned. "But I seem to have a proclivity for it."

"Then it would be best to learn to laugh at yourself, don't you think?"

She gazed into his eyes and momentarily forgot what she was going to say. All Phoebe could think about was how much she wanted to touch his face. Instead, she forced herself to turn away.

"I was hoping to ask you about the orchestra," she said, brushing nonexistent lint from her sleeve.

"What about it?"

"I wondered if your mother was in charge. I mean, it appeared to me that she was leading the group."

Dalton nodded. "Mother has always had a great passion for music. She said her violin has been the friend she's known the longest."

"I can well understand. I play the flute and feel the same."

"My father and I play guitar. You probably saw him among the musicians."

Phoebe remembered the man, although she'd never met him. "Yes. I was very impressed with the quality of their performance. Especially with so few members. Do you suppose your mother would be at all interested in attaining another musician?"

Dalton chuckled. "She would be delighted. She always bemoans the fact that there are so few people with an interest in such things. You should definitely approach her about it. They practice whenever time permits and are generally asked to play at every gathering."

"Well, that would certainly excuse me from dancing," Phoebe said without thinking.

"And why would you want to do that?" he asked. "I thought you were quite skillful at it."

Phoebe shot him a glance. "You saw me?"

"Of course. Yuri and I were discussing your arrival and decided you were by far and away the prettiest addition to the party."

His statement took her off guard. It wasn't that Phoebe hadn't heard men boldly speak their minds before, but she somehow hadn't expected it from Dalton Lindquist. She quickly changed the focus of their conversation.

"Who is Yuri?"

"He's my friend. I work with him and his father building boats."

"Was he the tall blond man?"

"So you noticed him, eh? Now I'm jealous."

"You needn't be. I couldn't help it. I . . . uh . . . well, I was looking at your mother and the orchestra, and then you went up

74

to speak to her. Later, after you left, you were talking to the blond man."

"Oh, so it was me you were watching."

She felt her cheeks warm again. "I . . . well . . ." What could she say?

"Come on, the dancing is about to start up again," someone announced behind Phoebe.

Other people rushed past Dalton and Phoebe as the melody of a familiar waltz began. Phoebe didn't know what to do. If she headed back inside, she would have to continue dancing.

"Shall we join them?" Dalton asked.

"What?" Phoebe wasn't exactly sure what he was saying.

"Would you like to dance—with me?"

Phoebe felt as if she'd swallowed her tongue. All she could do was nod and accept Dalton's arm as he led her back into the building. She trembled as he pulled her closer. She placed her hand on his shoulder and marveled at Dalton's firm muscles.

He said nothing as he maneuvered her around the room, weaving in and out of the other dancers. Phoebe wanted the moment to go on forever but knew it wouldn't. Even now, Dalton's friend Yuri was approaching to take her away from the only man with whom she wanted to dance.

"My turn," Yuri said, tapping Dalton and stepping into his place.

Phoebe took hold of Yuri and watched as Dalton moved aside. She tried her best to mask her feelings.

"I'm Yuri Belikov," the young man announced. "My mother is your housekeeper."

"Phoebe Robbins," she replied, amazed that no one stood on ceremony in this tiny town. The rules of society were observed but hardly imposed.

"You do realize that you're the most beautiful girl in the room," he said.

She wasn't sure what to say. His comment made her feel uncomfortable, but she knew he was only being nice. "Thank you. I'm not at all convinced that it's true, but you are very generous to say so." She immediately regretted her words, hoping that he wouldn't think she was seeking further compliments. Phoebe quickly asked, "Is Belikov a Russian name?"

He smiled. "It is. My family is originally from Russia. My father and mother came here when they were just married."

"Have you ever been to Russia?"

He shook his head. "It's often been discussed. My mother would like to go back. Her mother isn't well, and her sisters want her to come home."

"And will you go?"

A man was approaching them and Phoebe knew she would once again be handed off. Yuri apparently was unwilling to lose her company just yet and whisked her in the opposite direction.

"I'm sorry about that, but I've not had you for more than a few moments. He can wait his turn. Besides, I happen to know he smells like fish and doesn't dance well at all."

Phoebe suppressed a giggle. She had not expected such a comment, and it somehow put her at ease with this friend of Dalton's. She glanced up to find his blue eyes watching her. She smiled. "So I asked if you would go with your family to Russia?"

He gave her a rather wicked grin. "Not if there's a reason to stay."

Dalton couldn't help but notice the smug look of satisfaction that Yuri wore. He'd managed to keep Phoebe with him throughout the rest of the waltz and only now had relinquished her to another man.

"So did you see us dancing?" Yuri asked. "I think we make a great pair, don't you?"

A twinge of jealousy sliced through Dalton's heart, but he ignored it. His sister Evie had just joined them, and he didn't want her questioning his attitude. Rather than reply to Yuri's comment, he turned to Evie.

"You look tired."

"I'm exhausted. I can't believe how many times I've danced. I'm more than ready to return home, but I know I'd never get away with it." She smiled at Yuri. "How are you doing?"

"I am well. We were just talking about Miss Phoebe Robbins."

"She is quite pretty, don't you think?"

"I do indeed," Yuri answered. "I was just telling Dalton that I thought we made a great pair."

Dalton couldn't shake the growing sensation of wanting to hit Yuri in the mouth. Evie glanced at Dalton, but he looked away as if needing to tend to something else. If she saw his expression, she'd know his feelings readily enough, and he didn't want to have to explain. Besides, how could he explain when he didn't understand, himself?

"You still haven't danced with me, brother of mine."

Dalton was surprised by this. "I thought you were exhausted."

She took hold of his arm. "Never too tired to dance with my brother."

They set out onto the floor and began to join the others. Evie smiled conspiratorially. "You looked like you needed a reason to get away from Yuri."

Dalton wasn't sure what to say on the matter. "Sometimes he talks too much."

"He seems interested in Phoebe Robbins."

"I suppose so."

"Dalton, if you like her, you had best fight for her."

He looked at Evie in complete surprise. "What are you talking about?"

She laughed and motioned to the door. "Come with me."

Dalton followed his sister outside, more than a little curious about what she would say. He waited until they'd walked a few steps from the front entry before asking, "Why did you say that?"

Evie stopped and turned. "Dalton, it's clear that you are, at the very least, fascinated with Miss Robbins. And it's further evident to me that she's more than a little taken with you. If you are interested in her, you need to fight for her instead of just handing her over to Yuri."

"Who said I was handing her over to him?"

His sister smiled. "You need to make sure that Yuri knows you are interested. He's done nothing but bait a reaction from you. It's time you took a stand. If she means nothing, then let it drop."

Dalton shook his head. "I don't know what I feel. I like her looks, and she's nice to talk to." He knew there was something more, but he wasn't yet ready to say what that was.

Evie smoothed the skirt of her gown. "You don't have to be ready to propose marriage in order to challenge Yuri's comments. Simply let him know that you are interested in Phoebe, as well, and that you don't intend to stand idly by while he tries to win her over for himself." She gently patted Dalton's arm. "Look, finding the right person to spend your life with is so important. My own miseries are proof of that. Please don't let the chance for true love pass you by."

Her voice was so intense, so full of emotion, that Dalton couldn't help but put his arm around Evie. "I'm sorry that you didn't have a chance for love. You are one of the most beautiful, special women I know. Your heart is pure gold."

She smiled up at him. "I have missed the romance, but not

love itself. I have you and the rest of the family. I might never have known that, and my life would be much poorer."

"Haven't you ever heard from . . . him?" Dalton asked hesitantly. "I mean, in all these years, hasn't your husband ever sent you a single letter? Any word at all?"

"No," Evie admitted. "Our sister Jeannette sometimes writes me about him." She tilted her head. "I'm so sorry there have been so many secrets between you and me. Jeannette is a rather disastrous person. She has never been happy—even as a child. I find her annoying and ridiculous in most everything she says and does." She shrugged. "But she does keep me informed about things. She loves to gossip, and it seems to serve her purpose to write to me. I write her back from time to time, but never in detail and not very often."

Dalton dropped his hold. "Our family is so disjointed—so strange." He walked a little ways farther and stared out at the fading sunlight on the water.

Evie reached for him. "Let's get back to the party. You need to make your intentions known to Yuri."

Dalton allowed her to pull him along, but he still wasn't convinced. "What do I say?"

She laughed. "Well, the next time he comments on what a great couple they'd make, tell him you don't think so. Tell him you think you and Phoebe make a better pair."

Once they were back amongst the festivities, Dalton didn't have long to wait to say just that. Yuri was determined to goad him. It was as if he knew how his friend felt and couldn't resist adding to his misery.

"I danced again with Phoebe. I think she's just about the most beautiful woman I've ever seen."

"I agree."

This seemed to amuse Yuri. He turned to face Dalton. "I knew it. I knew you liked her, too."

"Of course I do. She's not only pretty; she's charming and smart."

Yuri moved in closer. "She looks better with me."

"That's your opinion." Dalton shrugged. "So now what? We both like the same girl. Do we take it outside and let our fists decide?"

Yuri laughed out loud. "You couldn't whip me. Besides, where's the fun in that? I say we make a bet on who can win her. After all, you're the rich man now. Surely you can afford to spare a little for a friendly wager."

"Since when do you gamble? My mother would never let me hear the end of it if I did such a thing," Dalton countered. "Your mother would be the same."

"Our mothers don't need to even know about it. We're men, and men gamble."

"Not all men."

"Men who aren't tied to their mother's apron strings do."

"So you are gambling these days?"

"I do what I like. I'm grown up now—who should say I can't do this or that?"

"Some things are just sensible, Yuri."

With great exasperation, Yuri waved his hands in the air. "So we don't say it's a bet. Let's call it a contest. I believe I can win Phoebe Robbins for myself by the time the winter ball comes round."

"I'll have her for my own before first snow," Dalton declared. He knew it was a foolhardy move. He should never have agreed to any kind of challenge where Phoebe's feelings were concerned.

Yuri rubbed his chin thoughtfully. "The winner gets Phoebe, while the loser . . ."

He said nothing for a moment. Dalton could only imagine the

misery of being the loser. He didn't like the way this conversation had turned out at all. Evie had said to take a stand, and all he'd managed to do was concoct a game of hearts.

"The loser doesn't," Dalton said before Yuri could add anything more.

His friend looked at him oddly. "What do you mean?"

"You said the winner gets Phoebe. I'm saying that the loser won't get her. That's loss enough. I don't like the idea of playing games where such important matters are at stake."

Laughing, Yuri gave him a playful punch on the arm. "You're just afraid that I'll win."

Dalton said nothing in reply. He was afraid. Afraid he was already losing his heart and had no control over the outcome.

"Now come on. I know where we can get something stiffer to drink than this punch."

"Yuri, you know I don't drink. My folks don't drink, either. We're pretty much temperance people, if you want to know the truth."

"You're missing out on a great deal of fun," Yuri assured him. "But have it your way."

"Your folks won't approve," Dalton interjected.

"My folks don't have to know. Besides, I am a man. I make my own decisions."

Chapter 7

*T*he arrival of the steamship *Corona* was reason for excitement in the town. Dalton knew there would be a crowd to contend with, but he had promised his mother that if the ship arrived he would bring the mail home with him that evening. He waited his turn at the post office, glad that he'd not come earlier. The sorting of letters and packages was done with meticulous attention to detail, much to the frustration of those who'd come as soon as the mail had been delivered. Everyone was anxious for information—for word from home or loved ones. It was cause for celebration in this island town.

When Dalton was finally handed a stack of letters, he had to fight his way back through the crowd of people. Once outside, his focus was immediately drawn to the letter on top. The return address indicated it was from Mrs. Jeannette Stone. His sister.

Here was a woman he didn't know—had never met—yet she was as much a sister to him as Evie. He touched the letter, lingering over the feminine handwriting. Who was this woman? Did she ever think about him—wonder about the brother who'd been born to her stepmother?

He frowned. So many unanswered questions. Would there ever be a chance to set it all straight?

"Dalton?"

He looked up to find Phoebe. She smiled, and he couldn't help but feel guilty for the conversation he'd had with Yuri. What was he thinking, agreeing to a contest of hearts?

"Hello." He felt rather tongue-tied.

"Mother came to see if the ship brought the rest of our things," she offered.

"I came for the mail."

For a moment, neither one said anything. Dalton noted the blue of Phoebe's eyes and the way her nose turned up just a bit at the tip. She had the most charming face—rather like an angel. He shook his head. This was getting him nowhere.

"I had a nice time at the dance," she said, breaking the silence. "You dance quite well."

"Uh, thanks. I suppose it's because my mother insisted I learn. How about you?" *What a dumb question*, he thought. She's going to think me an absolute bore.

"I learned to dance in Vermont. It came in handy when two of my friends married earlier this year."

Dalton nodded, uncertain what else to say. He wanted to ask if she had a suitor—if she'd considered marriage. He wanted to know how she had learned to dance, and what her life in Vermont had been like. Instead, he glanced down at the mail. "I guess I'd better head on home."

"Good day to you, then," she told him rather formally. Without another word, she turned and walked back up the street.

Dalton wasn't sure if he'd offended her or if it was just her way. Picking up speed, he headed the opposite direction. He was just passing the sawmill when Joshua stepped out the door to his private quarters.

"Are you heading home?" he asked Dalton.

"I am. What of you?"

"I'm going your way. If you'd like a ride, I have the wagon ready and waiting. I have some wood to deliver to your father. It's for the smokehouse."

"He'll be glad to get it, I'm sure. I know Mother and Aunt Zee have been anxious to get that project finished up so they can smoke fish."

They walked around to the side of the building, where two lanky Russian boys were securing the load. Joshua's large draft horses pawed anxiously at the ground. Dalton rubbed the velvet muzzle of the horse nearest him.

"Easy, boy. We'll soon be on our way."

The horse bobbed his head as if in agreement. Joshua climbed atop the wagon to inspect the load, then instructed his help to clean up inside before heading home. Dalton climbed onto the wagon as Joshua came forward to take his seat.

"How are the roads between here and home?" he asked Dalton.

"A little wet in spots, but not too bad. I don't think we should have too much trouble—not with these boys."

"They were well worth the money I paid to bring them up from Seattle," Joshua said, releasing the brake. He gave a gentle slap of the rein. "Come on now, get up there."

The horses pulled against their harnesses with minimal effort and began the slow plodding walk from the alleyway to the street. Dalton was glad for the ride and grateful for Joshua's company.

"So, how goes the boat building business?" Joshua asked.

"Not too bad. There hasn't been a big demand of late, and that has Mr. Belikov worried. Then, too, his wife's family has been nagging her to go home to Russia. It creates a source of frustration for him, which tends to trickle down to Yuri and me."

"Funny how that works," Joshua said with a grin. "When the boss is out of sorts, everyone suffers."

Dalton nodded and turned to study the harbor for a moment. "I've given a lot of thought to what I want to do—especially if he does close shop and head back to Russia."

"And what did you conclude?"

"I really enjoy making boats. I'd like to open my own shop. I've been thinking that with more and more folks heading up our way, it can't be too long before it could be quite profitable. I'm wondering, however, if maybe I should keep my sights low—make smaller launches and such. Then if someone wants to commission a larger boat, that would be bonus income."

"And the smaller boats would, no doubt, sell more easily."

"And if not here, then possibly in Juneau or elsewhere," Dalton added. "Mr. Belikov tends to be short-sighted when it comes to planning for the future. Maybe it's because he knows they will sooner or later return to Russia and he doesn't want to commit to too lengthy a project."

"I suppose I would be of the same mind," Joshua replied. "It wouldn't do to promise a product and be unable to make good on it."

"Still, there is great industry here. I've heard talk about additional canneries—and, of course, that will require larger catches of fish."

Joshua gave a shrug. "An island town will always need boats, my friend."

"And if things slow down, my father is always willing to have my help."

"Kjell has found himself much busier this summer, what with the new governor and his people. I heard there are plans for several new homes."

"It's true," Dalton confirmed. "Father put together several teams to assist him, but finding quality laborers has been difficult. He takes great pride in his work and refuses to simply slap together a place for the sake of finishing it."

"I've always admired that about him. Your father has a sense of honor and responsibility that has given him a well-earned reputation. No doubt, that is why the governor and his people have gone to him for help."

They rounded the bend and took the turn for the Lindquist property. Dalton glanced down again at the letters in his hand.

"You were here when my mother came to Sitka."

Joshua startled and laughed. "Yes, but what does that have to do with building houses and boats?"

"I'm just now learning the details of what happened after I was born. Mother being shot and my brother taking me."

"Your father mentioned that you were asking questions. It's been suppressed for so long that I've forgotten many of the details."

He frowned. "What do you remember?"

"That your father lost his heart the first time he laid eyes on your mother."

Dalton had often heard his father comment on meeting his mother and how she fainted dead in his arms. He'd spoken with great fondness of the memory, and how this was when he first fell in love with her. Dalton thought of Phoebe Robbins and their first encounter. The similarities were not lost on him.

Dalton could see the house ahead and hear his sisters at play. He turned to Josh. "What about when I was taken?"

"It nearly killed Kjell. He loved you both so much, and for Lydia to be so close to death . . ." Joshua shook his head. "They thought for a time that you were dead. The men had planned it that way—the ones who took you."

"Probably my brother's plan."

"I'm sure it was. I never understood how he was able to avoid paying the price for his part."

"Mother says that with enough money, you can buy yourself in or out of nearly everything."

"Kjell wasn't able to leave her side," Joshua continued. "He turned the sawmill over to me, and I doubt he ever gave it another thought. He only wanted to know that she would be all right. Then when she did recover but couldn't remember anything, well, it broke his heart all over again."

The girls came running as Joshua drove the wagon back to the workshop. Kjell appeared in the doorway as they brought the horses to a halt.

"We can talk more about this another time," Joshua told Dalton before turning to Kjell. "I've got that lumber you asked for. Where do you want it?"

Dalton climbed down from the wagon wishing they'd had more time. His father took Dalton's place. "Let's take it on down behind Zee's. We'll just stack it there."

"I'll be down to help after I take in the mail," Dalton told them.

"Did I get anything in the mail?" Kjerstin asked as the wagon moved out.

Dalton tugged one of her pigtails. "Now, why would you ask such a question? Have you ever received any mail?"

She gave her head a slight shake and lifted her chin in a pose of exasperation. "But that doesn't mean I never will. Someday I might get a whole bunch of letters."

"And who would be sending those letters, missy?" he asked playfully.

"A boy," Britta interjected. She giggled and covered her mouth.

Kjerstin was unconcerned with her sister's teasing. "I might get a letter from a boy. You just never know."

Dalton laughed and reached out to hug his sister close. "You will probably get more letters than you can keep up with. I shall have to watch after you very carefully when the men come to court. I won't stand for any nonsense."

————

Evie looked at the letter from Jeannette and sighed. She started to put it aside, then thought better of it. It was nearly dinnertime, but Lydia and Zee had things well under control. She opened the envelope and pulled out the single sheet of paper. How strange that there was so little news. Jeannette usually filled pages with all manner of gossip.

> *Genevieve,*
> *You must return to Kansas City at the earliest possibility. Your husband is gravely ill and is not expected to live.*

Evie reached for the nearest chair and sat down before continuing.

> *He has asked for you multiple times and begs for us to send you to him. I know this letter may not reach you in time, but you must come. We've arranged a train ticket to be waiting for you at the station in Seattle. The journey will no doubt be quite arduous, but there seemed no other choice.*

*No matter the past, you must come. You are his wife and it
is expected that you should be at his side.*

The letter ended there. Nothing more—nothing to state what
illness had befallen Thomas Gadston. No mention of why he had
asked for her.

"You look as though you've swallowed a fly," Lydia said, coming
to set the table.

Evie looked up, and Lydia immediately sobered. "What's
wrong?" There was fear in her voice.

"It's Thomas. He's dying." She straightened and folded the letter.
"At least that's what Jeannette says. He's asking for me."

Lydia put the dishes on the table and sat down beside Evie.
"When was the letter written?"

Opening the letter again, Evie noted the date. "June sixth."

"That's over a month ago." Lydia shook her head. "You don't
suppose he's still . . . well . . . alive?"

"I don't know. She doesn't say at all what's wrong with him, and
given Jeannette's penchant for exaggeration, who can know if she's
even telling the truth. He might not have anything more serious
than a cold. She could be trying to trick me into coming home."

Lydia folded her hands and considered this for a moment. "But
to what purpose?"

Evie wished she knew. She couldn't help but feel as though
she were drowning. Her chest was tight and air seemed unable to
pass to her lungs. What was she to do? Should she go home? If
she did, would she be able to return to Sitka?

"I don't know what to do," she murmured. "Jeannette says a
train ticket has been arranged for me in Seattle." She looked up
at Lydia. "I don't want to go."

Lydia reached out and put her arm around Evie. "I don't really see how you can avoid this. Even if he's already passed, you have an obligation to settle his affairs."

"Surely he has people for that. I've been gone for eighteen years. No one would even imagine that I'd return."

"Your sister would," Lydia reminded her.

Evie looked at the letter and tossed it aside. "I don't care what Jeannette wants. She's such a ninny. No one thinks like she does."

"I don't know what to say." Lydia dropped her hold. "He's your husband, and he is asking for you. He may well be hanging on just to see you again. Perhaps he hopes to apologize."

Getting to her feet, Evie looked at Lydia in disbelief. "Apologize? Apologize for never loving me? For hiring his secretary to seduce me? Perhaps he should apologize for never uttering one word to me in nearly a score of years." She began to pace. "I see no reason to adhere to his request. He cannot simply snap his fingers after all these years and expect me to come running."

"You're upset, and with good reason. You need to take some time to think this through before making a decision." Lydia stood. "Evie, don't be rash about this matter. You might well make a choice that you'll end up regretting for the rest of your life."

"Like allowing my father to force me into a loveless marriage? Oh, that's right; I had no say on that point. Neither did you, as I recall." Her snide tone caused Lydia to wince, and Evie immediately regretted her attitude. "I'm sorry, Lydia. I'm so sorry. None of this is your fault, yet here I am taking it out on you."

Lydia embraced her. Evie resisted at first, then fell against her as her last bit of strength fled. "Why couldn't Jeannette simply have written to say he was dead? Why couldn't the matter be settled without my participation?"

"Evie, God has a plan and purpose for everything. We cannot always see it or understand why it should happen. Usually, that isn't even as important as remembering that we can trust Him to see us through."

"I want to trust Him," Evie admitted. "I don't want to be so weak and frightened in this. I really don't. I just don't know what to do."

Lydia pulled back and smiled. "Often admitting our weakness and fear is the first step to finding rest in God. Our trust in Him isn't conveyed through superhuman confidence, as much as it comes in the way of a childlike reliance on Him."

"But I don't know how to do that."

"I think very few people fall into it naturally. I found that I had to pray a great deal to learn to let God take charge. When we don't know what to do, we must pray. Not as a last resort, but rather as the first step to finding true understanding and peace."

Evie nodded. "I know you are right. I know you are." The tears began to fall. "I just don't know what to even say. I don't know what to pray."

"Then we will ask God for that, as well. We will ask for His will to be done—for His direction to be revealed. We will give it over to Him and trust that the answer will be made plain."

Chapter 8

*A*t breakfast the next morning, Evie announced she would go to Kansas City. Though it went against everything inside her, it was the only way to put an end to the past. If her husband had already died, then she would be truly free. If he hadn't, she could at least hope to make peace with him and then return to Alaska.

Kjell picked up his coffee mug and before sipping said, "It seems to me that this would be the perfect opportunity for Dalton to meet the rest of his family."

Evie felt as if the air had been sucked from the room. Kjell continued, "I think it would give Lydia peace of mind to know that Evie is with him, to offer protection of a sort. And he can do likewise for her."

Lydia looked down at her plate. "I suppose it would be the sensible solution."

"What do you think, son?"

Dalton looked to his father. "I guess I wasn't supposing an opportunity would present itself so soon." He glanced at Evie. "Would you want my company?"

"I would value it greatly. It's a long, arduous trip back to Missouri—not for the faint of heart. Of course, I've not made the journey in eighteen years, so perhaps it has improved." She smiled. "And though you don't remember it, you were there. How strange. We made that trip together. I was your protector, and now you will be mine."

"A rather strange legacy," Lydia murmured. "But I have often found such completed circles in my own life."

"Would we stay long?" Dalton asked.

Evie shook her head. "Not if I have anything to say about it. I don't want to go in the first place, but I know it's expected."

"There will be legal matters to settle," Lydia mentioned.

Evie's head swam with thoughts of what would have to be done. "If Thomas is dead. If he's not, then I'll have to decide about waiting around or returning. I really have no interest in sitting by his deathbed."

"I think you'd hate yourself if you didn't go," Kjell said in a sympathetic tone. "A lot of times in life, we find ourselves faced with tasks we'd rather not do, but to leave them undone will only cause more discomfort in the long run."

"I know. I've considered all of that, and that is why I have decided to go back." Evie pushed her uneaten meal away and leaned back in her chair. "I think having Dalton with me might well give me the strength I need."

She turned to face him. "I can pay you for the time you'll be away from your job."

"It's not necessary. Apparently, I'm heir to a great fortune." He looked at his mother and winked.

"You mean like up in the air?" Britta questioned. She shook her head. "How can Dalton be up in the air?"

"Heir with an *h*, not air," their mother corrected. "It means that Dalton has inherited money."

"Where did the money come from?" Britta asked. "Is there money for me, too?"

Dalton reached over and pulled gently on her earlobe. "And whatever would you do with money, Miss Britta? All of your needs are provided for. Money would just get you into trouble."

"Well, I could have some pretty dresses and a new doll," she said. "And a horse of my own. I really want a horse of my own."

Everyone gave a laugh at this. Britta had been asking for a horse for as long as anyone could remember. Her father had tried to explain to her that livestock was expensive to keep on the island and that any such animal had to earn its keep, not merely be around to entertain young ladies.

"If I had lots of money, I could pay for his hay." She looked to her mother. "So do I have a air-a-tance, too?"

"We will discuss that at a more appropriate time. Right now, if you don't finish your breakfast, you'll be late for school. Zee is already hitching the wagon to take you and Kjerstin. Now eat."

"I need to get to work," Dalton said, getting up from the table. He looked down at Evie. "I will go with you to Kansas City. It seems to me God has opened this door to the both of us as a means to put our pasts to rest."

In that moment, Evie knew it, as well. She nodded. "We will need to leave right away."

She sat at the table nursing her tea long after everyone else had gone. Lydia cleared the table in silence, but Evie could very nearly hear her unasked questions. Looking up, she caught Lydia watching her. "He'll be fine. I won't let any harm come to him."

Lydia nodded and stopped what she was doing. "I just . . .

well . . . I worry that Marston and Mitchell will try to manipulate him."

"I know, but I'll fight against that happening."

"You'll have your own needs to see to," Lydia replied.

"But I'll have Dalton stay with me. We'll get rooms at a hotel." Evie frowned. "Unless Thomas is dead, and then we can go to the house."

She tried not to think about life in Kansas City. She had put that part of her life out of her mind for so long that Evie honestly didn't know how to deal with the matter. What would it be like to see Thomas again? What would her brothers and sister be like? Everyone had aged, no doubt, but what had the years done to their personalities and attitudes? She had given witness against her own brother. Marston wasn't one to easily forget that fact. He would no doubt hate her for her interference—for taking Dalton away from them.

"It won't be easy," Lydia said in a whisper.

Evie met her gaze. "No." If anyone understood the depths of this matter, it was Lydia.

"Perhaps you shouldn't go," Lydia said suddenly. "What if they mean you harm?"

"I don't know. I've considered that myself." Evie knew her brothers could be cruel, just as their father had been. She didn't trust any of them—not even Jeannette. "It comforts me to know that Dalton will be with me, however. He is strong, Lydia."

The woman sat down and leaned back in her chair. "Yes. Yes, he is. I've raised him not to hate, but to embrace life and do good. Part of the reason I never spoke of his brothers and Jeannette was because I didn't want him to hear the ugliness in my account of them."

"You did a good thing in that," Evie said.

"Still, there is so much anger and hatred in the facts of what happened. I know Dalton will go and meet them—see for himself who they are. And I don't believe they have changed." She leaned forward with a piercing look. "I know that sounds awful, but there are some people who simply aren't redeemable."

"I've no doubt that you're right. Jeannette's detailed accounts of the family and their doings proves that to me, if nothing else. Marston associates with many underhanded people. Mitchell too. They don't care about anything but themselves and the money they can make. That's why I'm not worried about Dalton. He won't be deceived by that."

"But they will show him opulence and power," Lydia countered. "It will be a completely different world to him. He will be tempted—everyone is."

"Then we must pray for his strength to be multiplied and his focus to remain on the Lord." Evie leaned forward. "Lydia, I don't think Dalton will be distracted by those things. He is searching not for possessions, but for an understanding of who his family was—who they are now. Marston and Mitchell won't be able to disguise their true natures for long. Even if they pretend to have the hearts of saints, Dalton will see right through them."

Lydia considered this for a moment, then nodded very slowly. "You're right, I know. He's a good man. He's young and inexperienced in the wicked ways of others, but he's intelligent."

"And so am I," Evie added. "And I bear the scars to prove how hard-fought that intelligence came. Together, we will be a force to be reckoned with."

———

Dalton hadn't expected to see Phoebe Robbins in town that morning, but there she was, like a ray of sunshine brightening everything around her. "Good morning," he said, feeling that same awkward sense of displacement he'd felt before.

"We always seem to meet at the most unexpected times," Phoebe said. She pushed back a single long braid of hair and smiled. "I have to say, it's a most pleasant surprise."

"I was thinking the same." He wanted to say something about the trip he would take but couldn't think how to bring up the subject. Instead, he thought of how lovely she looked in her flower-print dress. "You are very pretty, Miss Robbins."

She blushed and looked away. "That was a rather bold thing to say."

He laughed. "Well, I believe in telling the truth. Why play around with words when speaking what's on your heart is more important?"

Phoebe looked up just long enough to catch his gaze. "And what is on your heart, Mr. Lindquist?"

"A great many things," he revealed.

"I see. I must admit, I have a great many things on my heart, as well. Like a certain gentleman I've just come to know."

"Now who's being bold?"

She feigned confusion. "Why whatever do you mean? I was merely referring to Mr. Seymour."

"Arnie?" Dalton asked with a grin. "And what in the world placed Mr. Seymour on your heart?"

She shrugged. "He seems a lonely man. Has he no wife?"

"Women are at a premium around here. You'll soon learn for yourself that suitors will come calling in great numbers. Arnie might even give it a try."

"Oh, he's much too old for me, and not at all the kind of man I would fancy to court."

Dalton couldn't help but smile. "And what kind of man do you fancy?"

She tapped her finger against her chin thoughtfully. "I prefer the type who are industrious, creative . . . educated, but not too educated." Phoebe paused and shrugged. "I can't really put it into words, but I'll know him when I find him."

"So you are looking."

"Looking?" she questioned.

"For that one man—that industrious, creative, educated man—the one you would fancy to court."

Phoebe smiled and toyed with the edge of her bonnet. "It's possible, Mr. Lindquist. Quite possible. I am eighteen, and many of my friends are already married. I wouldn't want to be an old maid."

He laughed heartily at this. "I seriously doubt you will have that problem, Miss Robbins. I, for one, cannot even imagine the possibility of that occurring."

"Phoebe?" her mother called from just up the street. "Come help me with this material."

She gave him one more smile. "It was wonderful to see you again. Good day, Mr. Lindquist."

"Good day, Miss Robbins."

It was only after she'd gone that Dalton remembered that he was leaving. Would she care that he'd be absent from the island for several weeks, maybe even months? He thought to call after her.

"What can I say?" He stared after Phoebe and her mother as they moved down the street. "I can hardly tell her that she's bewitched me and that I'd like very much to be that industrious, creative, educated man she wants to court."

———

Later that day, Dalton explained everything to Mr. Belikov and Yuri, even offering to bring back any needed supplies from Seattle. "We probably won't return until September, but I would be happy to take your list with me."

"That would be good," Mr. Belikov said, nodding. "There are

some things a person would like to have handpicked instead of merely ordered. Don't worry about a thing, Dalton. You will have a job waiting here for you when you return." He pulled off his leather apron. "I will go see what we need."

Yuri leaned over Dalton's shoulder as his father left the room. "You might still have a job, but if I have anything to say about it— you won't have a girl."

Dalton turned. "I can't worry about our contest with this on my plate. My sister needs me. And, to be honest, I need this trip, as well."

Yuri's smile faded and he took hold of Dalton's arm. "You *will* come back?"

"Of course."

"There will be many excitements down there. My father says there is much pleasure to be had in the big cities."

"There is also much danger," Dalton replied. "My father has told me that, as has my mother. But it won't tempt me to stay."

"Why not? Because of Phoebe?" Yuri asked, letting his lips curl into a grin.

"She's a part of it, I suppose." Dalton walked to the boat they'd been sanding all morning. "But my life is here. I feel as if . . . well, that it's a part of me."

"But you also want to be a part of something more? You said earlier that it was important to meet your brothers."

Dalton turned back and looked at his friend. "Yes. That's impor- tant, but not because I would want to trade this place for them. I need to know who my people are. You know about yours. You have family in Russia, along with an entire culture. Your mother keeps that alive with photographs and traditions. If you choose to embrace your heritage, it is because it holds value to you. I have no way of knowing what, if any value, there is in my past."

Yuri nodded. "I can understand. In fact, I wish I could go with you." He grinned. "We would, no doubt, get into much trouble."

"That's exactly why you cannot go with me," Dalton said, laughing. "It would completely defeat the purpose." He drew a deep breath and began to gather his things. "I will return as soon as I can. As for Phoebe . . . well, I shall pray that you make no progress with her."

Yuri laughed. "You'd best pray hard. I find that I like her more every day."

Dalton ignored his friend, but on his long walk home, he fought the desire to go back to town to see the young lady in question. They'd only seen each other two times since the dance and the encounters had been merely by chance. He'd never dared to say a word about his interest in her. Maybe he should write her a letter before going.

Maybe . . . maybe he should explain how he wanted to know her better—that she had, in a sense, charmed him—that he thought about her all of the time.

"But what good would it do?" he questioned. "I won't be here."

Dalton made it home in record time and found his mother waiting for him on the porch as if by an earlier agreement. He could see that she had something on her mind.

"I just knew you would be coming home early," she told him.

"Father came by the shop and said that Evie had gotten us transportation to catch up with the *Corona*. I figured I'd best get home and get packed."

His mother nodded. "First, I need to talk to you about your inheritance."

He saw the concern on her face. "Of course." He put his tools on the porch by the door. "Where would you like to do this?"

"Come inside." She led the way to her favorite rocking chair and took a seat. "Sit here by the fire. There's a chill in the air today."

Dalton followed but didn't mention that he hadn't noticed any chill. Suddenly his mother seemed so very small and fragile. The thought of his older brother trying to hurt her ignited a smoldering rage deep within his heart. What would he do when he encountered the man who had tried to kill his mother?

"I know that you realize you have an inheritance from the Gray family."

"You said that you had kept the money given you by my grandfather and some of the money from my father."

"Yes." She folded her hands and drew a deep breath. "Dalton, you are a wealthy young man. The money has grown considerably over the years. I've had good men watching over it, and they have sent me periodic reports to make sure that I know exactly what is happening."

"Wealthy?" He couldn't grasp the thought. They lived comfortably in Sitka—better than most—but he'd honestly never imagined that they were rich.

"You won't come fully into the money until you reach your majority at twenty-one," she continued. "However, I am sending you with papers that will allow you to draw funds now. You can see to any need you or Evie have while in Kansas City. You can even arrange to transfer money here or to purchase anything you want to bring back with you. There is more than enough—more than you could ever imagine."

"Why are you telling me this now?" he asked.

She looked at him, unable to conceal the worry in her expression. "Because I am afraid for you. I fear what your brothers will do. They will know you are well off. They have their spies who will have informed them of the exact totals of your wealth. They have always been greedy, and I have no reason to believe they have changed."

"Everyone changes, Mother. Who knows if that means they've

become worse or better." He smiled. "Please try not to worry. I am not a child."

"But they will come at you like wolves in sheep's clothing. They will try to convince you to join forces with them. They will suggest that together you can make the mighty Gray empire they have always dreamed of building. They will appeal to your desire for connecting to the family. They will seduce you."

Dalton frowned. She was serious. His mother believed his brothers were in league with the devil himself, and that they would somehow have power over him because of this.

"Mother, I will be careful. God will be my guide."

She shook her head, and her eyes welled with tears. "I'm not at all sure that God lives in Kansas City."

Chapter 9

August 1889

Dalton marveled at the Kansas City skyline. He had read about multiple-story buildings that defied gravity but had never figured to see them. The sight was impressive, along with the crowds of people everywhere, all in a hurry.

Wiping his brow, Dalton was grateful for what little breeze they picked up as the carriage made its way through town. The heat was unbearable and already he'd shed himself of the new suit coat they'd purchased in Seattle. Evie fanned herself furiously and seemed more than a little unsettled.

"I'd forgotten how awful it could be—the dampness with the heat just makes a person long for winter." She shifted uncomfortably. "We used to take a lot of tepid baths, as I recall."

"It is amazing. It almost seems one can see the heat in the air itself." He peered out the opposite side. "I must say, this trip has been quite an eye-opener for me."

She looked at him oddly. "In what way?"

Dalton leaned back onto the thickly upholstered leather of the hired cab. "I feel almost startled to realize how the rest of the world functions outside of our little Sitka. We have truly been isolated and hidden away from the sorrows of the world. Of course, we have our own, but our troubles seem so small and insignificant in comparison. I mean, just look around. Hear it all. There is so much noise—so many people."

Evie glanced out the window. "It's as if they're all fighting for air."

"It's very much like that," Dalton agreed. "I did like the vast open spaces of the western states. The trip through the area they call Montana was quite beautiful. And it amazed me to find such open prairies—miles upon miles of wheat and corn as we drew closer to Kansas City."

"And now here we are," Evie said with a sigh. "I grew up here, you know. Of course, it's all changed. I would bet it has tripled in size."

"I can't even imagine. The train station alone held more people than on all of Baranof Island."

Evie laughed. "I'd never thought of it that way, but I'm sure you're right."

Despite her amusement, Dalton could see that Evie was worried. "Should we check into a hotel first?"

She drew a deep breath and shook her head. "I told the driver to take us to the house. We'll see what news there is of Thomas. If he has already passed, we will stay there. No sense in renting rooms elsewhere until we know."

"Do you suppose they will be expecting us?"

"There's no reason they should. It's been two months since

Jeannette penned that note. She had to realize that the distance would make it difficult to get word to us quickly, and then just as difficult for me to get here in any timely manner. I'll send one of the servants from the house to take word to our sister. She doesn't live far away. In fact, she now lives in the house where I grew up."

"I remember you mentioning that." Dalton pulled his collar. "What if they've changed, Evie?"

"What are you talking about?"

He shrugged. "What if our brothers are better people now? What if Marston really regrets what he did?"

"What if he does? It doesn't change the fact that he did it."

"No, I realize that. But you and Mother only remember him from long ago. They could all be very different now. I mean, think of how you've changed over the years."

Evie considered this for a moment. "Anything is possible, Dalton. I just wouldn't get my hopes up."

He frowned. He wanted so much to believe there might be some tiny shred of goodness in his heritage. After all, Evie was a wonderful person. *But she isn't a man,* Dalton reminded himself. Gray men were vicious and underhanded, to hear it told.

The carriage turned off of the busy avenue and made its way via a series of twists and turns to a more residential area of town. Here, the traffic thinned considerably and a large canopy of trees lowered the temperature a bit.

Dalton studied the architectural styles of the palatial homes and tried not to think so much about his family. The estates were large and plush. Such houses were not even imaginable in Sitka. Glorious arrangements of marble, brick, and limestone rose up from immaculately kept lawns like shrines to the owners.

"Oh, I wish there were more of a breeze," Evie grumbled. She, too, had purchased a few more formal clothes in Seattle so that she might better fit in with the society of her family. Dalton could see that she was every bit as uncomfortable as he was.

They finally turned down another long avenue of homes, even grander than the others. "We're nearly there," Evie announced. Her brows knit together, and she bit her lower lip.

Dalton couldn't help but reach out and touch her gloved hand. "It will be all right. No matter the circumstance."

She nodded. "I just wish this day might never have come. I would have been more than happy to go on as I was in Sitka."

"But if you had done that," Dalton said in a teasing tone, "you might not have had the possibility of courting Joshua."

Her head turned quickly as she met his gaze. "What?"

He laughed. "I've hesitated to say this, but Joshua Broadstreet is enamored with you, and I'm quite sure you care about him, as well. You have both behaved admirably over the years, but if your husband has died, you'll be free to marry again."

"I hardly expected such talk from you."

"Why not? I see no reason to hide from the truth. I've always regretted that you two could not be together."

She relaxed a bit and lowered her head. "I have missed out on so much. I hardly dare to hope that I might yet know true love."

"Well, I think it's entirely possible." Dalton cleared his throat rather nervously. "Do you believe in love at first sight?"

Evie shrugged. "I don't know why it wouldn't be possible. People form instant attachments to things, so why not people?"

"I don't know. I just . . . well . . . I keep thinking . . ." His words trailed off. Maybe he shouldn't even talk to Evie about it.

"Is this about Phoebe Robbins?"

He snapped his head around to meet his sister's amused expression. "Why do you ask that?"

"Because I think you have fallen for her."

"Again, why?"

"I can't really say. There's just something about the two of you together."

"See, that's the way I feel. I know we haven't been together but a few times, but I think about her constantly, and when Yuri told me he liked her, well, I wanted to punch him."

His sister laughed and patted his knee. "Violence won't win her heart."

"Neither will being down here in Kansas City. Yuri intends to go out of his way to steal her affections. I just keep thinking of how they'll have all this time together, and I won't even be around to make my feelings known."

"If she's the one for you, and it's meant to be," Evie said in a sympathetic tone, "it will happen. God has a purpose and will for each person. If you are to share your life with Phoebe Robbins, Yuri's attentions won't mean a thing." She sat up straighter. "We're here."

Dalton looked out at the massive three-story brick house and tried to forget the image of Phoebe's gentle smile. "It's huge. I can hardly wait to see the inside."

The carriage came to a stop and a uniformed man came down the steps to open Evie's door. The young man looked up and offered his hand. "Ma'am?"

Evie squared her shoulders and gave Dalton one last glance. "I suppose there is no sense putting it off." She allowed the man to help her from the carriage. "I'm Mrs. Thomas Gadston."

The young man's eyes widened. "The mistress of the house?"

"Yes. I realize you do not know me. Are there any servants still in employment from eighteen years ago?"

"There are. I will take you to them."

Dalton bounded out of the carriage to walk behind his sister. He heard her hesitate and clear her voice before asking about her husband.

"I'm sorry, ma'am. He is no longer with us."

"It's just as I presumed," she replied in a formal tone.

The front door was opened by an older gentleman. He looked at Evie for a moment, then nodded as if in approval. "Mrs. Gadston, welcome home."

She nodded and looked around the foyer. Dalton did likewise. It was a wonderment to behold. A heavily ornate marble and gold table with a large arrangement of flowers graced the entryway. Beneath this, a plush, but slightly worn rug of golds and reds accented the room's crimson wallpaper.

"When did Mr. Gadston . . . die?" Evie asked as the butler took her gloves and hat.

"The thirteenth of June," a man answered from somewhere to their right. The pocket door slid back to reveal the source.

"Trayton Payne," Evie whispered.

"One and the same. I wasn't sure you would recognize me after all this time. The years have not been nearly as kind to me as to you. You could still pass for seventeen."

"Hardly that," she replied. "As I recall, you were the one who knew every detail of my husband's business dealings. I will need a full accounting."

Dalton was stunned at the way she got right to business. She instantly became someone Dalton had never known. Was this the Mrs. Thomas Gadston from the past? Had she always been like this when it came to running her household? Or was this the woman who was borne out of years of encasing her heart in stone?

"Is this still my home?" she asked.

"Indeed. However, there is a great deal of business to discuss if you are up to it." Trayton smiled in a way that made Dalton feel possessive of his sister. Evie, however, seemed unimpressed.

She turned to the butler. "Would you have our things unloaded and see that Dalton is shown to the room next to mine? Also, give the driver this and dismiss him." She handed some money to the man and turned back to Trayton. "I will discuss matters with you now."

"I can stay," Dalton told her. He was still uncertain it was wise to let her be alone with this man.

"It's all right. You go and rest. I'll be up directly to let you know everything."

He exchanged a look with Payne and nodded. "And you will send for me if you need me?"

She smiled. "Absolutely."

Evie knew she was showing far more security in her position than she truly felt. Being in this house again threatened to steal away her breath. She followed Trayton through the sitting room to the back of the house, where Thomas had kept his office.

"You'll find very little has changed over the years," Trayton told her. "Thomas liked keeping things as they were."

"What took his life?"

Trayton turned, looking surprised at her question. "I presumed you knew. He developed consumption of the lungs."

"I see. There has been much of that in Alaska, as well."

She watched Trayton as he moved to one of the large leather chairs in front of her husband's desk. "Please have a seat. I will try to answer all of your questions. Would you care for refreshment?"

"Tea would be most welcomed."

"Have you tried it iced? Sally makes the most marvelous iced tea with lemon and ginger."

"Who is Sally?"

"She's been the cook's assistant for about four years."

"It sounds wonderful." Evie took the chair while Trayton rang for the maid.

A young, attractive woman appeared and nodded eagerly at

Trayton's instruction. He introduced her to Evie, and she curtsied ever so slightly. "This is Miss Dahlia Cummings. She is one of the household staff."

Evie nodded while Trayton finished explaining who Evie was and why she had come. The young woman seemed enthralled. Perhaps there had been a great many stories about Evie and her exploits. She could only imagine. Wives did not often run away from home and never return.

Well, I suppose it's not a matter of never returning, she thought. *I am here now.*

Trayton took a seat at the desk and reached into one of the side drawers. "Your sister told me that she had the highest hopes you would come. I've tried to keep things readied for just such an occasion. I have remained in your husband's service as his personal secretary all these years. I know his business dealings probably better than anyone, save his lawyers. I know his personal dealings better than even they do."

He placed several files atop the desk. "Where would you like to begin?"

"Why did Thomas ask for me? After all these years of silence— why did he ask Jeannette to send for me? Or did he even do that? Was that just a fabrication of Jeannette's to entice me here?"

"He did ask for you," Trayton assured her. "While on his death-bed, he dictated a letter to me, which was for you. It was his one and only bit of unfinished business, and he could not rest until it was concluded."

Evie couldn't suppress a laugh. "Unfinished business, eh? That's exactly how I thought of Thomas. It's the only reason I'm here. I need to put the past to rest once and for all."

Trayton studied her for a moment. His gaze captivated her, and Evie immediately remembered the seductive manner in which he'd controlled her so long ago. Her own husband had hired Trayton

Payne to keep her entertained. The thought sickened her even now.

"Why did you leave, Evie? I mean, I understand that you wanted to return your brother to his mother, but why not come home after that?"

She thought to rebuke him for asking her such a personal question, then decided against it. "I had no home to come back to. You know that as well as anyone."

"Thomas would never have denied you anything. He gave you all this and more. Why shame him just because he couldn't be the husband you desired?"

"I never intended to shame him," she replied. "He shamed himself. He never wrote to me—never attempted to come to me. He never loved me."

Trayton didn't deny this. Instead, his expression changed to one of discomfort. "He did bring great shame upon himself. Most of society was too fearful of his power to question him on it or to shun him, but they suspected the truth all the same."

"And what truth would that be, Mr. Payne?"

He met her fixed stare. "That he had taken a lover even before his marriage to you. That his lover was not another woman, but rather a man."

Evie felt the warmth drain from her body, leaving her icy and numb. Her sister had often suggested the possibility of such a liaison, but Evie had never been able to believe it of Thomas.

"And how do you know this?"

He leaned back in the chair. "Because, as I said, I know everything about Thomas Gadston's personal life. It was my job to keep the public from ever knowing, but I did that job poorly."

"It's abominable to even imagine such a thing. Why do you tell me this now?" Evie tried desperately to conjure up feelings of sympathy or regret for her dead husband, but there was nothing but a blank void where her heart should have been.

"I tell you this because of the will. Thomas's will leaves his wealth and properties divided between the two of you."

"His lover and I?" she murmured.

"Exactly so. He left this house and its contents to you. The gentleman in question—we shall call him Mr. Smith—has been given another residence." Trayton opened one of the files. "You are otherwise provided for in separate settlements. Each portion is enough to leave you both quite comfortable."

"I see."

He produced an envelope and handed it across the desk to Evie. She stared at the outreached letter for a moment before taking it.

"This will explain Thomas's desire that you make no public scandal regarding the matter. He further hopes that you will not oppose his wishes and create a scene where his will is concerned."

"I see," she repeated. She could hardly form the words. Looking down at the letter, Evie couldn't bring herself to open it. Not yet.

"Evie, I know all of this is difficult for you. I am sorry. I think in his own way, Thomas did care for you. I think he was greatly disturbed to know you were so miserable and unhappy. The letter will say as much."

"How sad for Thomas." She got to her feet, unable to think about the situation anymore. "I believe I will go to my room and rest. Please have those refreshments brought to me there."

Trayton was on his feet immediately. He came to her and took hold of her arm. "Evie, I know my words may come as something of a shock, but I have never stopped thinking of you. You surely know that my interest in you involved more than following Thomas's instructions."

She looked at him and saw the same appealing expression

in his face. That same look that had so captivated her as a young woman—barely a woman.

"Are you not married?" she asked.

"I was once. It was long ago. She died in childbirth."

Evie saw a glint of sadness in his eyes. "I'm sorry."

"She was the only woman who ever took my thoughts from you, and when she was gone, you came back to haunt me in a fierce way. I could not pass through this house without reflecting on our time together."

What sort of spell did he cast on her? Evie pulled away, hoping to distance herself from the emotions of the past. She walked quickly to the door only to find him there, just ahead of her.

"Evie, please don't reject me now. We both know there was never any love lost between you and Thomas. Now that he's gone, you are free to love me. Free to do what you like. You handled yourself most admirably in not divorcing the man, but now he's dead. There is no shame in remarriage."

She looked at him for a moment. He seemed so very sincere. It almost made her laugh. Here, she and Lydia had been worried about Dalton and the temptations that Kansas City would offer *him*!

He reached out to touch her cheek. "Just give me a chance, Evie. I'm certain I can convince you to feel something for me."

"I'm going to go rest now." She walked away without another word, terrified that if she spoke, she might say the wrong thing. The fact of the matter was, she wasn't all that sure that Trayton Payne couldn't convince her to feel something, and that frightened her a great deal.

Chapter 10

Phoebe put away her flute and smiled, a sense of satisfaction washing over her. It was so fulfilling to be a part of a musical group, especially one that enjoyed playing the works of many of the great composers.

"You are coming along quickly," Lydia told her. She had just seen the other members of the little orchestra out. "We will make quite the ensemble at the winter ball."

"I very much enjoy the pieces you have chosen. I am particularly fond of Johann Strauss the elder's pieces, but his son's 'Blue Danube Waltz' is also a great favorite of mine. I know all of them will be perfect for the dance."

"We shall have to make certain you get a chance to dance, as well as play your flute," Lydia said. "I know most of the men in town would be sorely vexed with me if I had you sit out the entire ball."

"Does Mr. Lindquist mind not getting to dance with you?" Phoebe asked. She had observed the couple, and she loved the way Mr. Lindquist attended to his wife. Watching them at the practice sessions, with him playing his guitar and Lydia her violin, left Phoebe longing for a love like that of her own.

"No, we found long ago that we preferred the music we could make together to dancing. Music binds us in a way that nothing else can."

The older woman's words pierced Phoebe's heart. How wonderful it would be to feel so connected to another person. "I truly hope for that one day, myself." She smiled at Lydia. "Whether through music or something else."

Lydia nodded. "So how are you adapting to life in Sitka?"

"Participating in our little orchestra helps, for sure," Phoebe replied. "Otherwise, I feel a bit out of sorts. I don't seem to fit in well, though I'm trying to adjust. Mother and I are working on the candles, and I love talking to Zee about the Tlingits. I've learned so much."

"Have you and your mother considered opening a little shop to sell your candles?"

"Mother said the cost of such a thing would prohibit us making even enough money to cover supplies. We have always made them at home. I like it that way, I must say. It's a tradition in our family, you know."

"Your mother mentioned something about all the generations of women who had made candles. My own lineage is so steeped in controversy and heartache that something more productive such as chandlery would have been welcome."

"It hasn't stopped us from having our share of controversy and heartache," Phoebe replied without thinking. She quickly put her hands to her mouth.

"You needn't fear saying the wrong thing to me," Lydia assured her. "I won't mention it."

"It's just that . . . well, my father has suffered politically for things over which he had no say. He prefers no one know anything more about him than what the present moment offers."

"It's hard when choices and decisions are made that cause us grief, even years later. Our family is definitely not without scandal. My own grief started when my father contracted my hand in marriage as part of a business arrangement. Please believe me when I say I understand—you needn't fear gossip coming from me on the matter."

"Are your mother and father still living?"

Lydia shook her head. "No, they died some time ago. My only family is what I have here. Kjell and my children, and of course, Zee."

Glancing around, Phoebe used the opportunity to bring up the question uppermost on her mind. "I haven't seen Dalton lately. I suppose he's been working hard."

"Actually, he's not here. He accompanied his sister Evie to Kansas City."

"He's gone? When?" She didn't mean for the questions to sound so urgent, but she was surprised. No one had said a word about him leaving and he had certainly never said anything about going away. Not that he owed her any explanations.

"He left about three weeks ago. I'm surprised you hadn't heard."

"Well, I asked Yuri when he came over one evening to say hello." Phoebe felt her cheeks flush slightly. "I asked about Dalton then, but he just said something about him being extra busy."

Lydia gave a light chuckle. "Yuri hopes to keep you all to himself,

I'm sure. I've no doubt he thought if he made it seem Dalton held you no interest, you would easily give your heart to him."

Phoebe was surprised by Lydia's words. She lowered her head and looked at the flute case she held. She couldn't think of anything to say.

"You will have many suitors in this town, as I'm sure you've already come to realize. You needn't be embarrassed, nor think to keep such matters to yourself. Sitka is a small town and people will talk."

Gathering her nerve, Phoebe looked up and found Lydia watching her with a motherly gaze. "Do you suppose . . . that . . . well . . . that Dalton would want to be one of those suitors?"

Lydia grinned. "If I know anything of my son, it is that he has a great appreciation for members of the opposite sex. He admires beauty in all shapes and sizes—be it in people, art, or even the boat he works on. I will not speak for him, but I believe he found you quite fascinating."

"I treated him terribly the day I arrived. He saved my life, and I acted like a complete ninny. Since then, I've tried hard to be pleasant and kind."

"Dalton isn't one to hold a grudge." Lydia paused and looked rather upset for a moment. "I think we should put aside such talk, lest I speak out of turn. Dalton hopes to be home sometime in the next few weeks. He and his sister did not plan to be gone long. It will give you plenty of time to focus on learning the songs we'll play at the winter ball."

"Thank you again for allowing me to join you in this," Phoebe said. "I'm sure it will help me to pass the time."

———

That night Phoebe surprised her mother as they saw to the supper dishes. "Do you believe in love at first sight?"

"What?" Her mother looked at her rather startled.

"Can a person fall in love with another person after meeting them only once or even twice?"

"Why do you ask that?"

Phoebe shrugged. "No reason. I just wondered. Didn't you once tell me that Father fell in love with you after meeting you only once?"

"I suppose I did," her mother replied. She turned back to the dishes. "But such things are rare."

"But entirely possible?"

"I suppose so. I mean, I very nearly lost my heart to your father just as quickly. Still, I think it is better in this day and age to get to know one another before deciding such important matters. Taking a relationship slow and steady is far more reasonable."

"I suppose so," Phoebe replied with images of Dalton Lindquist dancing through her head, "but reasonable isn't always how my heart sees things."

———

Evie looked at the letter once again. Thomas's dying words were full of apology and regret. He wrote that he had never intended to marry at all, but Floyd Gray had offered such a lucrative deal and that, coupled with his own father's demands that Thomas take a wife, determined his choices for him.

He further commented on the man he'd come to care about. They had been friends since boyhood, and now the man was crippled and unable to work to make his own living. Thomas begged Evie to understand and not protest the will.

"He has no one and no hope of seeing to his care without this gift from me," the letter read.

Evie couldn't begin to understand the relationship Thomas had with this man, but she felt sorry for both of them. Folding the letter, she put it away and determined to settle her other affairs as soon as possible. She longed for her home in Sitka, and there was clearly no reason to remain in Kansas City.

Gazing into her vanity mirror, Evie pondered how the evening might go for them. She had sent invitations to her brothers and sister, asking that they come without their spouses and join her for dinner. Replies had come from all, assuring her that they would be present promptly at six.

The clock revealed that there was less than twenty minutes until this affair was to take place. Evie drew a deep breath and picked up a decorative comb, placing it in her thick blond hair. She studied the effect in the mirror. Her appearance was elegant, but not overly stated.

She stood just as a knock sounded. "Yes?"

"It's me, Dalton."

Evie quickly opened the door. Her brother had dressed in his new suit, but there was still something out of place about him, an air about him that he would never be completely comfortable in such elite settings.

"Are you ready?" she asked. "Prepared to meet your siblings?"

"I'm plenty nervous about it, but yes. I want to get this over with."

"Just remember to be on your guard," she warned. "They all have a way about them that can be quite charming."

Dalton frowned. "Believe me, I've wrestled with my feelings on the entire matter. I would like to believe they could have changed, but the fact remains they caused my family great harm. Given that, I seriously doubt there is anything that will charm me about them—especially my brothers."

"Marston was always a great actor. He is wily and skillful, and I have reason to believe that those abilities have only improved over the years."

"Don't worry, sister of mine. I will be careful."

"They will certainly be surprised when they get here and realize you have come. I said nothing about your arrival. Unless one
of the servants has slipped out to speak to them, we will have the
upper hand."

Through her open bedroom door, Evie heard the front bell ring.
She glanced at the clock on her mantel. "That will be Jeannette.
She always arrives ten minutes early. She likes to be the first one
so that she can corner the hostess and learn all the new gossip
without anyone else interfering." She smiled at Dalton. "You might
like to watch them arrive from the larger sitting room. I will open
the connecting doors so you can hear the conversation and see
them. Then when you feel like joining us, do so."

"I would like that. It will give me time to assess the situation."

"Then let us be about our business." She led the way down the
back servants' stairs. "This will allow us to sneak in." Evie threw
him a conspiratorial grin. "We Grays are good at knowing how to
slip around unnoticed."

Evie took Dalton to the sitting room. "Stay here. I will leave
the doors open and greet Jeannette," she whispered. Dalton nodded
and Evie swept past him and through the connecting doors to the
smaller parlor, where her sister was already fussing with the butler
over the care of her shawl.

"Jeannette."

Her sister turned to greet her. The years wore themselves like
an old companion on Jeannette's face. Her sister looked haggard,
perhaps even sickly. She had plumped out in a most matronly fashion, but even this had not caused her to discontinue her penchant
for dressing in flamboyant gowns and jewelry.

"Genevieve! I can scarce believe you've finally come home."
She approached Evie with open arms. After embracing her rather

123

stiffly, Jeannette pulled back and shook her head. "You are much too thin."

Evie smiled. "It's good to see you, Jeannette. How is your family?"

"They were quite vexed that you had not extended this evening's invitation to them, as well. Of course, the boys are back East in school, but Minnie and Meredith would have loved to attend. Minnie would like for you to meet her husband."

"Perhaps before I leave we can arrange that."

"Leave?" Jeannette looked aghast. "What are you talking about? You just got here. Why would you leave again?"

"My home is in Sitka," Evie replied. "I have no desire to remain here. Once I attend to selling the house and finalizing the business matters, I plan to return home."

"But you can't. You belong here. This is your home. Now that Thomas has gone—God rest his soul—there will be more opportunities for you. I know that Marston and Mitchell will never tolerate you leaving."

Evie kept smiling. "They have nothing to say on the matter. At least nothing of significance to me. Now, tell me about Minnie's wedding." She knew that changing the subject to the glorious affair of her niece's marriage to one of Kansas City's finest families would persuade Jeannette to move on.

"Oh, it was like nothing you can imagine. I thought we had lovely weddings, but this was the event to top them all." Jeannette rattled on about the guest list and the importance of each person invited. She was starting in on the flower arrangements when the butler announced the arrival of Marston and Mitchell. Apparently, they had come together.

Evie hadn't realized how worried she'd been about seeing them again until this moment. Suddenly, she felt like a little girl—helpless and uncertain. This would never do. Her brothers could sense fear from miles away. They would pounce on her like an animal to its prey if she wasn't careful.

"Brothers," she said casually. "I see you have journeyed here together."

They stopped abruptly to study her for a moment. Mitchell seemed quite surprised, while Marston narrowed his eyes as if studying a specimen under glass.

"You are a stunning beauty," Mitchell declared. "You look exactly like our mother at your age."

"Our mother didn't live much past my age," Evie replied.

"But nevertheless, you look remarkably like her portrait. You'll have to see it for yourself. It hangs in Jeannette's main sitting room at the family house."

"I think she's too thin," Jeannette interjected.

Marston stepped forward. "You would," he muttered, his gaze never leaving Evie.

She couldn't help but wonder if he still held her a grudge. No doubt he would. He was, after all, a Gray man, incapable of forgiveness when betrayed. Not that she truly needed to be forgiven.

He reached out and took hold of her hands. Evie didn't stop him. "You are quite lovely. You will turn many heads in Kansas City." He pulled her forward to embrace her, then kissed her cheek. "I could have you remarried within the month."

"She says she won't be here that long," Jeannette announced. She was clearly frustrated that Evie held all of the attention.

Marston stepped back and Mitchell came forward to follow his example. He kissed Evie lightly, then questioned her. "What is Jeannette talking about?"

Evie steadied her nerves. "I am not remaining in Kansas City. My home is in Alaska now, and I intend to return as soon as my business affairs are in order."

"Unacceptable," Marston said, shaking his head. "We need you here."

"I see no reason to argue the point," she countered. "I will not change my mind. Now, I have a bit of a surprise for you."

"I'm not arguing any point," Marston said, crossing his arms. "You will stay. You've been gone long enough. You brought shame on this family, and by staying, you can erase a part of that. By marrying well, you can perhaps blot it completely."

Evie laughed out loud, surprising them all. "You haven't changed. None of you, really. But I have. I'm not the mousy little girl who left here so long ago. I will not be intimidated by your threats or demands, so before you further embarrass yourselves, please take that into consideration."

"I knew living with that woman would change you. Lydia has ruined you," Jeannette said in a huff. She moved to a chair and took a seat as if the entire matter was exhausting her.

"You will not speak out against Lydia if you intend to share my table," Evie said. She threw a look of warning at her brothers. "This is my house, and I make the rules."

Marston laughed. "Jeannette is right. You have lived under a bad influence."

"It sounds as if you are somewhat of an authority on bad influences."

Evie turned around at Dalton's comment. Her young brother strolled casually into the room. He came to her side, and immediately Evie felt stronger.

"Who is this?" Jeannette nearly shrieked.

No one said anything for several moments. Then Marston finally replied, "This is our little brother. Dalton Gray."

"Dalton Lindquist," he corrected.

Evie watched her sister's mouth drop, while Mitchell stepped around Marston to get a better look. She would have laughed out loud had the moment not been so intense.

"I thought it was about time we met," Dalton said, his voice strong and solid.

Evie was glad Dalton didn't appear the least bit intimidated by his brothers. She could see that he held their extreme interest—perhaps even their respect.

"I say the time is well overdue," Marston replied. "You are more than welcome to take your rightful place in our family—the place your mother deprived you of all these years."

Dalton stiffened and Evie put her hand on his arm in support. "I hardly feel deprived," Dalton said, "but perhaps if she did keep me from my rightful place, it had more to do with the fact that you tried to have her murdered."

Chapter 11

Evie could sense Marston's anger at the way Dalton had maneuvered the conversation to this undeniable confrontation. Evie knew her older brother was used to intimidating people—especially younger men. Funny it should be his own brother who broke the success of this habit.

Marston toyed with the cuff of his coat. "I'm sure you have had to endure many lies over the years."

Evie knew Dalton felt that there had been too many secrets and lies in his family, but she also believed he would never admit to such a thing. To say as much to Marston would give him power that Dalton wouldn't want him to have. She looked to her younger brother as he spoke.

"I know for a fact this one isn't a lie."

The smirk on Marston's face suggested he was enjoying the exchange. "Oh, you do? I find that fascinating."

"It's time," Evie interjected, "that we confront this matter and be honest."

"Does this mean we won't be having supper?" Jeannette asked. "I'm afraid I'm beginning to feel rather weak."

"I have no desire to keep you from eating," Evie told her sister. "Please feel free to go to the kitchen and get something."

"Me? Go to the kitchen?" Jeannette appeared to be completely shocked by the idea. She fanned herself furiously.

"Otherwise, you can wait until we've finished," Evie added. She then turned to Marston. "I have a few things to say, and I intend for you all to hear them. You might as well be seated. This will take a few minutes."

Dalton immediately extended his arm to her. As if by previous agreement, he led her to the two Italian throne chairs that graced the right side of the fireplace. He saw Evie situated comfortably and then took the chair beside her, as if they were king and queen holding court.

Mitchell and Marston exchanged a glance and took a seat on the large sofa. Marston studied the back of his hand for a moment, then glanced over to Evie. "Well, do get on with it."

"You will not lie to Dalton about the past. I won't have it. I have told him everything I know about the night you arranged to have Lydia killed. If you are uncomfortable with that, you have no one to blame but yourself."

"Killed?" Jeannette gasped. They now had her full attention. "Whatever are you suggesting?"

Marston didn't even acknowledge her question. Instead, he stared directly at Evie and Dalton. "I'm sure you told him what you thought you knew." Evie found the casualness of his tone quite annoying. How like him to respond this way.

"Why did you despise my mother so much?" Dalton asked. "It wasn't like she wanted to marry our father. She was forced into that by my grandfather. She tried to make the best of the situation, but you showed her nothing but hatred."

"This is the story your mother told you?" Marston asked.

Evie frowned. "You know it's the truth; why try to say otherwise?"

Marston fixed her with a hard look. "You were but a little child. What do you know about any of it?"

"I was old enough to know the truth of what happened to our mother," Evie countered. "I was in the attic when Father came upstairs. I hid so that I wouldn't get in trouble for being where I wasn't supposed to be. He didn't know I was there or he might have thrown me over the same railing as he did our mother."

"That's outrageous!" Jeannette declared. "How can you speak against our father that way? First you accuse Marston of trying to kill Lydia, and now this. It's entirely uncalled for!"

Evie could see Marston knew she was telling the truth. Mitchell, although surprised by her bold statement, didn't attempt to suggest she had been mistaken.

"Our father was an evil and heartless man," Evie began. "You may not want to speak ill of the dead for whatever superstitious notions you have steeped yourself in, but I do not have that concern. Our father was a very bad man, and you know it even better than I."

"You really don't understand anything," Marston said, his eyes narrowing. "Our father was a businessman, a man who went after what was important and fought his way to the top by doing whatever was required of him."

"Even if that requirement was murder?" Evie asked. "Our mother brought him great wealth when they married. It was her money that gave him the foundations for the business ventures he pursued. She served her usefulness to him, and Father simply eliminated what was no longer needed."

Her brother eased against the cushioned back and crossed his arms. "You are so sure of what you think you saw, but I believe you were just a terrified little girl, imagining that Father was involved because you couldn't bear the fact that our mother had killed herself."

"I was right there. I heard them talk. I saw Father lift her in his arms and throw her from the roof walk."

"I am completely aghast that you should fabricate such a story," Jeannette said, shaking her head furiously. "If this were the case, why did you not speak out?"

Evie was ready for this. "I was afraid of being Father's next victim. After all, if he'd known there was a witness to his act, do you really suppose he would have let the matter go unchallenged?

All this time, Dalton had remained silent, but at this point he reached over to pat Evie's hand and spoke. "I see no reason for Evie to lie to us about this."

"Just as you believe her incapable of lying about my trying to have your mother killed?" Marston questioned.

"Oh, there are records that show as much," Dalton stated nonchalantly. "You hired two brothers, Anatolli and Ioann Sidorov, to kill my mother and bring me to you. They tried and failed, but only because my mother's will to live was too strong. I want to know what you hoped to gain by such a heinous act."

"I never wanted your mother killed," Marston countered. "I wanted you to be protected from further harm. You weren't in a proper environment, and I feared for your safety, just as I told the judge. I did nothing out of selfish ambition, as you suppose."

"What of the fact that I stood to inherit a great deal of money and part of the family business? I suppose that had nothing to do with your motives."

Marston gave him a sardonic smile. Evie had seen her brother take on this stance before. He was sizing up his adversary and preparing to deliver a deathblow.

"Your mother robbed us of our inheritance, or did she fail to tell you that? The complications of our father's will were manipulated in such a way that she was able to steal a good portion of what he had worked so hard to gain. Knowing her to be capable of that, who could say what her ambitions might be as your mother? We genuinely feared for your safety."

Evie watched Dalton as he considered what Marston had said, confident he wasn't fooled. She suddenly realized that Dalton would be able to stand his own ground without any trouble. He was incredibly sensible and intelligent. He wouldn't allow Marston so much as a foothold.

"So you are saying that our father was either too stupid or remiss to deal properly with his will and business arrangements, and this is somehow my mother's fault."

Mitchell leaned forward. "You have no right to speak in such a manner. You are still but a child, and you weren't even born when our father was alive."

"He's right," Jeannette said in a seething tone. "You weren't even born. Why, we don't even know for sure that you are our father's child."

Dalton grinned. "I would just as gladly not be. My father, for all intents and purposes, is Kjell Lindquist. The man has shown me nothing but love and purpose for my life. But that isn't what I want to discuss at this point." He looked back at Marston. "You managed to finagle out of any responsibility for what you did to my mother. There's a part of me that would love to exact revenge on her behalf, but she doesn't want that."

"How gracious of her," Marston said, the sarcasm dripping from his voice. "Your mother—the one who stole our family's fortune, the one who did everything in her power to keep you from knowing your true family—she's the one who wouldn't want you to exact revenge?" He laughed. "That's only because she's already taken her revenge. She doesn't need any help in that matter."

"If my mother had had her revenge, as you suggest, you would be in prison and this family wouldn't have received a penny of inheritance." He noted Mitchell's reaction. "Oh, didn't you think I knew about that? My mother wasn't forced to give back any of the money or properties she inherited from our father, and yet she did. This woman you accuse of being selfish and deceitful was actually quite merciful, as I understand it."

"Perhaps that is just the problem. You don't understand anything," Marston countered.

"I understand enough. I read the account of the kidnapping trial. I saw how you got off without so much as a fine for murdering Anatolli Sidorov. You did as you have always done—you bought your way out of trouble." Dalton looked at Evie. "I can see this is an utter waste of time."

"Why, because it doesn't suit your idealistic nature?" Marston gibed. "You two are such dreamers. Our father would be sorely disappointed in the both of you. You have no understanding of what he had to go through in order to build the Gray fortune. He provided us with an opulent way of life—one you enjoyed as a child, Evie. He even managed to arrange your union to a very wealthy man, and then you deserted the marriage."

"Dalton, you're right. This is a waste of time." Evie got to her feet and looked down at Marston and Mitchell. "You are both like Father. You believe that anything is acceptable, as long as it accomplishes something you want or believe you need."

"Everyone is that way, Evie. Why can't you open your eyes and see that?" Jeannette surprised them by interjecting. "Why can't you simply appreciate what you were given?" She, too, got to her feet. "You are spoiled and indifferent to our needs, and I quite resent that."

"Just as I resent having to carry the burden of knowing our father to be a murderer. Has it never occurred to any of you that if he would kill his own wife, he was capable of killing anyone? There were probably others, and you are fools if you think otherwise."

"You take that back!" Jeannette rushed forward. "You take that back now. Our father . . . our father . . ." She swayed as though she would soon faint. "Oh dear." Jeannette stumbled back toward her chair. "Oh, you've caused me a state of apoplexy. You may well . . . have murdered me." She put the back of her hand dramatically to her forehead and moaned.

"If you're going to die, do it quietly," Marston said. Jeannette's eyes flared open for a moment, then she sank with no great grace into the chair and appeared to be unconscious.

Evie had seen her sister pull such theatrical productions years ago, although she didn't remember them being quite so dramatic. She looked to Dalton, who was frowning, and gave him a wink. She crossed the room and rang for the maid.

"Well, aren't you going to do something?" Mitchell asked Evie after she talked briefly with a young house girl.

"About what?" she asked casually. She didn't so much as acknowledge her unconscious sister.

"About Jeannette, of course. Are you completely heartless?"

"I have never been heartless. You, however, are hopelessly mired in having your own desires met, even at great price to others. You have no concern for your fellow man, and your spirits are corrupt."

Just then, the maid returned. Evie went to her and took the pitcher that the girl held. Without regard to her brothers, she marched directly to where Jeannette was pretending to be in a faint. She poured the contents of the pitcher on her sister's head, soaking her in cold water. Jeannette shot up from the chair, screaming obscenities that Evie hadn't heard in years.

"What in the world is wrong with you? You've ruined my hair—my gown!"

"I'm sorry, Jeannette, but you fainted. I've found over the years in Alaska that water seems to bring people around better than anything. In fact, the doctor has even told me that the shock is good to invigorate the heart. I was hoping to postpone your death." Evie smiled and walked back to her housemaid with the pitcher. "Thank you."

Dalton was suppressing a smile, but Marston didn't even bother. He pretended to applaud Evie as she returned. "Handled like a true Gray."

She glowered at him. "Think what you will, but I have no desire to relate myself to that name."

"I can see that my mother was exactly right in her assessment of them," Dalton told Evie. He shook his head sadly. "In fact, I believe she spoke most kindly of them, given the truth of the situation."

"Your mother knows nothing but her own selfish ambitions," Marston stated, getting to his feet.

"Does no one care that I am drenched in water?" Jeannette asked. "I will probably catch my death."

"Oh bother, Jeannette," Mitchell said. "It's still at least ninety degrees. I doubt it will do anything but make you a bit cooler than the rest of us, so do be quiet."

"I'm going home," she said in a huff. "I hardly need to remain here and be insulted by you four." She headed for the door, glancing once over her shoulder as if waiting for someone to stop her.

"Good evening, Jeannette," Marston called after her. "Give my regards to your husband."

Evie might have applauded him as he had her earlier, but at this point, she wanted only to put her brothers in their place, once and for all.

"I want you both to hear me and hear me well," she said, focusing her attention on Marston and Mitchell. "I am hiring a lawyer to see to the sale of this house and its contents, as well as to handle the transfer of the inheritance Thomas left me. I plan to return to Alaska as soon as my responsibility to these matters is complete."

"I forbid it," Marston said angrily. "You have selfishly not even thought to ask how we are doing, but I will tell you anyway. Mitchell and I have suffered great financial loss. We are barely able to keep to our obligations. Your husband owed both of us money, and I intend to see you pay us with interest." He stepped forward in a threatening manner, but Dalton took hold of Evie possessively. Marston stopped.

"As for you," Marston said, narrowing his eyes as he considered Dalton, "you would do well to realize that just because my financial situation is stretched, it doesn't mean I don't still have friends in places of power. I would hate for your misplaced notions of playing the hero to get you hurt."

"Are you attempting to threaten me?" Dalton asked, not once looking away from Marston's enraged glare.

"I'm not threatening anything. I'm making observances." He smiled, and Evie felt a chill run down her spine as he added, "And often my observances lead me to action."

She'd had enough. Taking a step forward, she faced her brothers with a bravado she didn't really possess. "This conversation is done. I am not staying, Marston. I am not assisting you and Mitchell in any way. If you have debts with my husband, then see his secretary,

Mr. Trayton Payne. The man keeps meticulous records of all of Thomas's business dealings. The terms and conditions of your loan to my husband will be kept in his possession. I am certain Mr. Payne will settle the matter amicably with you both."

She held up her hand as Marston started to comment. "Enough. I won't hear any more threats or 'observances.' I will, however, issue one of my own: You will leave Dalton alone. You will leave his family alone. You will have nothing to do with any of us. If you should so much as step foot in Sitka again, I will go to the newspaper and tell them every painful hidden secret that this family has, and then some." She smiled, feeling her strength grow. "You and your families and businesses will be in ruins once I finish explaining all of the details."

"You wouldn't do that," Marston declared. "It would ruin you, as well."

"And see, that's the nice thing about living in Sitka," Evie said, looking from Marston to Mitchell and back again. "No one cares about the scandals of people a world away. I've got good friends and family in Alaska, and it won't matter to any of them that my father murdered my mother, that my brothers instigated a plot to commit multiple murders for money, or that my husband had a male lover." She paused. "They won't care, but all of Kansas City society will stand on tiptoe to hear the latest and juiciest bits of Gray-Gadston gossip. So you had better consider my words carefully."

"And you have the gall to tell me you're nothing like us," Marston said, laughing. "You are the worst of us."

Evie felt the words pierce her only momentarily. She squared her shoulders. "If you cross me, you'll see just how painful I can make your life, and it won't require me to tell one single lie or kill anyone." She turned to Dalton. "I believe I've worked up an appetite. What say we have supper now?"

She took hold of Dalton's arm and started to walk away, but paused when they reached the door. "If you are hungry and willing to behave yourselves, you are still welcome to join us. Otherwise, I bid you good-night."

Chapter 12

September 1889

The first of September dawned rainy and overcast, but by the time church concluded, Phoebe was happy to see that the clouds had cleared and the sun shone bright. She greeted some of the people and thanked the pastor for his sermon before seeking out her mother.

"I'm going home now," she told her in a low tone. She didn't want anyone overhearing and questioning her as to why she wasn't joining her parents for lunch.

"I wish you would reconsider. The governor and his wife will be disappointed that you aren't there. They might even think that you are snubbing them."

"Just explain that I had a previous engagement. Yuri asked me to go on this picnic two weeks ago. We were just waiting for a nice day, and this is it. I made him a promise."

"I think Mr. Belikov has been paying a great deal of attention to you. Perhaps too much," her mother warned.

"Perhaps, but I find him good company," Phoebe replied. "If Dalton Lindquist would ever return, I would enjoy his company, too." *If he ever comes calling,* she thought. Mrs. Lindquist seemed convinced her son liked Phoebe, but of course, he was still on his trip south.

"Very well. I shall make your excuses. Do practice discretion and modesty. I wish I could send Theodore or Grady with you."

She glanced heavenward at her mother's comment. "I intend to be the model of decorum. Sitka's residents hardly worry about the same rules of etiquette that bind folks in the south." She smiled, realizing she'd found something to appreciate about Sitka.

Phoebe moved off down the street, glad to be free of her family for the day. Lately her brothers had been unbearable in their sullen dispositions. After a summer of doing most everything their hearts desired, the school year was upon them. Phoebe had argued with them just the day before about why an education was so important. Not that they listened to her any better than they did their parents.

At home, Phoebe quickly changed clothes. Her simple brown wool skirt would serve her much better than her Sunday best. She found a decent shirtwaist and the skirt's matching jacket and donned those quickly before rearranging her hair. She let down the blond mass and began braiding it into one tight plait to hang down her back. When this was accomplished, she traded out her Sunday leather shoes for a sturdier pair of boots. Yuri had said they would hike a little ways up the mountain and visit his favorite spot. From there, she could look down on the harbor for a beautiful view.

She thought of Yuri with a smile. He was amusing and charming. She loved to hear about his relatives in Russia and of his exploits on Baranof Island as a child. Most of all, she liked to hear him tell about the adventures he and Dalton had shared over the years. Sometimes they were boyish accounts of camping trips that turned complicated. Other times they were accounts of life at the boat shop, where they worked together to learn the trade. No matter what the story, however, Phoebe felt she got to know both Dalton and Yuri a little better. Today he had promised to tell her a little more about the Russian Orthodox Church. She had been fascinated by the green domed church and its priest. The man, Father Donskoi, had a reputation throughout the town of being compassionate and giving. The Tlingit loved him, Zee had told her, because he showed them respect and treated them as equals.

Phoebe heard Yuri approaching. He was singing a song in Russian, one she'd heard before. Sitka was a blend of many cultures, really—Russian, native Alaskan, and American—a sort of stew created of people and their traditions.

She grabbed her walking stick, a gift Yuri had made, and met him at the door. "Good afternoon," she said.

Yuri grinned and turned to reveal his knapsack. "I have our lunch packed and ready."

"Wonderful. I must say the day has turned out quite pretty." She secured the door and held up her walking stick. "I am looking forward to using this."

He shifted his rifle to his left hand, then offered her his right arm. Phoebe hesitated. She didn't want him to get the wrong idea and believe her to be more interested than she was. Instead, she stepped ahead of him and turned to ask, "Which way?"

He took no offense at her actions and quickly joined her. Together, they walked away from town. "There is a wonderful little path just beyond the lake. Not too far. The view is very nice."

"Have you been hard at work this last week?" Phoebe asked. "You look rather tired."

"It has been busy. Several repairs. We definitely could have used Dalton's help."

She was glad for the introduction of Dalton to their conversation. "Have you heard anything from him?"

"No. We didn't really expect to. He was hoping the trip would be relatively quick. There probably wouldn't be enough time to get more than one or two letters up here, and they would have had to be mailed early. Otherwise, they probably would have come here together on the same ship."

"I do marvel at the time it takes to get correspondence," Phoebe replied. "I have had as many as ten letters show up at once, and then nothing for such a long time."

"One day, I believe we'll get weekly service."

She remembered her home in Vermont where the mail came daily and sighed. "That would be wonderful."

"Now that I have told you about my week, what was yours like?"

"Mother and I managed to get some candles made. They turned out quite nice, in fact. I will soon need to braid more wick, but we had enough for what we made."

"My mother certainly enjoys working for your mother. She said she's never known a more organized woman."

Phoebe laughed. "My mother believes everything has a place and should be in that place unless being utilized by one of us. When I was a little girl, I remember mimicking her. I would line up my dolls and their clothes. I would make their little beds and arrange them just so."

"A fellow doesn't really think about such things."

"Oh, I find that hard to believe. Do you not carefully arrange your tools? Is your work area not set up the way you desire?"

Yuri grinned and his blue eyes seemed to twinkle. "You are

describing Dalton, but not me. I'm more of an 'as-you-go' kind of man. I use a tool and put it down where I finish."

"But what happens when you need it again?"

"Then I go in search of it."

Phoebe shook her head. "But doesn't that waste a great deal of time?"

"If you haven't noticed, there isn't a real sense of urgency here. We move at a nice steady pace but certainly never rush ourselves. Unless, of course, a storm is bearing down without warning or a grizzly has come to feed off our scraps. I've never lived in a city where people are constantly scurrying about, but I've heard enough stories. I suppose you know well about such matters."

She thought for a moment. "Yes, my life moved at a faster pace in Vermont. There was always something that needed our attention, and we had meticulous schedules to see that things were done in a timely manner."

"I wouldn't want to live that way. I enjoy my life here."

"So you never plan to leave?" Phoebe questioned.

Yuri threw her a smile. "Not if I have a reason to stay."

"You said that once before. What do you mean by that exactly?"

Yuri slowed their pace as they approached the lake. "My parents want to return to Russia. My mother's sisters write her every month to plead with her to come home. My grandparents are aging and in need of more and more help, and Mother's sisters want her to share the responsibility. My father knows he can build boats anywhere and doesn't seem to mind the thought of leaving, although I think he really does. Still, he will go if that is Mother's wish."

"It's kind of him to consider her needs before his own."

He nodded thoughtfully. "My father is a good man. He has always been good to the women in our family. He tells my brother and me that an honorable man watches over his family with strength and tenderness."

Phoebe thought such teachings to be admirable. "Your father sounds very wise."

"Careful where you step. The bears have been here," Yuri said, pointing to the ground. "They are searching for as much food as possible before they head higher and sleep through the winter."

She sidestepped the scat and frowned. "Will we be in any danger? Perhaps we shouldn't venture any farther from town."

"We'll be fine. I brought my rifle, and usually bears won't approach unless they are really hungry. There has been plenty of food available to them—berries, salmon, and such. We will keep watch, but not give up enjoying the day."

Phoebe felt nervous at the thought that they might well need to share their picnic with a family of bears. Her glance darted around the lake and trail.

"If it makes you feel better," he said, seeming to understand her fear, "we can simply have our picnic here. I think the bears have moved on and there are other people tramping about. The noise should discourage the wildlife."

"I think I'd like that, yes." She breathed a sigh of relief and gave Yuri a smile. "Thank you."

He pointed to a place by the lake's edge. Giving her approval, Phoebe watched as he quickly set up their picnic. First, he unrolled a square piece of oilcloth and spread it on the ground, and then surprised her by laying a wool blanket on top of it.

"I brought this for you to sit on, in case the ground was too damp."

She smiled. "That was very thoughtful." He was doing everything right, she had to admit. Perhaps she should give his attentions more consideration. He was a handsome young man, and his manners, while sometimes a bit crude, were generally delightful.

"Here, allow me." Yuri came to her side and offered her assistance. Phoebe sat down and waited for him to finish arranging their food. "Mother made us sandwiches and cookies. She makes the best cookies I've ever had." He looked at her and smiled. "Do you bake?"

"I do," she admitted. "I especially enjoy making cookies."

"That's good to know." He handed her a sandwich. "I heard from Dalton that your cookies were delicious."

She wasn't sure what to say. It was wonderful to hear that Dalton had bragged on her baking to Yuri. She shrugged. "Then you already knew that I could bake."

He laughed. "I suppose I did." He paused for a moment. "So, how do you like living in Sitka? You haven't yet experienced the winter here, but you needn't fear. Our winters are quite easy, compared to other places in Alaska."

"It's a nice enough place," Phoebe said, considering her words carefully. She didn't want to offend Yuri by telling him that she found the place unbearable at times.

"You don't sound very convincing."

She looked up and saw that he was watching her closely. "I'm sorry. I suppose it's still all very new to me. We haven't been here but a few months. It's much smaller and far more isolated than what I have known. It's hard to get supplies for the candles, and because of that, we can't make as many as we'd like. Not only that, but I left good friends in Vermont."

"You have managed to make good friends here," he offered.

"But my friends from home . . . I had known them from childhood and school. They were lifelong friends. I miss them very much," she admitted. "Then, too, my grandmother and other family are still living back there. Sitka is so far away from everything. Sometimes it's really . . . well . . . lonely."

Surprisingly, he laughed. "I would be happy to keep you from being lonely."

Phoebe frowned. "That was a rather forward thing to say."

Yuri shrugged. "I have to work quickly to win your heart."

"What happened to the slower pace of life in Sitka?"

"Dalton will soon return, and I will be forced to share you with him, unless I convince you to accept me first."

"Accept you?"

"Yes. As a possible husband."

Phoebe dropped the sandwich on her lap. "Why, I hardly even know you, Yuri Belikov!" She knew it was a lame excuse because she'd already considered how it might be to marry Dalton, and she knew him even less. "How can you even suggest such a thing?"

It was Yuri's turn to frown. "But I thought all women wanted to marry. Have you not even considered that this courtship is in the hopes of such a thing?"

"I never agreed to courtship. I thought we were two friends, enjoying a Sunday picnic," Phoebe replied. "I have given no thought to anything else." It wasn't exactly a lie, she told herself. She hadn't given thought to courting Yuri.

"Then you should. I know Dalton will have that on his mind when he returns. We have already discussed the challenge to win your heart."

Phoebe was embarrassed and angry. They had discussed her as a challenge? "You speak of love as though it were a game."

He smiled. "In a way it is. Dalton and I decided it would be our own little contest to see who could win you over. I am most fortunate that his family problems called him away to Kansas City. I get to work on winning your affection without his interference."

Jumping to her feet, Phoebe could see that Yuri was proud of the fact that he'd shared this information with her. Had he thought it would endear him to her?

"I am not the prize to be had in a game of hearts," she announced. Picking up her walking stick, she looked down at Yuri in as stern a fashion as she could muster. "You should talk to your father for further lessons on dealing with women."

Stalking back down the trail, Phoebe barely missed the bear's droppings. She was mad at herself for losing her temper. Yuri really hadn't done anything all that bad, but still it grieved her. He and Dalton had talked about her as if she were nothing more than a prize to be won. Somehow it cheapened her and the love she had thought might come her way.

"How dare they make it a contest!"

———

Dalton awoke Monday morning with Phoebe Robbins on his mind. It wasn't the first time he'd thought of her on this trip, but it was the most intense. He'd even dreamed about her, and this only made his longing to return home more acute.

Dressing quite casually in trousers and one of the white shirts Evie had given him from Thomas's closet, Dalton made his way downstairs. He was surprised to find his sister already at work. She was discussing something intently with the man Dalton recognized as her lawyer. Halting at the door to the dining room, Dalton started to turn away, but Evie motioned him in.

"We're just concluding. Please join us."

Dalton came forward and the lawyer stood. "Mr. Lindquist, it is good to see you again."

"Mr. Haskins." Dalton shook his hand, then took his seat at the table. One of the serving girls was immediately at his side, pouring hot coffee into a delicate china cup. Dalton was almost afraid to touch the thing. It didn't look strong enough to stand up to usage.

"We were just finalizing the details of the estate," Evie told him. "Mr. Haskins says he should be able to have all of the papers to me by tomorrow, and then we can leave."

"That is good news," Dalton said. The young woman returned with a plate of food and placed it in front of him. He smiled. The food in Kansas City had definitely been worth the visit. He had enjoyed the different dishes and marveled at the number of choices. Today he would dine on succulent sausages, fried potatoes, and fresh fruit.

Evie continued. "Mr. Haskins will also arrange our train tickets back to Seattle. If it is all right with you, we shall plan to leave on Thursday."

"The sooner, the better," Dalton replied.

The trip had really done nothing for him but affirm his mother's and sister's view of the Gray family. The desire to know his siblings and to better understand his past had proven rather futile. He had come face-to-face with their true character and what they were capable of doing.

Yet in spite of the disappointment where his family was concerned, his future was secure financially. Evie had arranged a meeting with his mother's lawyer, and the man seemed pleasant and very competent. He arranged for Dalton to have access to an amazing amount of money. For the first time, Dalton realized he had enough to start his own business or buy his own house, or both. And that was only a portion of what he would possess when he turned twenty-one. It was stunning.

"If you wish to purchase anything to take back to Sitka, we can go shopping later today," his sister announced. "I have a few things I'm going to pick up for Lydia, Zee, and the girls, and you might as well come along and see if there's anything you or Kjell might need."

"I would like that. I also have things to pick up in Seattle. Mr. Belikov gave me a list."

"We shall plan accordingly, then," Evie said with a nod to her lawyer. "Better arrange our stay in Seattle with an extra day or two for business."

The man nodded and took out a pencil and paper from his coat pocket. "I will see to it."

Evie smiled at Dalton. "We shall soon be home."

Dalton felt a sense of peace at the thought. He missed his family, and he longed to see Phoebe again. It seemed silly. They didn't know each other well enough for him to hold such longing. Still, he couldn't shake the feeling that this was the woman he would marry—would have a family with and make a life of their own together.

But first there were still a few things he wanted to accomplish here—the least of which was a private meeting with Marston on the morrow.

Chapter 13

"I find this rather annoying," Marston declared the next morning as he joined Dalton in Evie's front sitting room. "It serves no good purpose."

Evie had left the house an hour earlier to attend to some shopping, and Dalton was glad for the privacy. He didn't intend to play games with his brother.

"It serves my purpose," Dalton replied. "And that is all that matters to me at the moment."

Marston shrugged. "If that is how it's to be."

"It is." Dalton sat in the same chair he'd used the night he and Evie had spoken to Marston and the others. "I don't generally waste my time with godless men, but I find reason to give an exception this time."

"Godless? Just because I don't adhere to religious nonsense, you call me godless?"

Dalton stared at him a moment and waited until Marston finally took a seat. "I don't adhere to religious nonsense, either. However, I value honesty, humility, compassion, and forgiveness."

Marston uttered an expletive. "You sound like a naïve preacher."

"Be that as it may, I came here with one intent: to hear your side of what happened in Alaska between you and my mother."

His brother's eyes seemed to narrow to slits. "You seem halfway intelligent. Why do you suppose I will tell you anything? Men my own age do not speak to me the way you have. Why do you suppose I would allow you to do so?"

"You'll allow it, and you'll tell me what I want to know. Until recently, I knew very little about our father and nothing of you. My mother never uttered a word."

"I would have expected as much. Your mother is a liar and a thief. She isn't worth the dirt she walks on."

Marston's hateful words nearly caused Dalton to come out of his seat. He knew his brother was baiting him—trying to get him angry. *If I lose control,* Dalton told himself, *then Marston will take it.*

"You will refrain from speaking against my mother."

"You wanted the truth."

Dalton clenched his fist and then relaxed. "I want to know what prompted you to do the things you did. You will not malign my mother."

Marston laughed. "And if I do? What will you do about it?"

A slow smile formed on Dalton's lips. "In Sitka, when a man insults your womenfolk, the offense is often settled with a good punch to the face. Given you are an old man who does very little physically, and I am in my prime and quite strong, I believe I would have the upper hand. In fact, it might be extremely satisfying."

His brother studied Dalton for a moment, then shrugged again. "What is it you want to know?"

"I want the truth. It's just you and me, and I want to know why you did what you did."

Marston sat in silence for several long minutes before meeting Dalton's gaze. "I did it for the money. Pure and simple. You held the key to our family fortune. If I had you, I could have that, as well."

Dalton would never have admitted it, but his brother's callous words hurt him. He knew his mother had said this was Marston's reasoning, but he had somehow hoped the man might suggest otherwise. He hardened himself against the emotions welling within him, however. He needed to remain strong and clear-minded.

"Do you regret the things you did?" Dalton asked, knowing that his brother probably didn't have conscience enough for regret.

"I do."

His answer surprised Dalton. "Would you care to explain?"

"I should have simply waited until you were older, then enticed you to join Mitchell and me here in Kansas City. You really should learn about the family business, for we're the ones Father raised to take it. He had no idea you even existed. Your mother had been unable to give him children."

"Because he beat her badly enough to cause her to miscarry," Dalton replied. "Since he died, she was able to carry me to delivery."

"Your mother was difficult. Our father had to keep her in line. You weren't there, so it's easy for you to make her into some kind of saint. But believe me, she wasn't."

Dalton laughed. "I never said she was, but if any woman is capable of being such, she is. You don't know her at all."

"I know she had charges brought against me for murder and attempted murder—not to mention your kidnapping. I know she turned my younger sister against me, against the entire family. And her own husband."

"My mother did not turn her against any of you. Evie came to Alaska a broken, disheartened woman. When she overheard you admitting to your brother and her husband that you had tried to kill my mother so that you could raise me, it was more than she could bear." Dalton shook his head. "Just in talking with you, I realize that you care nothing about the pain and suffering you caused. My mother nearly died because of you, and even when she recovered, it was a slow and painful process. I suppose that brings you more joy than regret. I can only be glad that I wasn't influenced by your heartlessness."

"You are naïve," Marston said matter-of-factly. "You have a misconception of how the world functions. People get hurt. People suffer. People die. It's a simple cycle. Our father was a man of business and means. He craved power and respect, and he got both. These kinds of things are important to most men."

"My father has both, and I've seldom ever heard him raise his voice to anyone, much less commit murder to get them. I think you're the one who lives on misconceptions."

"Perhaps in your isolated little world, such things work. But not here. There are truly bad people in the world, Dalton, but I'm not one of them. It would behoove you to stick around and see that for yourself. I am hardly the same man I was then. Had I done things differently, you might be here asking me to teach you about the family business dealings. You would see the importance of bringing Mitchell and me back into what had always been intended for us.

"Furthermore, you would understand in time that the bond between us Gray men is a strong one—an unbreakable one. Just because your mother took you to Alaska and allowed a stranger to raise you doesn't change the fact that you're one of us. You have the same blood. We are brothers, Dalton. Nothing changes that. Not your mother's desires or the distance of miles. If you stayed here, we could build our business into an empire."

"I am your brother; that much is true. However, I feel no bond to you. Frankly, you disgust me with your excuses and contradictions. You are selfish, and that motivates you to serve yourself rather than others. I could never be in business with you. I don't trust you now, and I don't believe I ever could."

Marston gave out a loud guffaw. "So much for your Christian forgiveness and compassion. I thought practicing your religious values was what you held most dear."

Dalton got to his feet and stared at Marston for a moment. Everything his sister and mother had told him about the man was true. He was a liar and a cheat, a ruthless man who had no desire to play by the rules—either man's or God's.

"You should thank God that I am practicing my religious beliefs and values. Otherwise, I believe I would have killed you the first time we met—revenge for what you did to my mother. Instead, I'm glad to let God avenge her and me. Now I want you to go. There's no sense in your being here when Evie returns."

"But I thought you wanted my story about what happened." Marston's tone was taunting.

Shaking his head, Dalton moved toward the door. "I already know your story."

———

Phoebe made her way up the steps to the Lindquist house with their box of ordered candles tucked securely under her arm. She had thought to talk to Lydia about what Yuri said, but then realized it would be silly. Lydia probably knew nothing about the contest between the two friends, and even if she did, what could she say?

"Oh, I'm so glad you've come," Zee said upon answering the door. She ushered Phoebe inside. "I have some young ladies I want you to meet."

Lydia saw a circle of several girls; none looked to be much more than fifteen. She smiled and received their smiles in return.

"Girls, this is Phoebe Robbins," Zee announced. "She and her mother make candles, and she has brought some here today." She then introduced each of the girls, giving both their Tlingit name and the Americanized version. "Eleanor and Edith are sisters. Edith is sixteen and Eleanor is seventeen. Mary and Deborah are both fifteen, and Catherine is eighteen. They are each married and have come here to learn since they cannot attend the school."

Married? Phoebe was surprised by this news as well as the age of the girls. They were all quite small. *Of course, I'm not all that large myself,* she thought. Her petite frame and short stature had caused many people to misjudge her age. "I'm very glad to meet all of you."

"We're quilting today. Would you care to join us?" Zee asked.

"No, I can't stay long, but thank you for the invitation. My mother sent me with Lydia's order of candles."

Zee took the box from Phoebe. "Lydia is out back if you wish to say hello."

"I believe I will. It was nice to see you, Zee. I hope we can talk again soon."

"Perhaps sometime you could show the girls about candle making."

"I'll mention it to my mother," Phoebe replied. "I believe we could certainly plan something."

Zee smiled. "Until next time then."

Phoebe nodded and made her way out. She was just heading

around the side of the house when she spotted Lydia coming up the walk. "Hello, Mrs. Lindquist."

"I thought we agreed you would call me Lydia."

"I forgot," Phoebe admitted. "I brought your candles. Zee took them and said you were out here. I thought I would say hello."

"I'm glad you did," Lydia replied. "Come and talk with me a moment. We've had news. Evie sent a telegram to Seattle and arranged for it to be given to the captain of a vessel coming north. We got the message just yesterday. She and Dalton intend to be home in about two weeks."

"That's wonderful news. I'm sure you've missed them."

"I have. I can't help but admit my fear for their safety. But she says they are well. I'm sure we will hear all about it when they return."

"And . . . Dalton? He is coming back, as well?"

"Oh, most assuredly. Dalton would never leave Sitka for long. He loves it here. This is his home."

Though Phoebe was anticipating his return, she couldn't help but feel a sense of disappointment in Lydia's words. Sitka still felt unfamiliar. Now that fall was upon them, she missed New England and the wonderful colors of the trees in Vermont. She missed so many things about her home.

"You look upset. Are you unwell?" Lydia asked.

"No. Not at all," Phoebe said. "I've just not found a way to feel comfortable here. I envy you who have. How did you adjust to such isolation?"

Lydia gave a light laugh. "I never liked the city. It was noisy and smelly and there were far too many people. I suppose just as you hate the quiet, I craved it."

"It is a restful place," Phoebe agreed. "I pray and pray, however, that somehow God will give me a way to leave." She immediately regretted her confession.

Lydia gave her arm a pat. "But have you ever asked God to help you learn to love your new surroundings? So often, we pray for the wrong thing."

"Pray to love Sitka?"

"Why not? Instead of asking for Him to remove you, why not pray to find value and comfort in where He has taken you?"

Phoebe had honestly never thought of it that way. "I don't suppose it could hurt. But what then?"

"Who can say? Only the Lord can direct your steps. He alone knows where this will lead you," Lydia replied. "God's purposes sometimes seem strange, but He is a good Father, Phoebe. He wants to give good things to His children. Paul speaks in Philippians of it being great gain to learn contentment, no matter the circumstance. God can give it to you, if you truly want it."

Phoebe thought about it a moment and nodded. "I think I do. It would be wonderful to wake up in the morning and not long for another place. Sometimes I dread even getting out of bed."

"Well, I do, too, but for entirely different reasons. I find as I get older, I like to sleep just a little longer," Lydia said, laughing.

———

Well into the night Phoebe thought about what Lydia had suggested. In the solitude of her room she took up her Bible and searched through Philippians for the verses Lydia had mentioned. Finally, she found them in the fourth chapter.

"Not that I speak in respect of want: for I have learned, in whatsoever state I am, therewith to be content. I know both how to be abased, and I know how to abound: every where and in all things I am instructed both to be full and to be hungry, both to abound and to suffer need. I can do all things through Christ which strengtheneth me."

Could Christ give her a love for Sitka and the ability to be content, no matter where life took her? People seemed to always base their happiness or sorrow on the conditions of life around them. If loved ones died, their families were sad. If someone received a blessing, they were happy. Even the weather affected whether contentment could be achieved for some. Was it really possible to abound everywhere—in all things?

"It says right here that I can do all things through Christ which strengtheneth me. Not just some things," she whispered to herself. "All things."

Chapter 14

Y ou two run along now," Zee commanded. "The girls and I are going to have a nice supper together and then work on our quilt."

Lydia looked at Kjell and smiled. "Do you hear that? You and I actually get to have some time alone. That hasn't happened in a long while."

Kjell grinned. "I think I like the sounds of it, Mrs. Lindquist. I'll fetch the wagon." He gave her a quick peck on the cheek, then darted out the door like a young man about to court his girl.

Zee laughed. "You have a good time, Lydia. Enjoy yourself and try to put aside all your concerns. God has everything under control."

Lydia nodded. She couldn't help but dwell on the fact that her beloved son would come home a changed man. Whether that would be a good thing or not remained to be seen. She had done the best she could to raise him with a heart focused on God and the present. She often told her children that they couldn't change the past and they couldn't jump forward to the future. All they had was today, and they needed to live it in such a way that they wouldn't create just another regretted yesterday. Mourning the past was never productive—she knew this full well.

Having been chilled most of the day, Lydia took up her wool cape. "Thank you, Zerelda. How I appreciate the years we've had together. You've helped me in so many ways." She kissed her aunt on the cheek. "I think I'm even closer to you than I was to Mother."

Zee reached up and touched Lydia's cheek. "You are the daughter I never had, and Kjell is like a son. Your children are as precious to me as if they'd been my own. I'm the one who's blessed."

"When I think of coming here so long ago . . ." Lydia fell silent and shook her head. "My life is so different now, and I truly hadn't remembered much about my old life until Dalton took this trip south. I hope it won't damage him."

"You raised a good man, Liddie. Give him a chance to prove it."

"But you don't know how those people can be," Lydia said, frowning.

Zee grasped her hand. "I know the promises of God, and furthermore, I believe them."

Lydia nodded. "I keep reminding myself that. I'm trying to be at peace—to be content no matter the situation. I even reminded Phoebe of those verses in Philippians yesterday."

"Then take your own advice and remember that Christ will give you the strength to do all things. Even face the horrors of the past."

Lydia drew a deep breath and let it out slowly. Her aunt was right. She just had to be strong—not in her own strength, but in God's.

"Sounds like Kjell is bringing the wagon around." Zee pushed her toward the door. "Now, get on out of here. The girls and I have plans. I've sent them to find their quilt squares, and we will have a regular quilting party after we eat."

"I hope you have fun," Lydia said. "We won't be late."

She made her way outside as Kjell brought the wagon to a halt. He got down and helped her up onto the wagon seat, then joined her with a smile that stretched nearly from ear to ear.

"I have you to myself." He leaned over and surprised her with a passionate kiss. Lydia melted against him with a sigh, causing Kjell to chuckle. "Well, now that I have your attention, my dear, where would you like to go?"

"Anywhere, as long as you are with me." She smiled at him and looped her arm through his. "We can just take a nice ride, and then when the light is completely gone, we can have a bite to eat."

"I like the sound of that." Kjell slapped the reins lightly against the rumps of the horses. "Get along now."

Lydia enjoyed the view of the harbor as the road came closer to the coast. There had been a great deal of trouble some years earlier, when Sheldon Jackson had supposedly infringed upon the passage into Sitka. It was basically a property dispute blown out of proportion, but the truth of the matter was that Jackson had grieved some of the men in power, and they, in turn, had tried to see his reputation completely ruined. And they had nearly succeeded. The native school quickly emptied of children, and Jackson was arrested. But cooler heads prevailed, and the man was released. Most of the men who'd tried to rid Sitka of Jackson were now instead gone themselves.

"You seem deep in thought."

Lydia looked up at Kjell and nodded. "There's been a lot on my mind of late."

"Dalton and Evie?"

"Among other things," she replied rather defensively.

"Liddie, I know you pretty well after nineteen years."

"Well, I do think about other things and people," she replied with a sheepish smile.

"But Dalton is weighing down your heart. Come on, Liddie. Admit it."

Lydia pulled back. "Well, what decent mother wouldn't be worried? We know how evil Marston is."

"He could have changed," Kjell offered.

"Oh, you are the eternal optimist," she replied, crossing her arms.

Laughing at this, Kjell continued. "You are most likely right in assuming that Marston is the same. However, even if he's just as bad as he's always been, it doesn't matter. Dalton is a man who seeks God's heart. He won't be easily swayed. You have to account for the fact that he has grown up. He's able to look out for himself, Liddie."

She sighed. "I know what you say is true. He is a good man, and I have to trust that God has His hand on Dalton—no matter where he goes or who he encounters. God is faithful."

"Yes, He is. We have to remember that sometimes things seem wrong because they are out of our control, but they are never out of God's control."

"Do you think Dalton will be better for this trip?"

Kjell said nothing for a few moments, and Lydia could see he was giving careful consideration to her question. This was something he often did when matters were of the utmost importance.

Lydia looked out across the water at the sunset. There was such a peace about the way the water lapped gently upon the shore— constant, steady, reassuring.

"I think God allows us to go through so many things that don't seem likely to benefit us, but in hindsight, we can see where they did. Even the tragedies we've suffered over the years." He slowed the horses. "I think if Dalton will let Him, God will reveal important things about himself and life through this experience."

The words had a calming effect on her heart. "I know you're right."

"So what else has you concerned tonight?" He looked over at her with a grin. "You're not fretting over the girls, are you?"

"No, not really. Although I will say that Kjerstin has been making it quite clear she wants to be a nurse like Zee. That will require she go south for schooling."

"But not for another ten years or so. She might change her mind twenty times by then."

"I know, but the time will slip by faster than we think. But . . . well . . . there's actually another girl who's been on my mind a lot of late."

He raised a brow. "Who?"

"Phoebe Robbins."

"Why is that? Is there a problem with her flute playing? She still wants to perform with us, doesn't she?"

"Yes. I mean no, there isn't a problem, and yes, she still wants to perform." Lydia paused a moment before plunging ahead. "What has been on my mind—and please don't think me silly—but it has to do with her and Dalton."

His expression was one of pure confusion. "What are you talking about?"

Lydia's mind rushed with memories of Dalton and Phoebe, as well as her own prayers. "Before Dalton left for Kansas City, I could tell from some things he said that he found her quite interesting. Phoebe has also made it clear in our conversations that she misses him and she finds ways to ask me roundabout questions about him. Not only that, but I've long been praying for Dalton to find the right woman to marry someday, and the more I pray about it, the more I feel God laying Phoebe on my heart. I can't really say why, but I believe they are destined for each other."

As was typical, Kjell fell silent while he again considered what she'd said. They made their way into town, nodding or waving to those they knew. Kjell finally brought the wagon to a stop. "Let's walk a bit."

Lydia allowed him to help her down, and they strolled on a path near the main dock and held hands as the light faded bit by bit from the horizon.

"I think if God has really put this on your heart, Liddie, then you should seek His wisdom in what to do with it. Obviously the matter of falling in love will be between Phoebe and Dalton."

"But I'm worried about them doing just that. I like Phoebe a great deal and I think she's a lovely young woman, but she hates Sitka. You know Dalton loves it here. He's always said he would never live anywhere but here."

"Up until now he's never been anywhere but here. Now that he's seen the States and had a chance to experience life in the city, he may have a different opinion."

Lydia frowned to think that her husband might be right. Yet it was hard to imagine that Dalton would fall under the spell of the city. His love of solitude—which he could only seem to find up in the mountains—made even Sitka seem too big for him.

"What are you chewing on?" Kjell asked.

She shook her head. "I just can't see Dalton giving up this place. In fact, I could more easily see Phoebe coming to love Sitka than Dalton agreeing to move."

"A man will do strange things when it comes to the woman he loves," Kjell replied. "Look at me. I never intended to remarry, and I'd certainly given up on having a family. I figured I'd own the mill until I died. Then you came into my life."

He smiled at her in a way that caused Lydia's heart to skip a beat. My, but he was still the best-looking man she'd ever known.

"Dalton may come to realize, as I did with you, that nothing matters as much as loving Phoebe and being with her."

"I know you're right. When Phoebe told me how hard it was to be happy here, I reminded her of Paul's words in Philippians on contentment. I suggested she pray and ask God to help her find things to love about Sitka." Lydia stepped around a puddle. "I suppose I didn't want to suggest that Dalton could change his mind and desire to move away with her. Oh, Kjell, I think my heart would break if he left us."

Kjell put his arm around Lydia's shoulders. "I know it would be hard, but darling, we need to realize it's a possibility. We cannot put a harness on the boy. He will have to make his own decisions and seek the direction God specifically has for his life." He paused and pulled Lydia into his arms. "But don't be afraid. I'll be here with you every step of the way. I will bear this with you—you will never be alone. You and I have faced much worse than this." He kissed the tip of her nose. "We can do this together."

———

"You seem completely out of sorts," Evie said as she joined Dalton on the garden patio. The sun had long since descended from the Kansas City sky, but several gas lamps had been lit to softly illuminate the garden.

"I just don't feel like I accomplished what I set out to do in coming here," he said. "I had hoped to find a real connection to my father and my heritage. I expected to feel at least a slight attachment to the family. Instead, I feel nothing but sadness when I think of them."

Pulling a metal case from her pocket, Evie handed it to Dalton. "Open it."

He did as she suggested and looked down on a tintype of a man who very much resembled Marston and Mitchell. He glanced up at Evie with a questioning look in his eyes.

"That is our father, Floyd Gray. I thought perhaps you might like to have it."

Dalton looked at the picture again. "Do I look like him?"

"No. You don't look like him at all. You resemble your mother."

"He looks so hard—unfeeling. Just like Marston and Mitchell." He closed the case. "How can they be that way? Have they no heart at all?"

Evie sighed. "I think Father was raised with stern and unyielding temperaments. My mother was a gentle spirit, and her love and kind ways were my inspiration. Jeannette, however, was jealous of the attention Father gave the boys and she strived to do anything that might impress him—even if that meant becoming like him. Where our brothers could utilize that nature for business, it only served to make Jeannette appear shrewish."

"I'm glad you took after your mother," Dalton said with just a hint of a smile. He looked away and fixed his gaze on the lawn. "I suppose there will always be an empty place inside of me. Not knowing my father or understanding his ways leaves me with a void."

Evie considered something for a moment. "I know we will leave tomorrow, but the train doesn't depart until close to noon. I have an idea. I'd like to take you to the house where we grew up. Jeannette owns it now and much has been left as it was. I can even show you a painting of my mother. Everyone says I look just like her."

Dalton nodded. "I'd like that."

"Perhaps you will be able to see something of our father when you are there. Who can say? But no matter, I want you to be able to return to Sitka with a sense of accomplishment. I know this trip was important to you, just as it was to me."

He looked at her and frowned. "I hope this journey brought you peace of mind."

"It did. I find that so many doors can now be closed. I have a huge sense of relief in Thomas's passing. I didn't wish the man dead, but neither did I want things to go on as they were. I had planned to seek a divorce if I came here and found that he was really quite well and Jeannette had made up the entire story."

"I know that would have been very hard for you to do," Dalton said.

"Yes, but certainly no harder than what I'd already endured. To live all these years as a wife without a husband . . . well, that was difficult to say the least. Thomas didn't want me or the love I had to offer. Now I'm free to find someone who does."

"And I know just the man," Dalton said, his expression changing to amusement. "Poor Joshua. He won't know what hit him when you get home."

"Dalton Lindquist!" she declared in mock horror. "How can you even say such things?"

Her brother laughed heartily at this, and that made her smile, as well. She was glad to see he could find joy in something.

"All I know," Dalton finally answered, "is that Joshua is mad about you, and you are just as smitten with him. If you want my advice, Evie, don't waste any time with silly traditions of mourning or courtship. March right into Josh's office and tell him how you feel. You've waited long enough for love."

She felt her cheeks flush at the image she had in her head. What if she'd misread Josh's feelings for her? What if in her absence he had sought another? Evie forced the questions out of her mind. What if he had? She wouldn't know the answer if she didn't pose the question. Dalton was right. She needed to step up and try for what really mattered most of all.

Chapter 15

I must say this is short notice," Jeannette said, eyeing Evie and Dalton.

Dalton thought she looked like a nervous hen as she moved around the sitting room. Her lavender day dress seemed much too snug, adding to her awkward appearance.

"I'm sorry, but we leave in less than three hours," Evie told Jeannette. "That's why I called you last night."

"Still, it was a very brief warning."

"I didn't know that you needed me to warn you of our arrival. We aren't here on a hostile mission," Evie replied, pulling off her gloves.

"Why *are* you here?" Jeannette asked. "You said very little last night."

"Dalton wanted to see the home where his mother and father shared their life together."

"To what purpose?" She sounded suspicious.

Dalton smiled. "Just the satisfaction of connecting to the past."

Jeannette's expression was one of annoyance. She looked back to Evie. "I suppose if you must. I'll take you on a tour of the place and then we can have tea."

"If you don't mind, Jeannette, I'd rather take Dalton around on my own. We can stay out of any room you'd rather us not see." Jeannette looked offended, and Evie quickly added, "After that, we should have time to share tea with you."

"I . . . well . . . it's most unusual," Jeannette declared.

"We can leave if you'd prefer," Dalton told her.

"No!" Jeannette replied quickly. "I put all of my other plans aside for this morning. You might as well stay."

Jeannette seemed very lonely to him, and Dalton couldn't help but wonder if she really had had any other plans. She clearly didn't want their company, but she desperately needed someone.

"Go ahead and see the house. All of the rooms are open," Jeannette said. "I will arrange for our refreshments." She waited for Evie to nod before hurrying out of the room.

Dalton glanced around at the opulent room. The furnishings were a bit worn, but in every corner and flat surface there were a wide variety of knickknacks. He knew little about art or collectibles, but he figured their worth to be quite great.

"Are these things left over from your childhood?" he asked Evie.

"No. Jeannette has her own style and taste. Our mother liked things elegant, but not too overstated. I think the portrait is the only thing I recognize as hers," Evie said, studying the painting that still hung over the fireplace.

"I thought that was you," Dalton said in surprise. He looked again at the picture. "I noticed it when we came in. The resemblance is uncanny."

Evie was momentarily lost in thought. Dalton could see that the portrait had some strange affect on her. He said nothing more, waiting for her to begin the conversation when she was ready.

Evie clearly had adored her mother. The memories she'd shared proved as much. Then added to this depth of feeling was the fact that Evie had seen her father—their father—kill her mother.

"And years later his son tried to kill mine," he murmured.

Evie turned as if suddenly aware of him. "What?"

"I was just thinking about how our father killed her. Then years later his son—our brother—tried to kill my mother."

"It is a strange bond to share, don't you think?" Evie said, gazing into his eyes. "Funny, but I never shared a closeness with my other siblings. You are the only one who truly seems like a brother to me. You and I have these wonderful memories of good times and laughter. I have none of that with my older brothers. I don't even have it with Jeannette.

"I know that moving to Sitka saved my life in a way," she continued. "Not that I think anyone would have tried to kill me physically, but emotionally, every day they seemed to rob me of something precious. It was as if they knew they could take bits and pieces of my spirit, just a little at a time, and eventually they would have it all. I would simply fail to exist."

Dalton could see the pain in her eyes. He felt an overwhelming sorrow for Evie. Her life here had been a cruel hoax. There had been the pretense of a family but none of the love and joy that should have been present.

Evie hugged her arms to her dark blue traveling suit. Her gaze traveled back up to the painting of the blond-haired woman. "She was just a year older than I am now, yet she looks so ancient. Her eyes are haunting and hollow. This wasn't how she had been with me. This is a portrait she had made for our father. It was her Christmas gift to him. That and her death."

Putting his arm around Evie's shoulders, Dalton felt her tremble. "He can't hurt you anymore. None of them can."

She looked at him as if begging him to assure her. He hugged her closer. "We'll soon be home, Evie. We won't have to be influenced by any of them."

"I want to believe that," she said, giving the slightest nod. "It's just much harder than I thought."

"Coming here?"

"Yes."

"Evie, we can go. I don't need to see anything more," Dalton told her.

"Maybe not. But I do." She glanced upward. "I need to go back to the attic. I haven't been there since . . . that day."

"Are you certain you want to do this?"

She nodded. "I think I must. It will free me from the past."

"Then by all means, lead the way. I will go with you, and we will face it together."

Evie rambled about one thing or another as they made their way through the house and up the grand staircase. She told Dalton stories of playing on the stairs while the young maids polished the newels and banister. When they came to the second floor, she showed Dalton where Lydia's room had been.

"It's still very much as it was," she told him. "I think the bedding and rugs have changed, but the draperies look much the same."

Dalton could see there was great wear on the panels. "It would seem so." He fought back thoughts of his father beating his mother—of the horrible night he'd been conceived. How could any man be so cruel? Would he grow older and turn out to be like Floyd Gray? His brothers had mirrored their father's heartlessness. Was it hereditary?

"Are you all right?" Evie asked.

"Like you, I have my demons. Mother told me how cruel our father was to her. She said I was not conceived in love, but rather as the result of his attack."

It was Evie's turn to offer comfort. "I'm so sorry, Dalton. I cannot lie and say her life here was pleasant. I don't believe she ever knew a happy day here. If not enduring Father's temper, she had to contend with us—her stepchildren. Our brothers would not offer any respect, much less love. Jeannette hated her for taking our mother's place, but I loved her. Even then."

Evie's eyes welled with tears. "I was so young when Mother died, and the manner of her death filled me with despair and fear. I just knew Father would find out I'd seen him, and then he would do the same to me."

"My mother was so young when she married Father," Dalton said. "She must have been quite afraid."

"I know there were times when she was sorely abused, but Lydia always reached out to me. She knew that the others would offer her nothing, but I wanted her tenderness, and she needed my love. We couldn't be open about it, of course. Jeannette would box my ears whenever she found me in Lydia's company. She would drag me away on some pretense and tell me that I was in no manner to be kind to that woman. To love Lydia, Jeannette said, was to hate our mother. And if we hated our mother, we would suffer a great punishment from God."

"And did you believe her?"

Evie drew a deep breath and sighed. "I think I did at times. Remember, in the back of my mind was the fear that Father would kill me. Part of the reason I've wanted to be with Lydia these years is because she alone understands my painful life—the horror of being forced to marry a much older man, whom you didn't know, much less love."

They moved from the room and back toward the staircase. "Mother tried to make a pleasant home, but Father would have no part of it. Jeannette told me that Mother often tried to fuss over Marston and Mitchell. She tried to show them affection and tenderness, and Father accused her of trying to weaken his sons and make them into milk sops."

"It's so sad," Dalton said as they approached the third floor. "There but for the grace of God, it might have been me."

Evie nodded. "I've often thought of that, too. I'm glad God gave you a better father. Kjell is a remarkable man, and he's given me hope that not all men are vicious and cruel."

Glancing to the right, she pointed. "This floor was mostly for the servants." Turning to the left, she moved down the hall and Dalton quickly stepped to match her strides. When they reached the end of the hall she stopped. "To the left are the servants' stairs."

"And this?" Dalton asked as he pointed to the right.

She looked at the door and frowned. "This goes to the attic." Evie seemed to collect her thoughts for a moment. "When I was a little girl I loved to sneak up here. I would dig through the old trunks and crates and find all kinds of interesting things. I also liked it because it was so quiet and because my mother would also come up here."

Evie reached out and turned the knob. The door moaned and creaked as she swung it open. There was a glow of light at the top of the stairs. "Shall we?" she asked.

Dalton nodded and offered her a smile. "I'm right here with you."

They climbed the stairs, Evie moving with deliberate slowness. She seemed to be mentally preparing herself for what she would find at the top.

"I was playing up here, as I shouldn't have been. My mother came up. There was a little walkway on the roof. They called it a widow's walk. She liked to go there at times just to get away from her sorrows, I think." When they stepped onto the attic floor, Evie pointed. "It's just over there."

Dalton noted the door that led outside. There were several large oval windows that allowed light to flood the room.

"Mother was out there, and I didn't let her know I was here. Maybe if I had, she wouldn't have died that day."

"Or maybe he would have killed you both," Dalton said matter-of-factly.

"I know. I've often thought of that, too. I'd been caught in the attic before, and Father always whipped me soundly. He said the attic was for the servants to tend, not for a Gray's daughter to play in."

"What happened that day, Evie?"

"My mother was crying. She often did when she came up here. She would pace and weep knowing that no one would hear her. I always felt that in my knowing, it gave us a special bond. Mama wouldn't have wanted me to know, so I never said anything. But I knew that there was something that tied us together. Something much deeper than any of the others could possibly share with her."

Evie moved to the door and tried to open it. It stuck momentarily, then yielded to her firm hand. Crisp September air rushed in. Evie had said earlier that morning that it was unusually chilly for that time of year, and Dalton couldn't help but wonder what it must be like at home.

"I watched her for a while, then heard someone coming. It was Father. I barely hid in time. He went out there and embraced Mama, and just for a minute I thought maybe everything would be all right. When he kissed her and lifted her into his arms, I thought it so very romantic. Such a silly little girl notion." She turned back to Dalton. "It didn't last, because in the next moment he threw her over the side railing. She fell four floors to her death. I saw the entire thing from this window." She pointed to the large oval to her left. "I was so afraid. So certain someone would find out that I'd seen it all. I couldn't sleep for weeks afterward. The doctor told my nanny that it was not at all unusual for a child to mourn the loss of a mother in such a manner. They gave me laudanum, and no one else gave it a second thought."

"I'm so sorry, Evie. What a horrible thing for a child or anyone else to endure." Dalton came to her and took hold of her upper arms. "But it's over. You never have to worry about what you know—what you saw. You told me your mother loved Jesus most fervently. She has a place in heaven and knows real peace and joy now."

"Yes." Evie closed her eyes and nodded. "I think I can finally leave it here. All the sadness and regret. All my childhood sorrows." She opened her eyes again and smiled. "They can remain here with the rest of the unwanted things from the past."

"I believe you are right." Dalton hugged his sister. "Now let's go home."

———

Phoebe took herself for a walk along the shore, not far from the Jackson school for the natives. She loved the tall spruce and hemlock and the way they shaded the area, creating an almost protective ceiling of evergreen boughs. The scent was heady, clean, and refreshing. It was here that she could actually imagine coming to love Sitka.

A light misty rain was falling, but under the canopy of green she was sheltered. The pungent aroma of mossy earth mingled with the trees, beckoning her deeper into the forest. A totem, one of the artful creations of the Tlingit people, stood as a silent sentry, but otherwise there was no sign of man.

She found a rock to sit upon. The silence embraced her, and

Phoebe considered her circumstances. Yuri had come around, apologetic and begging her not to think ill of him or Dalton. He told her in an almost frantic manner that he and Dalton had made competitions and contests out of everything. They hadn't meant to show Phoebe disrespect by adding her to the mix.

Phoebe had agreed to forgive their indiscretion but told Yuri she didn't wish to see him for a time. She needed to let her heart figure out what it wanted. She needed time to adjust to her life in Alaska. He hadn't been happy about it, but he agreed that he would stay away until Dalton returned.

"He's due home soon," she murmured. She felt such joy at the thought that it seemed quite clear what her heart wanted. Still, there was that nagging reminder that Dalton loved this place and its solitude. He had no desire to ever leave.

"And I'll only be here as long as Mr. Knapp is governor," she reminded herself.

If the president should call him back or Knapp should fall ill and need to be replaced, they would leave the area, most likely never to return. Phoebe considered that thought for a moment. What if she did give her heart to Dalton and they married? Could she bear it when her family left Alaska?

"I'm being so silly. Dalton may return from his trip and have no desire to court me at all. He could have even met someone and married her."

She frowned. Surely he wouldn't have done that. Many men did go south to find brides, and a lot of them married much quicker than Phoebe found acceptable, but surely Dalton wasn't one of those.

Doubts lingered in her mind as she took up her walk once again. She made her way from the forest to the shore and watched as the water edged closer and closer. The tide was returning. Would it bring Dalton with it?

Chapter 16

"T his is lovely work," Zee declared, examining each girl's piecework.

Phoebe flushed from her praise. So many of Phoebe's teachers had been harsh, indifferent as to whether the students enjoyed their work. Zee seemed to understand the value of instruction that was surrounded by praise and enthusiasm for the task.

"You can make smaller stitches by not angling the needle so much," she told Eleanor. "See, if you keep the needle more vertical and just barely break the surface, you can bring it back up in a tighter fashion." Eleanor nodded and tried again. Zee smiled. "Much better."

To fill her empty hours, Phoebe had been spending time with Zee and her class of quilters. Candle supplies were sadly diminishing, and Phoebe and her mother had decided to save some supplies and not use up everything before the next shipment arrived. The next steamer was due to arrive around the twentieth, which was still a few days away. Hopefully, it would bring in their ordered supplies, as well as Dalton and Evie.

Phoebe tried not to think of Dalton's return but found her mind continually drawn back to him—and especially the way it felt to be in his arms as they danced. It seemed silly. They'd hardly had the chance to get to know each other before he left to go south. To think he shared her feelings . . . but there was Dalton and Yuri's contest. That had to mean something, and she couldn't help but feel flattered by their shared attention. She had never had many suitors back in Vermont, but here in Alaska, Phoebe could take her pick. Men had been approaching her father and mother at every turn. To have an attractive daughter with fair white skin and blond hair was something of a novelty in Sitka, and Phoebe felt like quite the belle of the ball.

The only problem, she mused, was that she had somehow lost her heart to Dalton Lindquist without him even being there to court her. She'd listened to the stories his mother told of his childhood, and Phoebe knew all about his desire to have his own boat-making business. Lydia had told her of his strong faith in God, and Phoebe, in turn, started to pay more attention to matters of faith. Where in the past she might have held only a token interest in the sermons delivered on Sunday, she now listened with new intensity.

She also enjoyed the spiritual aspect of her friendship with Lydia and Zee. Through them, Phoebe had come to understand that the Bible was so much more than just a book of rules given by God. Instead, through their guidance, she was starting to see it was rather like a love letter He had provided for His people so that they might know Him better. Lydia and Zee also had a wondrous way of praying, as if God were sitting right beside them and they were simply having a conversation. And at their urging, Phoebe had started memorizing Bible verses, as well.

"Are you daydreaming, Miss Phoebe?" Zee asked.

Phoebe looked up, rather surprised, and noted that the other girls were already putting away their quilt blocks. "Sorry. I do tend to get lost in thought." She tied off her thread and began to repack her things in a small traveling case her mother had given her.

The Tlingit girls bade them good-bye and headed back to their duties at home. Phoebe wanted to ask Zee if there had been any word from Dalton, but she knew better. There hadn't been a chance for more mail to be delivered. The regular steamer would be in port in a few days, hopefully bringing Dalton and rendering a letter unnecessary.

I'm too impatient, she told herself. *I must practice patience.*

"I can't wait for Dalton and Evie to return," Lydia said as she bustled into the room. "I am hardly good for anything but thinking about them."

"She's right on that account," Zee said with a wink at Phoebe. "Yesterday she ruined an entire cake just because she wasn't paying attention to the ingredients."

Lydia blushed lightly and shook her head. "You needn't tell all of my shameful secrets."

Zee laughed. "Well, I haven't mentioned how you can't sleep and so you pace the floors all through the night. I didn't say a word about how you sewed the sleeve closed on that shirt you were making for Dalton."

"Oh stop," Lydia said. "I won't have our Phoebe thinking so poorly of me."

"It would be impossible for me to think poorly of you or Zee," Phoebe assured them. She very much liked the way Lydia claimed ownership of her by saying *our Phoebe.* It made her feel as if she were already a member of the family. "I admire you two more than I do any other woman, save my mother."

"I find your mother's company refreshing," Lydia told her. "She is quite sensible and intelligent, and I like that in a woman. So often women try not to appear intelligent, in case they dare offend the men around them. Your mother doesn't seem to worry about that."

"Indeed, she does not. She says it was one of the things that attracted my father to her. He heard her making a speech about women's rights. In fact, she made such good points that he asked her to come and speak to his men's group. He told her they were a collection of progressive thinkers, and Mother was intrigued. She said they were very possibly the most intelligent group of men she'd ever met. They weren't intimidated by the idea of women having the right to vote, or of giving them rights to own property and businesses. She said she fell in love with my father at that meeting."

"How romantic," Lydia said. "What a wonderful story to tell your children."

"Better than meeting because you fell out of a boat and nearly drowned," Phoebe replied, then covered her mouth with her hand. She felt her face grow hot.

Lydia and Zee couldn't help but laugh. They didn't tease her or chide her bold statement; instead, they encouraged her thinking.

"Why, I think it a wonderful story. How marvelous to have had your true love rescue you from death," Lydia offered.

Zee nodded. "And the fact that you scolded him for it only makes the story better."

Phoebe moaned. "Oh, you must both think me awful."

"Nonsense." Lydia reached out and patted her arm. "I think you delightful and charming. I couldn't imagine a better wife for my son."

Against her will, Phoebe's eyes widened and her mouth dropped open. "You shouldn't say such a thing."

Zee chuckled. "Why not? Weren't *you* thinking that way?"

Phoebe began to wring her hands. "I don't know what to say. I'm just . . . well . . . I'm a silly young woman, just as my father declares me to be."

"Again, such thinking is utter nonsense," Lydia countered. "I believe you and Dalton are well suited to each other, and I intend to encourage him to call on you when he returns—though I doubt I shall have any need. He was already intrigued when he left. If I know my son as well as I believe I do, the absence and distance will have only served to add to his interest in you. But now I want to suggest an entirely different subject."

Feeling there was no possibility of being any more embarrassed, Phoebe nodded. "What is it?"

"I wonder," Lydia began, "if you would like to help Zee and I plan a party for Evie and Dalton's return."

She smiled at the thought. "I would love to. What would you like me to do?"

Lydia took the seat beside Phoebe. "I think we should like to decorate. Maybe you could help us in that area?"

Phoebe considered that for a moment. "I don't know what you have in mind, but I would be happy to assist."

"Zee had thought we should keep it simple. Maybe we could trim the room with some spruce boughs and ribbon. Oh, and we'll use some of the candles I purchased from your mother."

"I plan to make a cake," Zee added. "And a nice pot of chicken and noodles. I've already picked out the intended donor. He's a nice fat cockerel. The meat should be ever so delicious."

"When will we plan to have the party?" Phoebe asked. "There's no hope of knowing a fixed date for the steamer's appearance."

"We already thought of that," Zee replied. "We'll simply have everything ready to go and take care of the details at the last minute." She grinned. "I can put the chicken in cold storage until needed."

"I'll make some invitations," Lydia told Phoebe. "We will want to make sure that folks know we'll have a celebration on the night the steamer comes into the harbor. Would you mind delivering them to the people in town?"

"Of course not. I'd be happy to." Phoebe's mind raced with thoughts. What would she wear to the party? Would that be when she had a chance to first see him again? The waiting was so very hard. What if she'd only managed to create something in her mind that could never be? What if her heart was wrong and she found Dalton to be someone she couldn't abide?

Oh, why couldn't the steamer arrive tomorrow and put her mind at ease?

Just then, the front door burst open, and Kjerstin and Britta burst into the house in a frenzy of movement and conversation.

"Mama, there was a fight at school today," Britta announced.

"It was bad. One of the boys got a bloody nose," Kjerstin added.

Phoebe watched as Lydia got to her feet to deal with the situation. "Well, hello to you, too," their mother announced.

"Joseph called Vasilla a smelly half-breed," Kjerstin added. "His mother is a Tlingit, but his father is Russian. Teacher said he was a Creole."

"But he wasn't smelly at all," Britta interjected. "He was just fine. I played with him, and he took a bath just last Saturday."

The girls were so caught up in their reiteration of the details that they didn't even seem to notice Phoebe. Britta explained Vasilla's bathing routine in more detail. Apparently the boy always had a bath on Saturday before they went to church the next day. His mother and father were members at the Russian Orthodox Church, and they were very meticulous about Vasilla being clean before entering God's house.

Kjerstin was more concerned about the injustice of it all. She seemed appalled that the other children, as well as the teacher, put the entire responsibility for the altercation at Vasilla's feet.

"They don't like him because he's not all white. They said he should go to the native school," Kjerstin announced. "I told them they were being silly, but they didn't listen to me." It was then that she seemed to notice Phoebe. "Your brother Grady called him a no-account dirty Injun."

"Well, my brother Grady will not go unpunished, I assure you," Phoebe replied. She was angry to think that her brother had played a part in this matter. "He was not brought up to speak that way or to hold such thoughts. Our parents will be appalled."

Kjerstin nodded, satisfied at Phoebe's response. She then looked to her mother. "Why are they so mean? They don't like the Tlingits, and they don't like people who are just part Tlingit."

Lydia shook her head. "They think the color of a person's skin somehow makes them less valuable, but we know that isn't true. God holds all mankind dear, and He's the one who made us— colors and all."

"They have been misguided," Zee threw in. "They don't understand the culture and it makes them afraid."

"They also don't bother to know it," Lydia added, "and that makes them ignorant."

"Can't they get to understand?" Britta asked. "I don't want there to be more fights."

"I wish there wouldn't be, either," their mother said. "Still, I think as long as we have differences, someone will be happy to point them out—to even condemn a person for those differences. Someone won't like blond hair. Someone else will think that being a girl is bad. Others might not like people who talk with an accent. There will always be something that displeases people."

Phoebe nodded. "And your mother and Zee are right. If the people would bother to learn about the cultures instead of condemning them, they might not be afraid." She considered the words for herself. How many times had she crossed the street just to avoid having to walk past a group of Tlingits sitting on the walkway? The men, in particular, frightened Phoebe. They seemed harsh and resentful. Maybe it was just her imagination, but they appeared almost angry that she should even be there.

"Hopefully in time, with enough people showing tolerance and kindness instead of judgment," Lydia told her daughters, "we will see this kind of temperament leave for good."

"Well, I don't like it," Kjerstin said, crossing her arms. "I'm going to punch Joseph in the nose tomorrow and tell him so."

"You'll do no such thing," Lydia cautioned. "You are a young lady, and young ladies do not punch people in the nose."

"Never?" Britta asked. "What if they punch you first?"

Phoebe couldn't help but smile. "Young ladies," Zee interjected, "should never be caught fighting."

"So if we don't get caught, then is it okay?" Kjerstin asked. " 'Cause I know a good place where no one would see me punch Joseph in the nose."

"Kjerstin, I don't want you punching anyone," Lydia admonished. "Why don't you pray for Joseph instead?"

"Well, he didn't pray for Vasilla. He punched him," Kjerstin countered.

Phoebe wanted to laugh. The little girl's reasoning seemed logical. Kjerstin, however, was now shaking her head; clearly her mother's wisdom did not meet with her understanding.

"So how did the situation get resolved?" Zee asked, changing their focus.

"Teacher said Vasilla needed to go home and take a bath," Britta replied. "But he didn't smell bad. He had a bath on Saturday," she repeated, as if they had missed this important fact earlier. "Teacher said he couldn't come back until he got cleaned up."

Zee frowned. "I believe I will come to your school tomorrow and have a word with your teacher. She's a good woman, but perhaps she misjudged the situation. There is no sense in letting the children belittle someone just because they are different."

"Good," Kjerstin said, as if this were at least a small compromise. "But don't be surprised if she doesn't listen."

"I'm never surprised when people don't listen," Zee replied. "I'm just saddened."

———

Phoebe thought about Zee's comment long after she'd relayed the event to her mother. Grady was severely chastised and refused dessert that night. He thought it quite unfair. After all, to his way of thinking, they were all dirty Injuns. They lived outside for a good part of the year. They didn't wear many clothes, and they were always sitting on the ground. How could they not be dirty?

Most people felt the same way. The Tlingit had been taught about hygiene from the American missionaries and teachers, but their way of living did not always provide for the same standards. Phoebe didn't think that made them bad people, however. She sighed. The world was cruel at times.

She was getting ready for bed when she couldn't help but hear her mother respond to something their father must have said. It sounded like "What are you saying?"

Slipping over to the door, she opened it just a crack to better hear. Her father was explaining something. ". . . it wasn't that I didn't suspect, but now that I know for sure, it will probably spell trouble."

"But why must you get in the middle of it?"

"I'm the one in charge. I have worked with this young man for over three years. I am his superior. Lyman will expect me to handle the matter."

Her mother sighed. "But he knows about your father."

There was a terrible strained silence for several minutes before her father spoke. "I won't allow him to damage Lyman's reputation. It may well mean the end of my career, but I can hardly let him go on stealing from the government funds. If he exposes me, I will simply resign and we will return to the States. Perhaps we can relocate to California."

Phoebe gasped and closed the door. "Relocate to California?" But what of Dalton? And what would this mean for their chance to get to know each other—to have a future?

Chapter 17

*P*hoebe fretted for days over the things she'd heard her parents say. On the twenty-fourth of September, the steamer was finally sighted heading toward Sitka. A fishing vessel brought the news to town, and it was all Phoebe could do to keep her wits about her. She went through her wardrobe at least a dozen times, trying to decide on just the right thing to wear. She narrowed the choices to a lovely embroidered cream-colored suit, a two-piece silk dress that she sometimes wore to church, and a beautiful crepe de Chine gown in a lovely shade of pale blue.

None of the gowns would serve her very well if she helped in the kitchen, but Phoebe was determined to present a stunning picture to Dalton. This would be their first encounter since his departure, and she wanted it to be memorable.

"But in a good way," she said aloud. "Not in the way I met him the first time."

She had already decided she would await his return at the Lindquist house. Lydia wanted to meet him at the dock, and Phoebe thought that would give mother and son time to discuss the things that had happened in Kansas City. Kjell would drive the wagon, and Phoebe and Zee would continue working to make sure they were ready for the party.

Finally settling on the crepe de Chine, Phoebe called for her mother to help her do up the buttons. She could hardly stand still, thinking of all she still had to do before heading to the Lindquists.

"Phoebe, I can barely take hold of the buttons for all your dancing about."

"Sorry, Mother. It's just that . . . well . . . I'm excited."

"About Dalton Lindquist returning?"

Phoebe pulled away and turned to face her mother. "I can't stop thinking about him."

Her mother smiled and moved her back into place so she could finish with the buttons. "He is a very nice young man, but you hardly know him."

"I feel like I know him quite well," Phoebe admitted. "I've spent so much time with his mother and great-aunt that I've heard all about his childhood and passions."

"That's all well and fine, but he doesn't know you. He hasn't had the same opportunity in his absence that you have. There, your buttons are secured."

Phoebe thought again of what her father had said about leaving Sitka. She didn't want to admit to her mother that she'd eavesdropped, but she longed for more details. "How would you feel if . . . well . . . what if I married Dalton?"

Her mother's mouth dropped open. "What are you saying?"

"I don't really know," Phoebe replied with a sheepish grin. "The times we had together were . . . wonderful. Even when I fell out of the boat and he saved me, I can't help but remember how it felt to be in his arms. He's kind and considerate, yet a man of decisive action."

"But, Phoebe, that's not enough on which to base a marriage. You need to know each other on a personal level. Give yourself some time. Once he's returned, he may very well come calling. That will give you both a chance to get to know each other. And what of Yuri? You seemed to like him well enough. I know you two had some sort of falling out, but you appeared to enjoy his company. How do you know that he might not make a better possibility?"

"How did you know Father was the man for you?" Phoebe asked. She didn't wait for an answer, but continued. "I know it seems odd. I don't have that much to rely on when it comes to validating my feelings, but I can't imagine a future without him. He's all I think about."

She shook her head and went to pick up her hairbrush. "Mother, I don't want to be foolish about it, but if your heart tells you that this is the one, shouldn't you listen?"

"I think it's important to hear what your heart has to say, but also to use your head a bit, too. Don't let your emotions carry you away. After all, you're young and there is time to find a husband."

"I'll be nineteen next March, and that's very close to being twenty. Most of my friends married this summer or will marry this winter. But even so, if I wanted only to marry, you know as well as anyone I could have had a husband many times over by now. Sitka is full of single men looking for a wife. It's only Dalton who's captured my thoughts and heart."

Stepping forward, Mother embraced Phoebe. "Then follow your heart. I did, and I've never regretted it. Not once."

Phoebe pulled back. "Not even with Grandfather's underhanded dealings and the way that worked to ruin Father's reputation?"

Her mother shook her head. "Not even then. I know the truth of who your father is. I don't care what anyone else thinks. I love him."

Her mother's words pierced Phoebe's heart. How wonderful to hold such a deep, abiding love for your mate after so many years. That's what she wanted. A husband she could grow old with—no matter the controversies and adversities they might face.

———

Such thoughts remained heavy on her mind even after Phoebe arrived at the Lindquist house to help. Her brother Theodore pulled the wagon to a stop and begrudgingly assisted Phoebe from the carriage.

"Remind Mother that they should be here by six."

"I don't see why we should have to come."

"Because there will be wonderful food," she teased. "You will enjoy Zee's cookies and cakes. She and Lydia are quite gifted in the kitchen."

He perked up a bit. "Do you suppose they will have chocolate?"

"I'm sure they will. Zee mentioned something about a chocolate cake."

This met with the fifteen-year-old's approval. "Then I guess it won't be so bad."

"Just don't forget to remind Mother to be here by six."

Her brother bounded back up to the carriage seat. "I'll tell her."

Phoebe made her way up the porch steps and to the door. She knocked lightly and wasn't at all surprised when Zee showed up to answer. "They've all gone down to await the ship's arrival," Zee told her. "My, but don't you look pretty. Let's get an apron on you straightaway so you don't get anything on that lovely dress."

"I wasn't sure what to wear. I wanted to look . . . well . . . nice." Phoebe stumbled over the words, not wanting to sound as though she were looking for a compliment.

"That you do. I'll change my dress after I get the cake frosted. You go ahead and start decorating. Everything we gathered is in the sewing room."

Phoebe nodded and took the apron Zee offered. The pinafore-styled white cotton had straps that crisscrossed in the back, so Zee quickly went to work buttoning these in place while Phoebe smoothed out the apron in front.

"There you are. I'll leave you to manage the ties," Zee declared.

Phoebe did just that as she made her way to the sewing room. She looked at the variety of boughs and smiled. Lydia had arranged for Kjell to cut spruce branches, and the scent filled the room and would soon engulf the house. Kjerstin and Britta had helped her the day before in joining the pieces together to make a decorative garland, so Phoebe now worked at arranging the decorations about the room.

Above the fireplace, Lydia had positioned a new watercolor painted by a local woman, Paulina Cohen. Phoebe liked the way the artist had captured the scenic harbor. The skies held just a hint of orange, suggesting twilight. Placing two candles on either side, Phoebe marveled at how the illumination brought out the colors in the painting.

"That's perfect," Zee announced. "I've finished the cake, so I'm going to go on over to my cabin and change clothes. I'll be back in a quick minute."

"Is there anything else I can help with?"

"No, just sit tight and enjoy the quiet. Soon there won't be any at all." She grinned and headed to the door.

Phoebe hugged her arms to her body and glanced around the room to make certain everything was in place. She suddenly felt anxious. What if Dalton had changed so much that he wasn't at all the man he'd been before? Lydia was worried about the influence of his family in the south. What if her worries were well founded?

"You've considered this same matter at least a hundred times," she reminded herself aloud. "You must trust God for the outcome."

Zee returned just before the first of the wagons began arriving. People poured into the house, soon filling every corner. Phoebe had long since removed her apron and was mingling among the townspeople. Some of them were members of her church and some were neighbors. Everyone seemed in a mood for celebration. But where were Dalton and the others?

"Don't worry," Zee whispered in her ear. "They'll be here soon. Lydia had Kjell purposefully stop by the mill to pick up Joshua. They'll delay there as long as they can to give folks time to get out here."

Phoebe breathed a sigh. "That makes perfect sense."

Her mother and father arrived with Theodore and Grady in tow. Neither brother acknowledged her. Grady was still angry at Phoebe for having told their parents of his actions at school, while Theodore wasn't giving her a single thought. He was, instead, taking himself to the food table.

Phoebe made her way to her parents. "Mother. Father."

"My, but there certainly are a lot of people here," her mother said. "Has Dalton arrived yet?"

"No, but he should most any time. They were trying to keep it as a surprise," Phoebe explained.

"The governor and his family were touched to be invited," her father announced. "They will be here later."

"Wonderful," Phoebe said, remembering that there was trouble in her father's situation with the governor and some other worker. "I'm sure the Lindquists will be pleased that he is attending."

"They're here!" someone yelled from the porch.

Phoebe felt as if she might swallow her tongue. She took a deep breath in an attempt to slow the rapid beating of her heart. Just then, the unmistakable sound of a dish breaking caught her attention. Excusing herself, Phoebe went toward the kitchen to find that an old man had dropped a plate.

"I'll take care of it," she told Zee, who had also come to see what had happened.

Relieved that the cleaning gave her something to do, Phoebe tried to remain calm as a cheer rose up from the partiers. There were shouts of welcome, and Dalton's name was called many times over, as was Evie's.

Crouched on the kitchen floor, Phoebe couldn't see anything but legs. She hurried to pick up all of the broken bits of china. The last piece was positioned on the dustpan when she heard a voice from behind her.

"Did you break that?"

Phoebe rose slowly and turned to face Dalton. He smiled at her and his eyes fairly twinkled. Goodness, but he was even better looking than she'd remembered. Phoebe fairly forgot about the dustpan in her hands, and had Zee not quickly interceded to take it from her, she might have needed to pick up the entire mess once again.

"I was just the one to clean it up—this time." She felt tongue-tied, at a loss for words as she stared up into his face.

"I'm glad to hear it. It seems like every time we're together something or someone gets hurt." The people directly around them chuckled, and Phoebe felt her face grow hot.

"Now, don't be picking on this poor girl," Zee said, returning to Phoebe's side. "She has been our right hand these last few weeks."

Dalton raised a brow. "Is that so? I suppose by now you've heard all my secrets—dreadful stories of my youth and mistakes I've made along the way."

Phoebe shook her head. "No. Your mother told me wonderful stories."

"I did indeed," Lydia announced. "And all of them were true."

Soon others pressed in, demanding Dalton's attention, and Phoebe went to find her flute, as Lydia's orchestra was to play several songs of welcome.

As the musicians awaited the arrival of the governor and his family, Yuri found Phoebe and without hesitation said, "I hope you're going to give me another chance to court you." His wide smile was confident.

Phoebe looked at him for a moment and realized that while she found him sweet and very kind, he did not stir her heart the way Dalton did. "I'm sorry," she said with a small shake of her head. "I don't think I can."

Yuri frowned. "Are you still mad at me?"

She wasn't sure, but she thought she smelled liquor on his breath. "You know I'm not. I forgave you and told you so," Phoebe replied. "It's just that I don't feel that way about you, Yuri. You are a good man, but . . ." Her throat seemed to dry up and words wouldn't come.

"But you want Dalton," he said in a tone somewhere between resignation and disgust.

She glanced up and nodded ever so slightly. "I'm sorry."

"Don't bother." He stalked off just as Lydia and Kjell returned with the others.

"Let's take our places," Lydia directed.

Phoebe could barely concentrate on the music. She knew she

risked making the entire group sound bad, however, so she willed herself to focus. When it came time for her to play a solo, she was taut with fear that her mind would wander, but she managed to make it through without a single error.

The governor spoke a few words after the orchestra concluded, but Phoebe was certain she had seen Dalton and Yuri slip outside. She longed to know what was being said between the two. Were they laughing at the memory of their little contest? Were they arguing over her? Yuri seemed upset after talking to her—what if his anger had caused them to come to blows? Suddenly Phoebe felt rather ill. She wanted to leave the party and go home.

What if I've truly made a mess of things? She couldn't help but feel that Yuri's anger would not bode well for his friendship with Dalton. Slipping from the room, Phoebe paused in the kitchen to figure out what to do. Maybe she should go and talk to them—try to help them understand her feelings. On the other hand, maybe she should just leave.

"But I can't just walk home. It's much too dangerous," she muttered. She would simply have to wait until her parents were ready to leave. If that meant embarrassment and humiliation, she would have to handle it.

"Can we talk a minute?"

Dalton stood only a foot or so away, and Phoebe turned, her eyes widening at the nearness of him. When had he come back inside? Had he overheard her comment? She forced a nod but couldn't form any words.

"I very much enjoyed your solo," he began. "I have always loved the music my mother and father make together, but I think I told you that once before. Anyway, the real reason I wanted to talk to you was to ask if you would be willing to see me tomorrow. I'd like to tell you about why I went away and what happened."

Phoebe nodded, feeling rather overwhelmed by Dalton's

presence and the way her heart accelerated when she was with him.

He smiled. "Good. I'll come to your house around ten, if that's all right. Maybe if the weather is nice you'll walk with me?"

"Yes," she managed to say before someone claimed his attention.

Her mind whirled about one question: Was this the start of their courtship?

———

Dalton was glad to see the last of the guests head home. He was weary from traveling and craved only his own bed. Excusing himself, Dalton made his way to his room. He was pleased to see that a fire had been laid in and started. No doubt his mother or Zee had seen to it. The room was warm and welcoming. The covers on the bed had been turned down, and a pitcher of water awaited him by the fire.

He sat on the edge of the bed and pulled off first one boot and then the other. He found himself thinking about how beautiful Phoebe Robbins had looked that evening. Her smile was so infectious he couldn't help but grin just thinking about it.

Yuri, however, had been a disappointment. He had cornered Dalton and all but dragged him to the porch to announce that Phoebe knew all about their contest. He further added that she had been none too happy about it.

Dalton found the words troubling but figured he could take up the matter with Phoebe tomorrow. A light knock interrupted his thoughts. No doubt his mother had come to check up on him.

"Come in." He smiled when he saw that he was right.

"I wondered if you needed anything," his mother asked.

"No. I'm fine. You already thought of everything. I'm just glad to be home."

"I missed you more than I can say." She came to sit beside him on the bed. "I tried not to worry, but I'm not very good at doing so."

"There was no need. I quickly saw for myself what everyone had warned me about," Dalton admitted. "My Gray siblings are selfish, manipulative people. Marston is just as you said—an evil man with self-serving ambitions and notions."

Lydia frowned. "Still, I hope you found the answers you were seeking."

"I found the truth," Dalton replied. "It wasn't exactly as I'd hoped, but at least I know for myself. I am grateful for the fact that God interceded to make me nothing like my brothers. I credit you, of course, but also Father. He's been the best man possible to raise me. I'm glad I'm nothing like my family in Kansas City."

Lydia patted his hand. "Kjell is a good man. He's loved you since he first knew about you." She smiled. "You have been a blessing to both of us, and we're glad to have you home."

"But, Mother, I still feel like I'm struggling to know myself. All of this has caused me to question what I really want out of life."

"In what way?" she asked.

He shook his head. "I don't really know that I can explain it, but I'll try." He was silent for a moment, then continued. "I can say that it reaffirmed my choice to be a Christian. Seeing what life is like for folks who don't value God or His Word—I know that kind of life is not for me. Same for valuing family. Those people don't have a clue about the strength and joy that can be had in loving each other and holding fast to the bond that connects one person to the other."

His mother squeezed his arm. "I'm blessed to hear you say such things."

He looked at her with a smile. "I will say I was surprised to learn the extent of my inheritance. I have plans that I hope you'll approve of."

"And what are those?" his mother asked.

"I'd like to hire Father to help me build my own business and house. I'd like to build boats, just as I have been doing. Maybe even make an arrangement with Mr. Belikov to expand his business and combine our efforts."

"I think that would be wonderful, but you know you needn't move away. This will always be your home."

"I know, but my wife might have something to say about living with her in-laws." He grinned at his mother's startled expression.

"Wife?"

"Well, I don't have one yet, but I have one in mind."

"Phoebe?" she asked softly.

Dalton nodded. "She was all I could think about. I know it sounds out of line, but—"

His mother held up her hand. "Say no more. I believe you will find Phoebe quite open to the notion."

"Why do you say that?"

His mother got to her feet. "I wouldn't want to betray confidences. But let's just say she spent the time you were away trying very hard not to ask or think about you. She failed miserably, if I'm any judge of the matter."

Dalton laughed. "Good. I'm seeing her tomorrow, and we shall discuss how we tried not to think about each other these last few months."

His mother paused at the door. "I like Phoebe very much, Dalton. I think she's a wonderful young lady."

"I have prayed a great deal about this, Mother, just so you know."

She gave a chuckle. "So have I, Dalton. So have I. I have a peace about the entire matter."

"That's good to hear," he said, thankful to hear that his mother agreed with his thoughts. He had worried that his family would think him strange for falling in love with a woman he hardly knew.

"Just trust God's guidance in the matter, son. Take it at His pacing."

"I will. I promise."

Chapter 18

S o you see," Dalton explained to Mr. Belikov the next morning, "I have the capital to either buy into this business, if you are of a mind to sell me a portion, or set up my own shop."

"That is remarkable news," Mr. Belikov said, rubbing his chin. "My wife and I have been discussing the possibility of leaving Sitka in the spring. This could be the answer we've been looking for. If you bought, say, half of the business and I gave Yuri the other half, you could be partners, and we would have the money needed for our trip to Russia."

Dalton nodded. "I'm not in a hurry. We can take this slowly and figure out what works best. I would, of course, want you to talk it over with Yuri. If he didn't like the idea, I wouldn't want you to impose it on him."

"Bah, you and Yuri are like two sides of the same coin. You've been friends for so long, it's hard to know where one ends and the other begins."

Dalton considered his employer's words for a moment. "There is a girl between us now," he admitted. "The woman I intend to marry."

"You what?" Yuri questioned from the door.

There was no way for Dalton to know how long he'd been listening to the conversation. Yuri stormed into the room.

"You haven't even been here this summer, and you're imagining you can just up and propose?" His blue eyes flashed with anger. "What kind of man are you?"

Mr. Belikov intervened. "Yuri, sit down and talk this out like friends. This is uncalled for."

"You don't understand," Yuri told his father. "I've spent the summer trying to court Phoebe Robbins. She and I were getting along pretty well, if I do say so."

"Until you opened your mouth and told her about our contest," Dalton threw in.

"What is this contest he speaks of?" Yuri's father questioned.

Yuri shrugged. "It wasn't important. We both found Phoebe to be attractive. We spoke of which one of us could win her over first."

"You wagered on this?"

"No," Dalton said. "We both knew that wouldn't be acceptable. Still, Yuri upset her by telling her we had talked about it like a game."

"Matters of the heart are never to be played in such a way," Mr. Belikov said.

"I agree. That's why I'm not playing a game anymore." Dalton got to his feet. "As far as I'm concerned, the contest is long over. Now if you'll excuse me, I have some work to finish before I leave.

You can let me know about that other matter when you've had a chance to discuss it with Yuri."

Dalton left, even as Yuri asked his father what that was all about. In time, he hoped Yuri would calm down and let go of his anger. Yuri had always had a quick temper, but usually he was good to let the matter drop once he reconsidered the situation. Dalton prayed this time would be no different.

He finished uncrating the things he'd purchased in Seattle and gave them a good inspection to make certain nothing had been damaged. Everything looked as it should, with the exception of one lamp fixture that had a broken chimney.

Satisfied, Dalton made his way from the building and headed for Phoebe's house. Yuri's demanding tone let him know he was still in discussion with his father, so Dalton hadn't bothered to say good-bye. He hoped that by the time he came to work the following morning, Yuri would have forgotten about Phoebe in the wake of possibly co-owning his own business.

———

Phoebe paced at the window, looking for some sign of Dalton. She was about to give up her vigil when she spied him strolling up to the house. He looked like he didn't have a care in the world. Her heart skipped a beat. She longed to run out the door and throw herself into his arms.

"Goodness, but wouldn't that be shocking," she mused.

She ran to the hall and made a quick assessment of her appearance in the mirror. Frowning, she wondered if she should have pinned her hair up instead of simply pulling it back in a casual braid.

"Will he think I don't care about my appearance?" She glanced down at the dark brown wool skirt. It was the same one she had chosen for her picnic with Yuri. Maybe that wasn't such a wise choice. Would it somehow taint her time with Dalton?

"Stop being so silly," she chided.

Dalton's knock put an end to her appraisal, and she opened the door to find Dalton waiting with a smile. "Hello." She suddenly felt very shy. "Let me get my coat." She grabbed the matching suit jacket and was rather surprised when Dalton reached out to take it.

"Allow me." He helped her into the coat, then offered her his arm as she turned. "Shall we?"

Phoebe nodded. She was almost afraid to speak. Dalton didn't seem to notice, however. He quickly picked up the conversation.

"I have so much I want to tell you," he began. "First of all, I'm sorry that I didn't have a chance to say good-bye before I went south. It was such a quick decision." He frowned for a moment as he looked at her. "It wasn't entirely a pleasant matter. We got word about my sister's husband being sick."

"I'm sorry to hear that. I suppose I didn't realize Evie's husband was still alive, what with her living up here."

"He died before we arrived in Kansas City. It's a long story, but it's enough to say Evie's marriage was never one of love. She only came here to bring me back to my mother." He shook his head. "I'm getting ahead of myself."

They walked away from the center of town and beyond the place where all of the fishing boats were docked. Phoebe could see that Dalton was struggling with what he wanted to share with her.

"There is quite a scandal in my family background. I think it's important for you to know about it."

Phoebe looked up to find him watching her closely. She couldn't help but smile. "You aren't the only one, you know."

"What do you mean?"

"With a family scandal." She had been forced to maintain

silence about the subject for so long that she immediately felt guilty for the comment. "But please continue."

Dalton nodded. He explained about his mother's tragic marriage and his birth. As he continued and gave her the details of what had happened the night he was kidnapped by his brother's hirelings, Phoebe was more than a little intrigued. This was far more exciting than her family history.

Leading her to a rock, Dalton suggested they sit for a time. "I felt I had to go to Kansas City with my sister because I needed to know about my family there. I learned a great deal, but not all of it was good."

"I'm sorry, Dalton," Phoebe said. "It must have been very hard on you."

He stared deep into her eyes. "It might have completely devastated me had I not had something—well, *someone*—else on my mind, as well."

"What are you talking about now?"

Dalton gave a light laugh. "I was thinking about you."

Phoebe looked away quickly. She had longed to hear him say as much, but now that he had, she was rather embarrassed.

"I know we haven't spent much time together, but you were often present in my thoughts. I started praying about you."

"Hoping God would get me out of your mind," she teased, still not looking at him.

"Hardly." He reached out and lifted her face. "Phoebe—"

"So you're just going to haul off and ask her to marry you?" Yuri interrupted. "I can't believe you are so bold as to approach my father and try to steal my inheritance, and now this."

Phoebe startled at the comment. Was Dalton really going to ask her to marry him? Dalton moved away from her to intercept Yuri. The two men halted within inches of each other.

"What's the meaning of this?" Dalton asked.

"You tell me. You offered my father money to steal what should only belong to me."

"I did no such thing. I discussed the possibility of buying into the business—to be a partner with you and your father. He told me of his plans to leave in the spring for Russia and said my timing was perfect. The money I could provide would allow him to move and would make you and me partners."

"I don't want to be your partner—you are a cheat. You went behind my back to dangle your newfound wealth under my father's nose. You wanted to rob me of what is rightfully mine."

Dalton shook his head. "You aren't even making sense, Yuri. I wanted to work *with* you, not against you. We're friends, Yuri."

"Not anymore." Yuri threw a punch that took Dalton completely by surprise.

Phoebe gasped as Dalton fell backward and landed on the ground by her feet. Yuri started to walk away, then returned and hauled Dalton back to his feet and pushed him away from Phoebe.

"I suppose you're telling Phoebe all about your money, as well. Well, I may not have money, but I like her, too, and you knew that. You talk about being friends, but then you do this." He walked up to Dalton and pushed him backward again. "You can't go around buying everything or everyone."

"I wasn't trying to buy anyone, Yuri. You aren't listening to me, and you aren't making sense. Calm down. We can talk about this later." Dalton rubbed his cheek. "Fighting isn't going to solve anything."

Phoebe fairly held her breath. The two men were nose to nose once again, and Yuri showed no sign of backing down. This time, however, when he raised his arm to deliver a blow, Dalton was ready for him.

"Knock it off, Yuri," Dalton said, taking hold of his fist. "I'm not going to fight you. This is ridiculous. You're just mad because I don't want to play games anymore."

"I'm mad because you're a liar and a cheat." He pulled away and paced back a few steps. Casting a glance at Phoebe, he addressed her. "Do you want that kind of a man for a husband? Are you going to let him buy your love?"

"I don't even know what you're talking about," Phoebe said, shaking her head. She looked to Dalton. "What is going on?"

"Oh, so you haven't told her yet, is that it? Did I come too soon?" Yuri asked sarcastically. "Dalton is rich—wealthy beyond his wildest dreams. His mother inherited a fortune and placed it in trust for him. Now he wants to buy my father's business and steal my inheritance."

"That isn't true." For the first time, Phoebe could hear the anger in Dalton's voice. "If you aren't going to be honest about this, Yuri, you might as well leave."

"I'll leave when I'm good and ready, and it won't be until after I knock some of that pride out of you." Yuri charged at Dalton, and the two crashed to the ground.

Phoebe let out a short yelp as if someone had stepped on her toes. Jumping down from the rock, she called for them to stop fighting, but neither one heard her.

"You can't act this way," she insisted. "This isn't right."

They were back on their feet, each throwing punches at the other. Sometimes they connected, but mostly they didn't. For this, Phoebe was relieved.

"Please stop!"

"I trusted you," Yuri shouted. "My father brought you in to teach you a trade, and this is how you repay us."

"You aren't thinking clear," Dalton answered, plugging his fist into Yuri's stomach.

Yuri doubled over with a groan but quickly recovered. He was charging back at Dalton when everything seemed to go horribly wrong, and Phoebe found herself somehow in the middle of the action. Without warning, she was thrown to the ground as the two men plowed past her and bounced off the rock where she'd been sitting only moments earlier.

For a moment, the wind was knocked from her lungs and Phoebe felt a sensation of panic. She swallowed hard and forced herself to breathe. Dalton and Yuri were at her side in a flash. Both looked mortified that she had been caught in the fracas.

Dalton reached down to help her up as Yuri began to apologize. "I'm sorry, Phoebe. Are you hurt?"

She felt Dalton's gentle touch on her back as he steadied her. Phoebe drew another breath and nodded. "I . . . don't think . . . so."

Dalton turned a piercing glare on Yuri. "You've caused enough trouble. You need to go."

"Me?"

"You're the one who started this fight. Now I'm finishing it. Phoebe could have been hurt—badly. You didn't even care that she was right here."

"Don't play the innocent one," Yuri countered. "You knew she was here, as well."

"Go." Dalton's tone left Phoebe little doubt he would finish not only the fight, but the friendship, as well, if Yuri didn't leave.

"Please go, Yuri. I don't want to see you two fight anymore," Phoebe begged.

Yuri glanced at her for a moment, then fixed Dalton with a hateful look. "You'll be sorry, Dalton. Wait and see if you aren't." He stormed off, muttering as he went.

Assessing Phoebe for a moment, Dalton asked, "Are you sure you're all right?"

She nodded. "I think I should go home. I'm sorry to have been the cause of all of this."

"You aren't to blame for anything," Dalton said as he walked with her toward the road. "Yuri is volatile in his anger. He'll calm down and feel really bad for how he's acted. He's just feeling put out right now."

"I'm sorry, nevertheless," Phoebe said. "You've been friends for so long. He told me about some of the great adventures you used to have together. I can tell he really admires you—cares about you. I'd hate to see you throw that away."

"We won't," Dalton replied. "He just needs time to think through things. I'm sure he's worried about his parents leaving for Russia in the spring. I had hoped that buying into the business and becoming his partner would give him a sense of confidence that he could remain here and do well. I guess I misjudged his feelings on the matter."

Phoebe nodded. "Well, I will pray for you both. Good friends are hard to come by."

Dalton said nothing more, and when they reached Phoebe's house, she invited him in. "Would you like to join us for the noon-time meal?"

He shook his head. "I wouldn't be good company. I'm sorry, Phoebe." His tone held something akin to regret.

"I'm sorry, too." But she wasn't entirely sure why. Had he been about to propose? That hardly seemed possible. He had only just returned from his trip.

"I would like to call on you again," he said, his expression softening.

Phoebe couldn't help but gaze deep into his eyes. "I'd like that very much."

He nodded. "Good day, then." Walking away, he didn't so much as turn back to offer her a smile.

She watched him for several minutes, longing to run after him. It was never easy to see friends at odds with each other, but the situation seemed even more painful because she was in the middle of it.

Turning to go inside, Phoebe was unprepared for what she found there. Her mother was in tears, and her father was standing in silence at the fireplace. She saw that Theodore and Grady were peeking out to watch from the hallway. What in the world was going on?

"Is something wrong?" she asked.

Her mother looked up most mournfully. "Your father . . . he . . ." She burst into tears anew and buried her face in her hands.

Phoebe turned to her father. "What is it?"

He looked at her as if his world had somehow crumbled. "I no longer work with the governor."

Chapter 19

"What are you saying, Mr. Belikov?"

Dalton looked at the older man with a frown. Belikov shook his head. His expression was one of sheer misery.

"I don't know what to say, Dalton. Yuri wants no part of a shared business with you. He's angry over that woman you both like—the one you want to marry."

"And that's a reason to throw away a perfectly good business arrangement?" Dalton was livid. Yuri had promised he'd be sorry.

The older man wrung his hands and shook his head again. "I can't dishonor my son by going through with something that will cause such division. He said he would walk away from the family business altogether if I sold you half an interest."

"This is ridiculous," Dalton said.

"It's . . . well . . . it's worse than just that."

Dalton eyed him suspiciously. "How so?"

"I . . . have to . . . you see . . ." He blew out a long breath and rubbed his forehead. "I have to let you go. You can no longer work for me."

Dalton stared at the man in dumbfounded silence. How could Yuri be so vindictive? They'd been friends since they were small. Why would Yuri be willing to just throw that away?

Mr. Belikov was going on about something, but Dalton couldn't hear the words for the racing of his own thoughts. What should he do now? It seemed no matter what direction he took, he found himself displaced.

"I cannot tell you how sorry I am," Mr. Belikov relayed. "Yuri is my son, however. I cannot lose him. He swore to me that if I didn't let you go, he would leave for the south and never be heard from again. His mother was in tears. She wants him to return with us to Russia." He muttered several incoherent words and raised his hands toward the sky. "I don't know what is to be done."

"I understand your position," Dalton admitted. "I just don't see how he can let this come between us. It's not like him."

Mr. Belikov nodded. "I'm sorry to say that while you were gone, he fell into bad company. His new friends are not a good influence on him. When Miss Robbins voiced her anger with him, Yuri . . . well . . . I'm afraid he took to drink."

Dalton felt a sorrow he couldn't explain. Yuri had always been the type to experiment with such things. As boys, they had been caught sampling some Tlingit hoochinoo or hooch, as most called it. Father had paddled Dalton soundly, then explained why it was so critical he stay away from such things. Dalton had never forgotten his father's words: *Alcohol has a way of taking hold of you. At first it convinces you of all the wonderful things it has to offer, but it isn't long before you are trapped by its seduction. Once this happens, getting away from it is not only difficult, it's often impossible."*

He had taken his father's advice to heart, but Yuri had always been a rebel. Dalton knew his friend had a drink on occasion. Was it possible that this was the real cause of his sudden change?

I haven't been here for a long time, Dalton realized. *And if I'm honest with myself, Yuri wasn't himself even before I left.* There were many little things that Dalton had tried to ignore. Yuri not finishing jobs. Yuri arguing more with his father. Yuri sneaking out from work to do who knew what. Yuri might well have given himself over to drinking, and maybe it had been for a lot longer than anyone realized. Seeing that Mr. Belikov was waiting for him to say something, Dalton offered him a smile.

"This isn't your fault. You have to be true to your family. I will be all right."

Belikov nodded. "I don't know what will happen. We most likely won't have the money to leave in the spring as I had hoped."

Dalton thought of the vast fortune he owned. He could already access a portion of the money, and it wouldn't be all that long before he turned twenty-one and all of the inheritance would belong to him.

"If I can help you, I will," Dalton promised. "Yuri doesn't need to know about it. You took me in and taught me a trade, Mr. Belikov. I won't easily forget that."

The older man's face contorted as he fought his emotions. "You are a good man, Dalton Lindquist. I am blessed to know you."

"I'll get my things and leave. I don't want to further upset Yuri. Maybe in time he will speak to me about this and what's really bothering him."

"I hope so."

Dalton gathered his tools and packed them neatly in a small crate. For now, he would take them over to the sawmill. Then when his father was available, they could come by and pick them up. He knew Joshua wouldn't mind.

His heart was heavy as he walked away from Belikov Boat Builders. He remembered the first time Mr. Belikov had put him to work sanding. The memory was a good one; he and Yuri had enjoyed the task. It hadn't seemed at all like work.

After leaving his things with Joshua, Dalton made his way on foot to the structure he knew his father would be working on. The house, not far from the coastline, was positioned a little higher on the side of the mountain. Father had nearly finished the place with the help of his Tlingit workers. Little by little, the Tlingits were returning to the village, and Dalton knew his father was happy to have them working with him again.

"I didn't expect to see you today." Kjell took one look at Dalton and asked, "What's wrong?"

"Mr. Belikov had to let me go. Yuri doesn't want me working there anymore. He doesn't want me to buy into the business, either."

"What happened?"

Dalton sat down on a nearby sawhorse. "I'm not sure I entirely know. It began when we both voiced an interest in Phoebe. But the stakes are much higher in this case than the adolescent competitions we once played at. I don't think Phoebe is the only reason it happened, however. Mr. Belikov said Yuri has fallen in with a bad crowd. He's taken to drinking."

"It's easy enough to do," Father said.

"Yuri has been slowly changing over the last year, but it's only now I've allowed myself to see it. I feel like maybe if I'd paid more attention, things wouldn't be so bad now."

"You can't be responsible for what Yuri chooses to do."

Dalton paced a few steps, slapping his hands against his sides. "I know that, but we've been friends for so long. Why is he letting this come between us? We've argued before, but it never lasts. But he's so angry this time, and I can't help but think that the difference is Phoebe."

"So what will you do?"

He stopped and looked at his father. "That's why I came to talk to you. I'm not sure what direction to take. I still want to have my own business, but I don't want to cause problems for Mr. Belikov or for Yuri."

"Perhaps Yuri's jealous, Dalton. You got the girl and a fortune. Maybe he's afraid it will change you."

"But he's the one who has changed," Dalton countered. "Not only that, but it started before Phoebe ever arrived. I can see that now."

"You could come to work with me for a time," Father offered. "It might give you a chance to clear your mind. On the other hand, maybe it's time for you to make your own plans."

"What do you mean?"

Two men moved past them carrying a door. "We hang now, yes?" one of them said to Kjell.

"Yes. Go ahead. I'll come check it when you're finished." The men nodded and moved on. Kjell turned back to Dalton. "It's nearly October. You could set up your own small place. I could help you build it. You wouldn't have the wherewithal to build the bigger boats, but maybe you could start small. Spend the winter building some skiffs or prams. Folks are always needing them around here."

"I don't have nearly all the equipment I'd need," Dalton told him. "I'd have to order up stuff from Seattle."

"Or go there yourself and get it," Father replied. "You might find the time by yourself will help you to see things straight."

"I suppose you're right, but having just come home, Mother won't be happy to see me go again."

Father brushed some sawdust from his trousers. "Your mother will understand. Besides, she has your sisters to keep her busy."

Dalton grinned. "That's a full-time job, to be sure." He looked at the house his father had been working on. "It looks good."

"We're finishing up today," he replied. "It's for the judge."

"Sitka has come a long way. We've got judges and a new U.S. marshal due any day. All sorts of law and order," Dalton mused. "Just like a regular civilized town."

"It's an exciting time. And just think, you get to start a business right in the midst of it all." Father got up and stretched. "Well, it's back to work for me. Are you heading home?"

"I wouldn't mind sticking around and helping you, if you don't mind."

Father laughed. "The more the merrier."

———

Phoebe sat down with her parents at the kitchen table. With her brothers off to school, she felt it was important to gain a full understanding of what was going on. Apparently there had been a discussion last night, and it had been determined that for the sake of the governor's desire to seek a higher office in the years to come, her father would sever their working relationship.

"He didn't ask me to do so," Father explained. "It's just that I can never tell when the past will rear its ugly head and expose me. It isn't fair to Lyman."

"But Lyman promised to stand by you," Phoebe's mother said, shaking her head. "How could he just let you go?"

"Like I said, he didn't want to." Phoebe watched her father stare sadly into his coffee cup. He seemed so lost—so confused.

"What will we do, Father?" She was terrified of the answer, but she had to ask the question.

"I don't know. My entire life has revolved around banking or politics. Now I cannot embrace either one."

Mother dabbed a handkerchief to her eyes. "It's so unfair. Why should we bear the marks of your father's misdeeds?"

"I've brought this shame on my family," Phoebe's father said, shaking his head. "I must be the one to deliver us from it."

"If I may be so bold, it seems God is the one who will do that, Father." Phoebe offered him a smile. "I don't know how or when, but God is faithful."

"God has deserted me," her father replied. "No, I should have borne evidence against my father at the trial. Had I made a better stand against what he did, people would not question my involvement. They wouldn't believe me to still hold the money my father swindled from them and the bank." He got to his feet. "My mind is made up."

"On what?" Phoebe's mother asked.

"I will go to California. You will remain here while I seek employment and a means to support this family. I will take the money we've managed to put aside and find us a small house. Once things are settled, I will send for you. It shouldn't be more than a few weeks. Lyman assured me he would see to your expenses during that time."

"You've already discussed this with Lyman?" Her mother's tone was edged with hysteria. "Why did you not discuss this with me first?"

"You always knew it was a possibility. I needed to make plans and have them in place before trying to explain them to anyone else."

Phoebe felt sick inside. Her father planned to move the family to California. What would it mean for her? She looked at her mother and felt awash in guilt. *Here I am worrying about what I will have to face, while poor Mother is enduring such a nightmare.*

"Mother, it may well be the only way. We will be fine. We have supplies once again for the candles, and we can support ourselves adequately for that short amount of time."

"I must go make arrangements. I might have to enlist the help of the navy to assist with my departure." Her father squared his shoulders and looked at his wife. "I am sorry, Bethel. This was not the life I planned for you and the children." He glanced at Phoebe and murmured, "I'm so sorry."

The house seemed horribly empty after he'd gone. Phoebe and her mother remained at the table, sitting in silence for some time. Phoebe longed to find Dalton and throw herself into his arms. She wanted his comfort and assurance that everything would be all right.

"I want to talk to Dalton and explain what has happened," Phoebe finally said.

"What does it matter now? We are ruined, just the same."

"Dalton won't care. His family is full of scandal and difficulties. He will not hold such a thing against Father or our family."

Her mother began to cry in earnest. "It's so unfair. Your father is a good man. All he needed was a chance. I don't blame Lyman— he has big aspirations. He might one day be president. Your father has known he would be a liability for Lyman, but we had hoped time and a reputation of doing good would resolve the matter. And now . . . now, even God has left us without hope or comfort."

"But, Mother, that is impossible. The Bible says otherwise. I memorized a verse while working with Zee and Mrs. Lindquist. It says in the book of John, 'I will not leave you comfortless: I will come to you.' Jesus was talking to His disciples about the fact that He would leave them and return to heaven. He promised they wouldn't be left alone. Lydia—Mrs. Lindquist—says we can trust God to never leave us alone. He has promised, and His promises are unbreakable."

Mother looked at Phoebe with tearstained cheeks. "I can scarcely believe that. I'm not sure I have the strength to endure."

"You don't have to rely on your own strength, Mother. Jesus will give you His, and He will see us through this." Phoebe reached out and took hold of her mother's hands. "You have only to trust Him for this."

For a moment, her mother said nothing; then she nodded. "I know you are right. I'm just so afraid of what this will mean for us."

"I have a confidence, Mother, that we will all be all right. I cannot say why, except that over these past weeks, I have learned so much about the character of God. He is faithful and worthy of our trust. He loves us, and that love is unconditional." Phoebe squeezed her mother's hands before releasing them.

"I'm going to go see if Dalton will stop by here after he finishes his work. I think the sooner I explain matters—and what this might mean for our family—the better."

Chapter 20

*P*hoebe didn't have to go in search of Dalton, however. He came to her. Seeing the troubled look on his face, she quickly agreed to go for a ride when he announced that he'd driven the wagon.

"I was hoping to see you. I had planned to walk down to the boat shop earlier, but time got away from me."

Dalton helped her into her coat. "I wouldn't have been there anyway. That's part of the reason I want to talk to you."

She looked at him oddly. "Is something wrong?"

"Yes and no. I'll explain it on our way."

Her mother had taken herself to bed and Phoebe hadn't seen her father since earlier that day, so there was no one to tell that she was leaving. Deciding to leave a short note of explanation, Phoebe positioned it in the kitchen near the stove. She had already prepared a stew for the evening meal, and no doubt her brothers would soon return to eat. Hopefully, they would see the note and let her parents know where she had gone.

"I'm ready now," Phoebe declared as she returned from the kitchen.

Dalton led the way and helped her into the wagon. Phoebe lowered her face and smiled at the sensation of his touch. She wanted nothing more than to scoot very close to him as he joined her on the seat, but propriety would never allow for such a thing.

"So why were you not at the shop today?" she asked.

Dalton moved the horses down the road before answering. "I lost my job."

Phoebe looked at him in disbelief. "Why?"

"Yuri. He's upset because . . . well, he knows how I feel about you. I think there's something else going on with him, but he won't talk to me."

Phoebe felt an odd sensation sweep through her at Dalton's declaration of having feelings for her. She wanted to hear more but knew it was best to wait for him to explain.

"I had offered to buy into Mr. Belikov's business," Dalton continued. "I love building boats, and I knew he was giving thought to leaving Sitka. I thought maybe it would be a good thing. Yuri and I could go on working together as we always have."

"Yuri doesn't plan to return to Russia with his family?" she asked.

Dalton shook his head. "He has always said he would remain here." He let out a heavy sigh. "Yuri is angry, though. He didn't want to share the business with me. He didn't even want me working there any longer, and his father felt he had no choice in the matter."

"What will you do?" Phoebe thought of her father also losing his position.

"That's why I wanted to talk to you." Dalton slowed the horses as they headed away from town. "I know Yuri mentioned that I have an inheritance. I had wanted to tell you about it myself, but it's of no matter now. The reason I bring it up is that I plan to take some of that money and build my own business. I will continue to build boats on my own, and with any luck, maybe I'll be able to hire someone who already has the necessary skills."

Dalton brought the wagon to a halt and set the brake. For several moments he was silent, and then to her further amazement, Dalton reached out to take hold of her hand.

Phoebe trembled from head to toe. She glanced up into his face, unable to speak. Dalton watched her with such intensity that she found it impossible to look away.

"I need to go to Vancouver or Seattle for the supplies I need. I didn't want to leave without letting you know—I've always regretted how I left the last time."

"You . . . you certainly didn't owe me an explanation." She fought to keep her voice steady.

"But I want you to have one," he assured. "It's important to me." He rubbed his thumb over the back of her hand. "Phoebe, I want you to wait for me."

Her eyes widened. "Wait for you?"

"Yes. I don't want you to court Yuri or anyone else while I'm gone. Would you do that for me?"

She nodded, knowing full well she had no intention of courting anyone else. "But you have to know something first," she said. Licking her bottom lip, Phoebe tried to think how best to phrase her confession.

"My family . . . my father . . ." She sighed. "I hinted at this the other day when you explained your past. There is a scandal in our family, as well. You might not want to get to know me better if you know the truth about it."

"You can't believe that would be true."

Phoebe offered a weak smile. "I don't . . . not really. But something has happened and everyone will soon know about it. My father lost his position with Governor Knapp. Actually, he resigned."

"But why?" Dalton tightened his hold on her hand. "What happened?"

Phoebe explained how her grandfather had once owned a bank and how her father had been the vice-president. "My grandfather swindled people and businesses, stealing thousands of dollars. It was a huge scandal, and Grandfather was found guilty and sent to prison. But the money was never recovered. My father was spared going to jail, since there was no evidence against him. Still, people believed him guilty by association, and it ruined his reputation. Especially when word got out about how the money was never accounted for. Many believed my father had it hidden somewhere. When Mr. Knapp suggested my father move away and work for him in Montpelier, it was an answer to my mother's prayers."

"So why did he resign?"

"Someone on the governor's staff knew about my father's past. He was caught embezzling by my father and threatened to make a very public affair of all he knew if my father didn't simply look the other way. Father refused. He went to the governor, explained the details of what he knew, and then resigned. Governor Knapp didn't want him to go, but Father felt he'd imposed enough on his friend. The governor would one day like to be president of the United States, and he doesn't need scandal in his background."

"Your father proved himself to be an admirable friend," Dalton told her.

"I know. But now he plans to leave. He's going to California to seek employment and to bury the past, once and for all."

"He'll most likely head out on the same ship I'll be on," Dalton said. "Maybe we can talk on the way down."

"That would be good," she said, considering her family's plight. "I'm sure he'll need a friend."

For several minutes, they said nothing. Finally Dalton reached over and touched her cheek. Turning her face gently, he asked, "So you will wait for me?"

She wondered what the question really meant. Was he asking her to marry him? Was he offering her a commitment of any type? It didn't matter. She knew her answer. She loved him. She would wait.

October 1889

October brought a damp cold to Sitka. The usually temperate air took on a bite that left everyone complaining. Evie's complaint, however, had nothing to do with the weather. She was tired of waiting for Joshua to declare his feelings for her.

Dressing carefully, she determined that if he would not speak up, she would. She was tired of waiting for love. Tired of being alone. If nothing else had proven itself to her on the trip south, it was that she was no longer willing to waste her life being alone.

"Are you ready to go?" Zee asked when Evie appeared in the living room.

"I am. Thank you so much for the ride into town."

"It's no trouble," Zee told her. "I was going anyway. I hope you don't mind we're taking the smaller wagon. Kjell took the big one and the draft horses. They were hauling wood today."

"The small one is fine. Sitting all stuffed together on the bench will keep us warm."

Lydia took one look at Evie and nodded. "He won't be able to resist you."

Evie laughed. "I've been home almost three weeks, and he's had no trouble keeping his distance."

"Men are like that sometimes," Lydia agreed. "Maybe he just needs your encouragement."

"Well, he'll not want for that," Evie replied.

Her resolve was a little less emboldened by the time Zee dropped her off at the sawmill. She had worked up a little speech in her mind, but now the words fled. Squaring her shoulders, she walked into the open workroom and glanced around. It appeared to be deserted. Maybe Joshua and his men were off working to help Kjell. She hadn't considered that possibility when Zee apologized about the small wagon.

"Hello?" she called. "Is anyone here?"

The door to the office opened and Joshua Broadstreet looked out. His brown hair was rather disheveled and the look on his face was one of pure surprise. Upon further inspection, Evie could see he had black smudges on his face, as well.

She smiled. "I see I have caught you hard at work."

"I was wrestling with the flue on the stove. It isn't venting as well as it should." He opened the door fully and stepped back. "Would you like to come in?"

Evie nodded and walked past him into the chilly office. Things suddenly seemed very strained. She didn't know what to say, and Joshua looked uncomfortable.

"Please sit," he offered. "I'm sorry it's so cold in here."

"It isn't all that bad," she said, taking a seat. Folding her gloved hands together, Evie tried to calm her racing heart.

"I was . . . well . . . I wanted to offer my condolences regarding your husband's death."

"Thank you," she said, frowning. The conversation wasn't exactly taking the turn she had hoped. "It's kind of you to say," she continued, "but you know there was no love between us."

"Yes. I suppose I do," he murmured.

Evie couldn't let things go on this way. She got to her feet and faced Joshua. "And there shouldn't be any games between us."

"What do you mean?"

He held her gaze, his brown eyes boring into her soul. Evie took a step toward him. "I want to know . . . I need to know . . ." Her breathing quickened and her chest felt tight. *This is it,* she thought—the moment she would know if her assumptions regarding his love for her were correct.

"I want to know what your intentions toward me are . . . now that I'm free."

She didn't even see him move, but without warning, he was there holding her, caressing her face. Evie let him tighten the embrace, not minding at all that he was nearly forcing the air from her lungs.

"Evie. Oh, Evie," he whispered against her ear. "I've waited so long. Loved you so long."

She nodded. "I know."

He pulled back and seemed to search her eyes for something. "Marry me?"

She smiled. "Of course. Why do you think I'm here?"

Joshua crushed her lips with his own. He kissed her with all of the pent-up longing they both felt. They clung to each other urgently, desperately. They had cared for each other but had respected the boundaries that kept them apart for all these years. Neither had ever crossed the line into impropriety. Now, Evie sighed and wrapped her arms around Joshua's neck, not caring if someone should walk in on them.

"I love you," she whispered as he trailed kisses along her jaw.

"And I've loved you since I first laid eyes on you."

Evie sighed as Joshua buried his face in her hair and did nothing but hold her for a long, long while. Evie didn't need words in that moment—she only needed his touch, his presence. She placed her head on his shoulder. This was what she had waited for all of her life.

———

The plan had been to marry as soon as possible, but Evie knew that even the best laid plans could be overruled by sickness. When the Lindquist girls, as well as Lydia, fell ill, along with a good number of other Sitkans, the wedding arrangements had to be delayed.

Zee had sent Evie to town to get several things while she remained home to nurse the family. As soon as Evie could return, Zee would go to the village to see about helping there. It appeared they were facing an epidemic of scarlet fever. If not treated, it would leave many weakened for life, if not dead.

A general quarantine was in effect, but it was difficult to manage the sales of much-needed items without some exposure. Evie had lived through scarlet fever as a child of three, and it was believed that once it had been survived, a body was forever immune. Quite a few people in town understood this, while others were all but boarded away in their homes, terrified of what exposure might bring.

Arnie, at the general store, had arranged a means of dealing with his customers. Those with sickness were to come to the back, where they would transfer a note with the needed items listed. He would fill the order and put the items in a box outside the door. They would then take the items and place them into their own bags or box.

Waiting her turn and doing exactly as ordered, Evie was glad to be done with the chore and headed for home nearly an hour later. The lines and frustrations of people dealing with this new manner of shopping had led to some ugly encounters. If things didn't calm soon, there would, no doubt, be fights.

"Evie, how are you?"

She turned to see Phoebe Robbins. "Keep your distance. We have the fever at home."

"We've all had it," Phoebe assured her. "Are the girls sick?"

"The girls, as well as Lydia. Poor Kjell was beside himself when Lydia took ill."

"And Zee?" Phoebe asked.

"She is there for now, but when I get home she plans to go to the Tlingits and see what can be done there."

"Could I come and help you?"

Evie considered this for a moment. With the girls sick, as well as Lydia, it would be nice to have some extra help. "Are you certain your mother can spare you?"

"Of course. I will go speak with her and pack a few things. I will come and stay, if that's acceptable to you. I don't know much about tending the sick, but I'm sure that I can help, even if it's to cook or clean up."

"Zee can teach you what you need to know. Why don't you climb into the wagon? I'll drive you home and we'll get your things."

Phoebe nodded. "Hopefully this will pass quickly and not result in too many deaths."

"I pray so. I can't imagine losing Lydia or either of the girls. I'm only glad that Dalton isn't here, as well."

"Me too," Phoebe barely whispered. "I pray he stays well."

Chapter 21

*D*alton approached Phoebe's father at the stern of the ship, hoping for a chance to spend some time talking before their ship docked in Seattle. Mr. Robbins had kept to himself throughout most of the trip, and this was actually Dalton's first opportunity to speak with him.

"Mr. Robbins?"

The man turned from the railing, where he'd been staring out to sea. His face contorted, and he looked quite distressed. "Yes."

"I know we've only met briefly." Dalton extended his hand. "I'm Dalton Lindquist."

Robbins nodded rather nervously and finally took hold of Dalton's hand. "Yes. You're the young man my Phoebe has spoken of."

"She's part of the reason I wanted to talk to you." Dalton leaned back against the railing, hoping his action would lend a less formal spirit to the moment.

Robbins gripped the rail and looked away. "My daughter thinks highly of you."

"And I of her," Dalton admitted. "In fact, I would like to seek your blessing to ask for her hand."

This caught Robbins' attention in an unexpected way. He jumped back as if Dalton had somehow wounded him. "Marriage? You speak of marriage?"

Dalton nodded. "I know it might seem out of order. We've only known each other a short time, but I'm not a man given over to frivolity or nonsensical notions. I do not take action without a great deal of consideration and prayer on any matter. Phoebe has touched something deep in my heart. I love her, and I want to marry her as soon as possible."

Robbins looked him over. "And you have the means to support a wife?"

"I do. I have an inheritance—a rather large inheritance—that I will take complete control of upon my twenty-first birthday. At this point, I have partial management of the money and intend to start a business in boat building."

For several minutes, Robbins said nothing. He turned back to look at the water, rubbing his chin as he contemplated this news. Dalton wondered if such an announcement had put the man's mind at ease or only served to further complicate matters.

"So you are not planning to simply sit back and live on this inheritance. You desire to work, as well?"

Dalton considered it an odd question, but responded. "I do. I have no intention of sitting idle. I wasn't brought up that way. I very much enjoy working with my hands. Building boats has been something I've trained to do since I was young. I will most likely hire people to work with me, as I'd like to make this a large business in the years to come."

"And where will you live?"

"In Sitka," Dalton answered. "It's been my home, and after a trip to the States, I am convinced it will remain such. I'm unimpressed with large cities and the problems they bring. I prefer our life on the island. Besides, there is a great need for boats all along the coast."

Robbins' shoulders seemed to slump a bit. Dalton couldn't tell if the man was sorrowed at the idea of losing his daughter or relieved. "You have my blessing to marry her," he said in a barely audible voice.

Dalton was troubled by the man's reaction and manner. He toyed with the idea of saying nothing more, but he felt compelled to speak out. "Phoebe told me about the past—about your father. I want you to know that it doesn't matter at all to me. My family has its own past and problems. All families do."

The older man stiffened. "It is a millstone around my neck. I doubt I will ever be free of it—at least not until I die."

Robbins straightened and turned to face Dalton. "You seem like an admirable young man. I have only heard good things about your family. It seems that taking care of one another is important."

Dalton nodded and smiled. "It is. Family is everything."

Sadness and defeat etched Robbins' expression. "Family is very important." Then, as if the topic had become too difficult, Phoebe's father changed the subject. "Will you debark in Seattle?"

"Yes. I have to arrange for my business needs. After that, I will return to Sitka," Dalton replied. "What of you, Mr. Robbins?"

"No. I will head south to California." He seemed to consider something for a moment, then added, "Since you will no doubt head back to Sitka before I can, I wonder if you might take a letter to my wife."

"Of course. I'd be happy to."

"Very well. I'll have it brought to you in the morning."

"Would you care to have supper with me tonight?" Dalton asked.

The man shook his head. "No. I have some matters to tend to, including the letter." He reached out to Dalton and took hold of his arm. "I pray you will treat my daughter well."

"I assure you, sir, I will."

Robbins' expression took on a look that Dalton could only think of as regret. "She was always the joy of my heart. As the oldest, she held a special place in my life. I will miss her."

"You could stay in Sitka," Dalton offered. "Perhaps even work with me." Dalton hadn't thought about it until just then, but Phoebe's father might be an asset to him. The man knew about banking and keeping books; perhaps he could work for Dalton in that capacity.

But Robbins shook his head. "I can't remain in Alaska. I would only end up causing my family more pain."

———

Yuri sat at the table and studied the cards in his hand. If he could get the queen of hearts, he would have a straight flush. The pile of money on the table would be his then, and he could prove to his father that he was just as capable of buying into the business as Dalton. Not that his father expected such a thing, but Yuri knew it had hurt him financially to be unable to sell Dalton half of the business. His father needed the money in order to take the family back to Russia, and with just a little bit of luck, Yuri could provide it.

"Give me one," Yuri said, tossing down a card.

The bearded man across from him smiled. "Just one? You must have a good hand."

Yuri stared at him, trying hard not to reveal his excitement. It was just one card—one card that would mean the difference between shame and his father's approval. Of course, if his father knew he was gambling, there would be no approval.

"Give him the card," the man to Yuri's left demanded.

The dealer shrugged and did just that. Yuri looked at his hand for a moment before retrieving what he hoped would be the answer to all of his problems. He drew in his breath and held it. The others played on, while Yuri added the card to the back of his hand. *This is it*, he thought. He'd put all of his money on this one hand. He didn't even have enough left for a drink—not that he needed another.

"The moment of truth, Yuri," the dealer called.

Yuri looked up to find everyone watching him. He tried to keep a relaxed expression as he turned back to his hand. Spreading the cards ever so slowly, he saw the situation for what it was. A losing hand. The king of spades almost seemed to laugh at him.

The dealer laughed as Yuri threw down the cards. "Maybe better luck next round."

Yuri got to his feet. He swayed for a moment, feeling the effects of the liquor he'd consumed. "Not tonight. I'm busted."

He stalked from the room and slipped into the darkness of the night. It was well past ten, and his folks would no doubt be worried about him. Yuri didn't care. His plan had come to nothing. He had only accomplished bringing shame on himself. Why couldn't he be as good as Dalton? All of his life, Yuri had wanted to be like Dalton Lindquist. Even as boys, Dalton had always seemed to accomplish anything he set out to do. Yuri envied him then, but especially now.

How was it that Dalton could just inherit great sums of money? Why was that fair? Yuri had worked hard all of his life. He'd enjoyed his father's approval and teachings. He'd been happy when Dalton had joined them in the business. But now Yuri just felt jealous—angry that Dalton should have it so easy.

He will make his own business, Yuri thought. *He will marry Phoebe and he will have everything he wants, while I have nothing.*

What was to become of Yuri after his father and mother left for Russia? Could he manage the business and keep a profit coming in as his father had? Yuri doubted his own ability to do so. He had never had a head for numbers, and even when his father had tried to teach him bookkeeping, Yuri had struggled.

Approaching his house, Yuri stopped and tried to clear his head. He couldn't risk his father knowing that he'd been drinking. He would never hear the end of arguments about why such things were foolish.

"I am a man," he said, shaking his fist at the house. "I can do as I please."

"Yuri?"

He started at his name being called. "Who's there?"

"It's me, Maxim," his brother answered. "I've been looking for you."

"Why?"

His brother approached, but darkness kept his face veiled. "I was worried about you."

"That's stupid," Yuri said in a gruff manner that he hoped would send Maxim back to bed. "I am a man."

"So I heard you declare," Maxim said. "You are also drunk."

"What of it? I have a right to do as I please." Yuri staggered forward and put his hands on Maxim's shoulders to steady himself. "You are but a child."

"I'm old enough to know the truth of what you're doing to yourself. Mama is so fretful. You have caused her great pain."

Yuri didn't want to hear the truth. He pushed away, nearly

falling backward. "I am going to bed," he announced. "You can stand out here all night if you like."

"No. I'll help you. Otherwise, you'll wake the entire house, and we'll all hear from Father on the dangers of hard drink." He pulled Yuri's arm around his shoulder and steadied him. "Come on. I'll get you to bed."

Yuri said nothing. He knew if he spoke he might well start to cry. He felt so broken inside, and it frightened Yuri to the depths of his soul.

———

"The sickness isn't as bad as we'd feared," Zee told Evie and Phoebe. "It appears to be a milder form of scarlet fever. The chills last much longer and the fever comes on in a slower manner. Many of the Tlingits have already had the disease and so are not succumbing."

"The doctor saw Lydia and the girls," Evie told her. "He felt they were making an adequate recovery. He suggested warm vinegar wraps around the throat for Lydia. For the girls, he told us to use this soap and wash them daily, then rub seal or candlefish oil over their skin." She took out a cake of soap and held it up.

Zee nodded. "We should lay in a supply. I'll talk to Kjell. Lydia is a few days behind the girls in this, so she'll soon need it."

"So the danger has passed?" Phoebe asked.

"Hopefully," Zee replied. "Yet there are sometimes complications. Scarlet fever can affect the heart and kidneys. We'll keep administering care and medicine; that's all we can do for the time being, besides pray."

"When can we expect the epidemic to abate?" Evie questioned, slipping the soap back into her apron pocket.

"I think another week or so will show a turning in the tide." Zee went to the kitchen counter and checked the milk pail. "Kjell will bring you more milk this evening. It's really the best thing we can give them. I wish we had a hundred milk cows instead of just one."

"Perhaps we can pray that God will multiply the milk as He did the loaves and fishes," Phoebe said with a smile.

Zee flashed a grin. "Perhaps."

Phoebe waited until Evie had gone to bathe the girls before peeking in on Dalton's mother. Surprised to see Lydia awake, Phoebe stepped into the room.

"Do you need anything?" Phoebe asked. "Are you warm enough?" She went to the fireplace and added a log.

"I'm better," Lydia said with a heavy breath. "I feel so tired and weak."

Drawing up the chair, Phoebe sat down beside Dalton's mother. She looked small and frail. "It's to be expected. You have made great progress, however."

"How are the girls?"

"They are much better. Evie is washing them with the soap given us by the doctor. It should help with the itching and the scaling."

Lydia nodded and closed her eyes. "I can't thank you enough for what you've done for us. I know Evie and Zee are grateful for your help."

"Zee says things aren't as bad as they'd feared in the village. Hopefully by the time Dalton makes it back, the sickness will be over and he'll be able to come ashore."

Lydia looked at Phoebe and smiled. "I know you miss him greatly."

"I do. But certainly no more than you do."

"He cares for you," Lydia murmured.

"I know. I care for him, as well. He asked me to wait for him."

She wasn't sure why she'd shared that with Lydia, but now that the words were out, Phoebe was glad.

"I thought he might." She gave a weak smile. "And what was your response?"

"I said yes, of course."

"So we will most likely have two weddings before the year's out," Lydia said, meeting Phoebe's gaze.

There was no need for pretense. "I certainly hope so," Phoebe replied. "I love him. I want you to know that. It happened quite suddenly, and I never expected to feel so much for another person, but I cannot imagine my life without him."

Lydia's expression betrayed her pleasure at Phoebe's announcement. "I'm so glad. Dalton is a good man, but he will need a strong woman to stand beside him."

"Just as Mr. Lindquist needed you."

"I suppose that's true, but I feel that I needed him ever so much more."

Phoebe could see that Lydia was tiring. "You should rest now. I will be back to check on you very soon."

Lydia reached up her hand and Phoebe took hold of it. "Thank you. I will pray that your marriage will be filled with all the blessings that God can bestow."

Phoebe smiled. Lydia had spoken of her marriage to Dalton so casually that she couldn't help but feel aflutter with excitement.

Oh please, God, bring him home safe and soon. I miss him so.

Dalton had been in Seattle for three days before he realized that one of the three letters Phoebe's father had deposited in his care was addressed to him. Mr. Robbins had said nothing about it, and Dalton had presumed the letter was for his sons.

He couldn't imagine what Robbins would have to say to him

in a letter. Perhaps he had felt it important to reiterate his approval about Dalton and Phoebe marrying. Opening the envelope, Dalton began to skim the contents. A cold dread crept over him.

And so it is with great regret that I must go. It gives me comfort to know that you will be there for my family. Knowing that you hold family dear, I believe I can count on you to care for them long after I'm gone.

Shaking his head, Dalton reread the letter from the beginning. What was Robbins saying? There was an odd air of finality to his words that left Dalton with a great sense of unrest. He looked at the other letters and wondered what Robbins had penned to his wife and daughter.

Dalton took the letters in hand and turned them over. Neither was sealed. Should he open them and read the contents? It would be an invasion of privacy, but Dalton felt almost frantic to know what Robbins had written.

"Maybe I'm assuming too much," he said aloud. He looked at his own letter again. There was a definite tone that suggested Robbins was bidding Dalton good-bye. "It's not my imagination." Dalton dropped the letter on the bed and took up the envelope that Robbins had addressed to his wife.

My dearest Bethel,

So long I have loved you, and for so long I have burdened you with my shame. You have suffered at my side, bearing more than any good wife should have to bear. I have loved you more dearly than any husband has ever loved his mate. You have been my all—my very breath. Please know that you hold no responsibility in the decision that I now make. Please tell my children that they were dear to me, and that I held great pride in them.

When I announced my resignation to Lyman, I knew that I

was making a decision that should have been made years ago. As I resign my life, I feel much the same. The decision should have been made a long time ago to save my family from the pain and sorrow that has haunted us these many years.

Dalton's hand trembled. It was exactly as he feared.

Forgive me, Bethel, for I am but a weak man and haven't the strength to go on. Dalton Lindquist has just asked to marry our daughter. I have given him my blessing, and I know that he will care for you and the boys, as well. It is the only thing that gives me any peace of mind in leaving you.

Feeling as though the wind had been knocked from him, Dalton sank to the bed and shook his head. Robbins meant to end his life.

"What is to be done?" The ship was long gone and Robbins with it. By now, the man might even be dead. Dalton wished fervently that his mother or father might be there so he could consult them. "Dear God," he prayed, "what should I do about this?"

Chapter 22

November 1889

*D*alton arrived back in Sitka on the twenty-third of the month. The new mail steamer, *The City of Topeka*, had provided him a comfortable journey on this, her maiden voyage to Alaska. Dalton had heard the crew say that this was only the first of many trips to come, as the ship would become their primary postal transport.

He also learned that scarlet fever had afflicted the town in his absence and prayed that his family had not suffered from the disease. He couldn't recall ever having had the sickness himself, and he feared for his little sisters. His biggest worry, however, was how to share the news of Mr. Robbins' death with his family.

He scanned the crowd of people who'd come to the dock. There was no sign of his father or mother, but then, they hadn't known he would arrive today. Dalton toyed with the idea of going home first. It was a cold, rainy Saturday, so perhaps his father and mother would be available to accompany him to the Robbinses' house. He hated the idea of going alone.

His own investigation of Mr. Robbins' trip to California had revealed he had succeeded in his intention: Dalton had it confirmed that he had jumped from the ship and drowned. Dalton was at a loss as to how he would break the news to Phoebe and her family. He had, in fact, thought of saying nothing—of hiding the letters Robbins had given him. But he couldn't abide the lies and secrets that had marred his own life. It would be painful for them to know the truth of what Mr. Robbins had done, but Dalton couldn't protect them from it. Soon enough the authorities would be in touch, and it was better that the news come from someone who cared about them.

"But what do I say?" There was no easy way to break news of this type. Maybe it would be better to seek advice from his family first.

Finally, Dalton decided it would be best to just get the matter out of the way. Phoebe's home was less than two blocks away, and with bag in hand, he walked the short distance, praying every step that God would help him to say the right things.

The gloomy day seemed the perfect backdrop for bad news. Dalton trudged through the muddy streets greeting those around him in an absent-minded manner. It wasn't until he saw Yuri from a distance that he pushed aside thoughts of his task.

"Yuri!" Dalton called and waved.

His friend glanced up but didn't return the greeting. He stared at Dalton for a moment, then turned and walked away. Dalton stopped and watched Yuri go. Apparently the time apart had not assuaged Yuri's anger.

There is nothing I can do about it right now, Dalton reminded himself. He was in sight of the Robbinses' house. The small building bore the same signs of weathering that most other places had, but Mrs. Robbins and Phoebe had done a good job of making it a home. Despite the wear of age, it seemed almost cheery with the lacy curtains that hung in the front window.

It will never be cheery after today.

Knocking on the door, Dalton prayed one more time for strength. There wasn't any way he could make this easier for the family. No matter what he said, Mr. Robbins would still be dead, and their loss would be acute. Mrs. Robbins opened the door and beamed him a welcoming smile.

"Dalton—we didn't know you were back." She stepped back. "Please come in out of the cold."

He did so and placed his bag just inside the door. Pulling off his cap, he looked at the woman. "I wonder if we could talk for a few minutes."

"Of course. Phoebe is here, as well. Let me get her. She's in the kitchen ironing. The boys have gone off with friends, so we should be able to speak without interruption."

Dalton let her go, knowing that she would need her daughter to help steady her through the sorrowful news to come. Maybe he needed her, too. With Phoebe sharing the moment, Dalton knew he wouldn't feel so alone. Still, this was her father, and the shock would be equally hard for her. Dalton ran his hand through his hair and silently wished he'd gone to get his folks first.

Phoebe stepped into the room at that moment and gone were all other thoughts. Her honey gold hair hung loose around her shoulders, and though her manner of dress was quite simple, Dalton thought she'd never looked more beautiful.

"I didn't know you were coming today. I would have been at the docks," she declared. She crossed the room to come closer. Her mother was right behind her or Dalton might have swept Phoebe into his arms.

"I'm sorry I couldn't get word to you ahead of time." He braced himself and motioned to the sofa. "I wonder if we could sit. I need to speak with you—both."

Phoebe smiled and nodded. "Of course. You sound so serious. Is something wrong?"

She took a seat, as did her mother. Both women looked to Dalton with such expectancy that he wanted nothing more than to bolt from the room. Instead, he pulled up a straight chair to sit directly in front of both women. He took Mr. Robbins' letters from his pocket but didn't hand them over.

"I'm afraid there is something wrong. I wish I didn't have to be the bearer of bad news, but it has fallen to me, nevertheless."

Mrs. Robbins' smile faded as she glanced at her daughter. Phoebe leaned forward. "What is it, Dalton? Tell us now."

"Your father . . . Mr. Robbins . . . I'm afraid he's . . ." Dalton struggled with the word. It seemed so harsh, so final. "He's dead."

Phoebe shook her head in disbelief. Her mother stared back at Dalton, eyes wide and mouth dropped open in shock. He wanted to comfort them both, but they had unanswered questions. Rather than wait for them, Dalton continued.

"I spoke to him on the trip down to Seattle. He gave me these letters for you." Dalton handed them over. "In fact, there were three letters, but one was for me. However, I didn't realize that until days after your father and I had parted company."

The women stared at the envelopes for a moment, then looked back to Dalton. Phoebe spoke first. "What happened? How did he die?"

"He jumped from the ship. A witness saw him, but by the time they were able to stop the ship and send rescue, there was no sign of him." Dalton paused and drew a deep breath. "Let me back up a bit. When I talked to him on the ship, he seemed burdened. He had kept to himself throughout most of the trip, so I wasn't even able to talk to him until the day before I debarked.

"I went to him to ask for Phoebe's hand," he said, looking at her apologetically. "I am sorry to mix such a wonderful event with so much sadness, but it's important for you both to know."

Phoebe nodded and looked to her mother. "We understand."

Mrs. Robbins had tears streaming down her face but otherwise remained silent.

"He asked me to bring a letter back to you, Mrs. Robbins. When he had your letter delivered to me the next morning, there were two others with it. I presumed, as I said earlier, that they were for you both and the boys. I went about my business paying no attention to the letters, until three days later. At that time I noticed that one of them was addressed to me. When I read it, I became alarmed. It sounded very much as if Mr. Robbins was giving the care of his family over to me. I was certain that he was saying good-bye. I feared that he intended to do himself harm and needed proof."

Dalton shifted uncomfortably. "I beg your forgiveness, but this, in turn, caused me to open your letters. When I saw what he'd written you, I went immediately to the authorities. They contacted the ship's captain and eventually learned that Mr. Robbins had died at sea."

"He couldn't swim," Mrs. Robbins said, speaking for the first time since hearing the news. "None of us can." Her voice broke and a sobbing gasp escaped her. "Oh, what are we to do?"

Exchanging a glance with Phoebe, Dalton reached out to take hold of Mrs. Robbins' hand. "I don't want you to worry about anything. I love Phoebe very much, and I believe she loves me."

"I do," Phoebe whispered.

He fixed his eyes on her. "Do you love me enough to marry me?"

She nodded most somberly. "You know I do."

Dalton looked back at Mrs. Robbins. "We will marry, and you will become my family. I will see to your needs. You mustn't be afraid of the future."

"But how can you take care of us? You're hardly more than a boy yourself," Mrs. Robbins said, shaking her head.

"I have money. My father left me an inheritance. It's been in my mother's care all these years. It is quite substantial and will be more than enough to see us through. I only ask one thing."

"What is that, Dalton?" Phoebe questioned.

"That you remain here in Sitka. This is my home, and my business has always been here. I do not desire to leave. So for the time being, I would ask you to stay. If later you think it best to return to Vermont or some other place, I will see you safely there and provided for, but Phoebe and I would stay on here."

"I can scarcely believe this," Mrs. Robbins said, clutching the letter to her breast. "I . . . I . . . need to be alone." She got to her feet and fled the room without another word.

For a moment Dalton and Phoebe sat in silence. He was glad the boys were not home. He thought it might be easier for them to hear the news from their mother—in private.

"I'm sorry," he finally said.

"Don't be. You did everything admirable and good," Phoebe replied.

"But you deserve better than a proposal in the same conversation in which you learn of your father's death." Dalton got up and joined her on the sofa. Slipping his arm around her shoulder, he pulled her close and breathed in the scent of her hair.

Phoebe clung to him and buried her face against his chest. It felt so right to have her there. Dalton longed to kiss her, but now was not the time.

"We should marry as soon as possible," he finally said.

"Yes. I agree." She straightened and met his gaze. "Dalton, where will we live? There's hardly room here for the four of us as it is."

"I hadn't really considered it, but I plan to build a business. I might as well build a house, too. I'll need to talk to my father. For the time being, maybe your mother and brothers can remain here, and you and I can take a small place nearby. We could even move out to my place, but that wouldn't keep us close to your mother."

"I suppose there will be time to figure it all out." She sounded so lost, and Dalton reflexively pulled her close again.

"I'm sorry that I couldn't have proposed in a romantic setting," he said. "I have thought of nothing but you the entire trip. How is it that you worked yourself so completely into my heart when I wasn't even looking?"

"I wanted to ask the same of you," she said, trembling in his arms.

"Are you afraid?"

She said nothing, and Dalton couldn't help but seek her face. "Look at me, Phoebe."

She pulled back just enough to gaze upward. Dalton took hold of her face and caressed her cheek. "Don't be afraid . . . not of me . . . not of the future. God has not forsaken us. He will guide our steps."

"I'm not afraid of you," she whispered. "I am . . . I am nervous— anxious. I want to be a good wife, but I . . . well . . . I've not even been kissed before. I'm afraid you will find me quite naïve."

He smiled. "I don't mind." He traced a line along her jaw. "And I intend to remedy that matter of the kiss . . . very soon."

She looked at him with such an expression of awe and delight that Dalton wanted nothing more than to kiss her then and there, but he held back. He wanted their first kiss to be just as special as their first night together. It was hard to hold off, but Dalton knew it would be worth the wait.

"Very soon," he promised.

———

"I'm so glad to know you're all doing much better," Dalton said. He looked at his mother now tucked under a blanket, sitting in her favorite rocker. "I had no idea you were so ill."

"We couldn't very well get word to you," Evie replied. She had just returned from seeing the girls to bed. "It all happened rather fast."

"And without Phoebe, we would have been much worse off," his mother added.

"She said nothing about it. Of course, my news to her was so overwhelming, she probably forgot all about it." Dalton had already told them about Mr. Robbins.

"I wish we could have helped you, but I know God was at your side," his mother said. "It's hard to imagine why someone would end their life like that."

"The man no doubt felt overwhelmed with the weight of all that had happened," Father said as he joined them in the living room. "The past has a way of stealing the joy of the present."

Dalton sighed and leaned back against the leather-upholstered chair his father had made. It was so good to be home. He longed for his bed and a long sleep.

"Were you able to get everything you had wanted to buy while in Seattle?" Zee asked.

"Yes, and then some." He grinned. "Part of it won't even be shipped up until later. But I brought the important things with me—like presents for all of you."

His mother laughed. "It's very nearly your birthday. You're the one who deserves the presents."

"I have arranged my own special gift," Dalton replied. "I proposed to Phoebe and she accepted. The timing was less than perfect, but I wanted to reassure her mother that I would take care of her and the boys, as well."

His parents exchanged a glance. "That was an admirable thing to do, son," his father said.

"I figure I'm carrying on a tradition in a sense," Dalton said. "You took on me and Mother, as well as Evie and Aunt Zee. I figure it's the least I can do for the woman I love."

His father leaned back against the fireplace mantel. "It's a big responsibility."

"When will you marry?" Mother asked, wiping a tear from her eye.

"Very soon. Within the week, if possible. I think it's important that we do this and offer the family as much security as we can."

"Where will you live?" Evie asked.

"Well, I think the best thing will be to build a new house." He looked to his father. "I was hoping you would be available."

"As if I would let anyone else help you," Kjell said, laughing. "In fact, while you were gone, I managed to secure a piece of property not far from here. It's a nice harbor location where I thought you might want to have your boatbuilding shop. It's definitely large enough for a house, as well."

Dalton grinned. "When can I see it?"

"How about tomorrow after church?"

He nodded. "Of course, it will be hard to put much together over the winter. I guess in the meanwhile, we'll probably rent something small in town. Her mother will want Phoebe close."

"I can understand that. I'm glad though that you'll be able to be off to yourselves at least for a little while," his mother said thoughtfully. "It will be an important time for you and Phoebe to get to know each other."

"I don't know if you've heard," Evie interjected, "but Joshua and I are to be married on the seventh of December."

Dalton laughed and reached over to give her a playful nudge. "It's about time. What took him so long to propose?"

Evie shrugged. "I guess he was just waiting for me to come give him a good push."

"Well, sister, I couldn't be happier for you." He couldn't help but think back on the pain and misery she'd suffered. No one deserved a happy marriage more than Evie.

His father stretched. "It's getting late, and we have church in the morning," He went to where Lydia was sitting and without so much as a grunt, swept her into his arms and headed for the stairs. "Now I'll have you all to myself."

Dalton heard his mother giggle and smiled at Evie and Zee. "I hope I'm just as romantic at their age."

Evie nodded. "I know I plan to be."

Phoebe sat on her bed, staring out into the darkness. Her father was dead. She had never admitted it to her mother, but Phoebe had feared her father might never return for them. Her initial worry was that he was running away from them—that he would leave for California and never send for them to join him. She wasn't even sure why she'd feared that. He'd never been the kind of man to leave his family to do for themselves.

"But he's done exactly that now," she whispered.

She hugged her knees to her chest and fought back tears. How could he be gone? How could such a thing have happened? Surely he knew the pain it would cause. His letter to her said as much. A wave of anger coursed through her. How could he have been so inconsiderate—so selfish? Her mother was inconsolable, and the boys . . . well, they were confused and grief-stricken.

"It wasn't right," she said, shaking her head. "What you did to us wasn't right."

Bowing her head, Phoebe tried to pray, but the words would not come. How should she even address the matter? Wasn't suicide a sin? Had her father lost his place in eternity because of his weakness? Surely God wasn't like that. God, above everyone, knew the pain and weight of the burden her father carried.

Her sigh echoed in the silent room. What would happen now? She knew she would marry Dalton, but beyond that her future seemed obscured. It seemed her family—her very life—was in pieces and she might never be able to gather them together again. Phoebe had never felt so alone.

"Oh, Dalton. I wish you were here now. I wish we were already married." She straightened and slumped back against her pillow. Pulling the covers around her body, Phoebe let her tears flow freely.

"Papa," she breathed, "I will miss you so."

Chapter 23

Phoebe looked down at her cream-colored suit. The dark brown embroidery work gave it a more festive look, but still it was quite simple. The lines of the piece had been designed for ease of travel and comfortable walking. She doubted the designer had ever intended it to be a wedding dress.

She glanced at the clock. In less than fifteen minutes, she would be Mrs. Dalton Lindquist. It all seemed like a dream. They had spent much of the past week together, even managing to find a tiny apartment above one of the stores. It wasn't much, but as Dalton explained to her, they didn't need it to be. Come spring, they would have a new home of their own   one large enough for her entire family.

"Are you ready?" her mother asked.

"I suppose I am." Phoebe looked up and smiled. "It's not exactly how I envisioned my wedding day, but in all honesty, it doesn't even matter. I'm marrying a man I love, and though Father isn't here to share the moment with us, I am happy."

Her mother nodded and reached for her daughter's arm. "He is a good man. His concern for our family is more than anyone could ever expect." Her mother's voice seemed to weaken. "I wish this day could have been different for you. I never imagined that your father wouldn't be here to give you away. I miss him so." She dabbed at her eyes. "I'm sorry."

Phoebe took hold of her mother's hand. "Don't be. I know how very much you loved Father. I wish he had not . . . had not . . . gone away. I hope you know I will always be here for you. My marriage to Dalton will not change that."

Her mother smiled sadly. "I know, but I also want you to have a life of your own. Your wedding should be a day of happiness and joy, focused completely on you and your husband. I don't want you to give this another thought. Not now." She squeezed Phoebe's hand. "There will be plenty of time for mourning after today."

Phoebe nodded. She followed her mother from the small room and into the sanctuary. She noticed the small gathering of people. Most were Dalton's family and friends. The governor and his wife, however, had managed to attend, as had a few of her father's other associates. Phoebe saw her brothers at the front, standing with Dalton. They seemed unhappy and out of place.

Britta tugged on Phoebe's skirt. "Are you ready?"

She looked down at Britta and Kjerstin. They were to be her maids of honor. Phoebe smiled. "I am. You go ahead and lead the way."

Someone began to play the piano, and Phoebe realized that her wedding had begun. Britta led the way down the aisle, and Kjerstin followed about six paces behind. Phoebe drew a deep breath and felt her knees begin to wobble. Upon meeting Dalton's blue-eyed gaze, however, she steadied.

He smiled, and Phoebe couldn't help but flush. She lowered her head, embarrassed that she was now truly a blushing bride. What would people think? She moved down the aisle slowly, keeping her focus on the floor just a few feet in front of her.

I can do this. It's just one step at a time. She couldn't help but smile as she remembered her Bible verse from Philippians. *I can do all things through Christ which strengtheneth me.*

She felt Dalton take hold of her arm. Trembling from head to toe, she was barely able to look up. Dalton winked, furthering her discomfort. He seemed more the mischievous prankster than the serious groom.

Tucking her arm close to his side, Dalton pressed in closer and whispered in her ear, "If you faint, they'll report it in the paper."

Phoebe's head snapped up. The preacher looked surprised, but Dalton simply held a matter-of-fact expression. Phoebe wanted to give him a hard whack in the ribs, but he was only trying to help. Still, there was something very wrong about a bride being teased in such a fashion. Didn't he know how nervous she was? Didn't he understand that she had waited for this day all of her life?

"Dearly beloved," the pastor began.

Phoebe licked her dry lips and tried to focus on the words of the ceremony. Dalton was about to become her husband. She was about to become his wife, and yet she barely knew this man. Why, they'd only come to Sitka less than six months ago. Maybe they were rushing this.

"Who gives this woman in marriage to this man?" the pastor asked.

For a moment, there was nothing but a stifling silence. Phoebe hadn't considered who might answer this question. Would her father's absence somehow cause the wedding to be less than legal in the eyes of the law and God?

"I give her in marriage."

Phoebe turned to find her mother standing to address the matter. She gave Phoebe a nod, then took her seat.

Turning back to the pastor, Phoebe couldn't help but ask, "Does that count?"

Dalton and the pastor chuckled, but Phoebe was quite serious.

The pastor leaned toward her. "It's absolutely fine." He straightened. "Do you, Dalton, take this woman, Phoebe, to be your lawfully wedded wife—to live together after God's ordinance in the holy estate of matrimony?"

The words ran together in Phoebe's head. She tried to focus on them, but her nerves got the better of her. *I'm being so silly,* she thought. *I must pay attention. I must listen to what's being said.* But the more she tried, the more she argued internally with herself.

"I do."

She heard Dalton's assent, and for a moment, the confusion cleared. Looking up, Phoebe found him smiling down at her. No, he was grinning like a child who'd gotten away with something he shouldn't have.

"And do you, Phoebe, take this man, Dalton . . ."

Oh dear. Now it's my turn. Why can't I stay calm? She tried to slow her rapid breathing. *I want to get married to him. I love him. Why do I feel so . . . so . . . terrified?* Her trembling intensified.

". . . forsaking all others, keep yourself only unto him so long as you both shall live?"

Phoebe swallowed hard. She knew it was her turn to speak. *I've forgotten the words. What do I say? I can't remember.* She looked at Dalton, feeling panic overcome her senses. "Yes," she said with a nod for emphasis.

"Say, 'I do,'" the pastor prompted.

Dalton gave her hand a reassuring squeeze. The look on his face was a mixture of amusement and compassion.

"I do," Phoebe whispered.

The rest of the ceremony seemed to pass quickly, and for this, Phoebe was grateful. She watched in mesmerized silence as Dalton slipped a ring on her finger and pledged his life and love to her. This was really happening. She was truly becoming his wife.

"I now pronounce you husband and wife in the sight of God and man," the pastor declared. "You may kiss your bride."

Dalton leaned down. "See, I told you I'd remedy this problem of yours."

Before she could answer, he pulled her into his arms and lowered his mouth to hers. The kiss was gentle and much too brief. Even so, Phoebe felt the wind go out of her completely. She gazed up into Dalton's eyes even as she felt her legs give way and the world go black.

When she awoke again, Phoebe found herself stretched out on a pew, several people gathered around her as if she were some sort of exhibit at the fair. Dalton was kneeling beside her. His worried expression quickly faded and the impish tease returned.

"I hope you won't do that every time I kiss you."

Everyone laughed around them, and Phoebe wanted to escape. She wished silently that God might reach down and pluck her up to heaven. At least that way, she wouldn't have to live down the embarrassment of fainting at her first kiss.

"Are you feeling better now?" Zee asked her.

Phoebe tried to sit up, but Zee held out her hand. "Just rest a moment. It's been a big day."

"I'm fine," Phoebe said. "Really I am. I'm sorry if I gave everyone a fright."

Apparently convinced that Phoebe wasn't about to perish before their eyes, Zee nodded and Dalton helped his wife to sit. He sat down beside her and put his arm around her shoulders.

"Are you sure you are all right?" her mother asked. She looked worried, which made Phoebe feel even worse.

"I'm perfectly fine. Honestly. You mustn't worry."

Her mother seemed to understand her discomfort. "Well, if you are certain." She leaned down and kissed her daughter on the cheek. "Congratulations." She turned to Dalton and kissed him, as well. "Welcome to our family."

That seemed to serve as the cue for everyone else to offer their best wishes. Phoebe smiled and made all the right comments, but she was ever aware of the man beside her. She belonged to Dalton Lindquist now. A smile crossed her lips.

And he belongs to me.

———

A week later, as Evie and Joshua exchanged a kiss at the conclusion of their wedding, Dalton couldn't help leaning over to whisper in his bride's ear. "See, she didn't faint. That's how it's done." Phoebe elbowed him hard, but he only chuckled.

Evie had chosen for the late afternoon wedding to take place at the Lindquist house, with a reception to follow. Friends and neighbors had come to join them, and while the setting was less formal than most ceremonies, Dalton thought it perfect for his sister.

Pulling Phoebe along with him, Dalton quickly congratulated the couple, kissed his sister on the cheek, and then slipped back through the crowd of well-wishers. He drew Phoebe with him and didn't stop until they were well away from the others. Then without warning, he kissed her with great passion.

"I think I'm getting the hang of this," she said as he pulled away. "I'm still standing."

Dalton laughed and kissed her again. "I think you're quite adept at the fine art of kissing."

Phoebe gave him a coy look. "I do rather like it."

Dalton felt his heart skip a beat. "What say we skip the recep tion?" he said with a grin.

She rolled her eyes but didn't otherwise protest. Dalton made their excuses to his mother, then found their coats and hurried Phoebe outside.

"What did you say to her?" Phoebe asked, pulling on her cloak.

"I told her we needed to check in on your mother," he replied innocently. "Why, did you think I had something else in mind?"

Phoebe played right along. "Of course not. I couldn't imagine you having any other thought. My mother will be so very touched at your consideration."

He drew her close, his breath warm against her ear. "I'm a very considerate man."

They began the long walk home arm-in-arm. "I thought Evie made a very pretty bride," Phoebe said in a thoughtful tone. "I hope she will be very happy."

"I think for the first time in her life, she is." Dalton pulled Phoebe closer. "But I doubt anyone could ever be as happy as I am."

"Unless it's me," Phoebe countered. "Oh, Dalton, I do love you so."

He stopped and glanced down the road before lifting her in his arms. "And I love you." He twirled her in a circle and declared, "I love you more each day, each hour, each minute."

She giggled and squealed. "Put me down. I'm getting dizzy."

"I like it when you're dizzy," he said, laughing. "Then you need me to help you stand." He stopped and planted her feet back on the ground.

With a look of love that completely pierced his heart, Dalton heard her whisper, "I'll always need you to help me stand."

"And I always will," he promised. "Now, we really should pick up our pace. It's cold out here. I rather fancy snuggling with you by a warm fire."

"After we see my mother and brothers?" she asked in a most innocent tone.

It was Dalton's turn to gaze heavenward. "Of course," he replied, "after we see your family."

The visit to Phoebe's mother took longer than Dalton had planned. She first needed him to help Theodore and Grady repair one of the back steps. Then she offered them supper, and Dalton figured it wouldn't be polite to refuse. Afterward, Mother Robbins, as he'd come to call her, wanted to discuss the handling of her husband's estate. Apparently the governor had given her some information regarding the situation, and she wanted to talk about it with Dalton and Phoebe.

By the time they started for home, it was nearly nine. Phoebe pressed close to his side. "It was so good of you to help Mother that way. I know you wanted to leave, but the fact that you stayed only endears you to me more."

Dalton smiled and put his arm around her. "And that's why I do it. So that you will love me more and more."

She giggled and looked up to meet his gaze. "Can we still snuggle by the fire?"

"I have thought of nothing else all evening."

Just then a commotion rose from one of the drinking establishments. There was some shouting and a bit of scuffling as one man was thrown out the door to land in the street not but a few feet away from Dalton and Phoebe.

"And stay out until you can afford to pay your tab," the man at the door declared.

The man in the street muttered a slew of obscenities and struggled to his feet. It was only after he was standing that Dalton realized it was Yuri.

"Are you all right?" he asked his friend.

Yuri looked at him with contempt. "What do . . . do you care?" He weaved a bit, and Dalton could smell that he'd been drinking.

"I do care, and you know I do."

"Right. You care so much."

Dalton shook his head. "Yuri, why don't you come home with us and have something to eat? That will help you to sober up before you go home."

Phoebe seemed to shrink back behind Dalton. He immediately wondered if he'd overstepped his bounds by inviting Yuri without first talking to his wife.

"I don't need your help, Dalton. I'm a man. I don't need anybody." Yuri started to stagger off toward the next saloon.

"Stay here," Dalton told Phoebe. He rushed after Yuri and made the mistake of taking hold of his arm.

Yuri twisted around, bringing up his fist and nearly connecting with Dalton's jaw. "I said I don't need help."

"You also don't need another drink," Dalton told him.

Yuri seemed to consider this a moment, then laughed. "You don't know what I need." He looked past Dalton to Phoebe. "Neither one of you knows what I need." He pushed away from Dalton and headed back in the opposite direction.

For a moment, Dalton just watched. He hoped that Yuri was headed home but somehow doubted it. What had happened to his friend? What had caused him to sink so low? It had to be more than simply losing Phoebe's affection. To hear Phoebe tell it, she'd never encouraged anything more than friendship.

"I'm sorry, Dalton," she whispered, coming to his side. "If

you need to go after him, I can just go home by myself. It's not that far."

"No. He's right. I don't know what he needs. In fact, I don't think I know anything about him at all."

Chapter 24

March 1890

"I wish you weren't going away," Britta said to Yuri's little sister, Illiyana.

Phoebe noted the mournful look of the two children. The Belikovs had announced they would leave for Russia at the end of April. She knew Dalton had helped finance the trip. Mr. Belikov hadn't wanted to take the offering at first, but once it was agreed that it could be a loan, he was less inclined to reject it. His wife's mother had grown ill and Darya was desperate to reach her. Illiyana was less enthusiastic.

"Perhaps you girls could write letters to each other," Lydia encouraged. "You share all about the things you are doing in Sitka, and Illiyana can teach you all about Russia."

"But we couldn't play together," Britta said with great sadness. Illiyana nodded in an equally morose spirit.

"We've been friends all of our life," Britta continued. "You can't just make two friends stop being together like that."

Phoebe felt sorry for the girls. She knew what it was to move away and leave beloved people behind. "Your mother is right. I write letters to my friends in Vermont. I miss them terribly, but the letters are a good way to keep the friendship alive."

"I can't write very well," Illiyana admitted. "And I'll have to learn to write in Russian when we go there."

"And I can't read Russian," Britta threw in.

"You two will simply have to keep up your English correspondence then," Lydia replied. "Or Britta will have to learn Russian. That wouldn't be such a bad thing. Dalton can read and speak Russian, as can your father. He could teach you."

Phoebe noted the time. "I'd better get back to town. Dalton will be coming home for lunch. He and Kjell have certainly gotten a lot accomplished with the house. I'm so excited to think that soon we'll have a place of our own."

"It will be very special for all of you."

"Oh, and thank you again for these recipes. I hope I can do them justice."

Her mother-in-law smiled. "You are very welcome. Dalton tells me you are a wonderful cook, so I'm sure you'll have no trouble at all."

She tucked the pieces of paper into her pocket and collected her wrap. "When I get good at them, I shall invite you to eat with us." Frowning, Phoebe added, "But it will probably be after the new house is finished. Our apartment barely has enough room for two people."

Lydia laughed. "That will be soon enough. Kjell tells me it won't be long. The mild winter helped them to accomplish a great deal more than they had originally planned. You shouldn't have long to wait now."

Phoebe imagined the glorious log house that was being built. It excited her more than she liked to admit, to know she would have a brand-new house that no one else had ever lived in. She gave the girls a wave and headed down the long drive. It was a beautiful day and she was glad for the time alone to sort her thoughts.

Dalton had been rather moody lately, and it had more and more to do with Yuri. Frequent rumors were circulating about Yuri, and Dalton feared for his well-being. Phoebe had tried to encourage him to talk with Yuri, but whenever her husband had approached his friend, Yuri had refused to even listen.

Men can be such ninnies. Why, if I had a problem with my girl friend, I would simply go to her and demand she hear me out. Phoebe began to get an idea. *What if I went to Yuri? He would have to listen to me—it wouldn't be polite to do otherwise.*

Her mind set, Phoebe strolled past the Sitka Industrial and Training School, where Sheldon Jackson had set up classes and living quarters for the Tlingit children. The positive proof of Jackson's approach seemed clear. The children were learning a great many new job skills—there was a carpenter who taught the boys about building furniture, houses, and boats, as well as women who were teaching the girls housekeeping and sewing. This would definitely give them an advantage in joining the American work force in Sitka and elsewhere.

Phoebe approached Belikov Boat Builders, determined to speak to Yuri and insist he stop this nonsense. Whatever was wrong in his life, it wasn't Dalton's fault. There was no sense losing a good friend over issues that perhaps they could work through together.

"Hello?" Phoebe called out as she entered the shop. "Is anyone here?"

"Be right there," Yuri called from somewhere deep in the building. When he came out and realized it was Phoebe, his smile faded. "Why are you here?"

"I want to talk to you," she replied.

"Well, I don't want to talk to you."

"Isn't that too bad." Her comment surprised him, but Phoebe didn't stop there. "You have long had your own way, Yuri Belikov, and now it's my turn."

He frowned. "I don't know what you think you have to say, but be done with it and go."

Phoebe crossed her arms. "You and Dalton need to resolve whatever the problem between you might be. I know it isn't me."

"Oh, and how can you be so sure? We both liked you, and he stole you away from me."

"Be reasonable, Yuri. You and I were nothing more than friends. I'd like to be your friend now. You are important to Dalton. He speaks about you all the time. He doesn't understand what's happened to you."

Yuri shrugged and pretended to busy himself at one of the tables. Phoebe came to stand directly in front of him. "Yuri, what is wrong? Is it your mother and father leaving for Russia?"

"They can go. I hardly care. I have this shop now. My father sold the last of his big boats, and he has the money he needs to leave—so let him go."

"But you will miss them. Having your family move away is not an easy thing to bear."

"I don't care. Now if that's all you've come to say—"

"It's not," she interrupted. "I'm not leaving until you are honest with me about this. I don't have to share your thoughts with Dalton, but I do demand you tell me why you are no longer willing to be his friend."

"Why should it matter to you?"

"Because I love him," Phoebe replied matter-of-factly. "And, believe it or not, I care about you, as well."

"You lie."

"Why should I?" She shook her head. "I owe you nothing. Don't you remember the pleasant times we spent together? I'm sorry that you took offense that I could not turn our friendship into something more, but I never played false with you."

Yuri heaved a sigh and his shoulders slumped forward. "No, you never did."

"I'm glad we can at least agree upon that."

"Still, it hurt that you gave your heart to Dalton so easily."

"And for that I'm sorry," she offered. "Not that I gave my heart to Dalton, but rather that I hurt you. I never meant to cause you pain. I can't explain what happened to me when I first met Dalton. It was like nothing I had ever expected. I fell for him from the first moment."

"He's a lucky man."

Phoebe heard the weight of sorrow in his voice. "But that isn't what this is all about—is it?"

He met her gaze. "No. I suppose not. It was just one more thing."

"What do you mean?"

Yuri walked to the open workshop door. The water lapped the shore not but about twenty feet away. Phoebe could smell the strong scent of seawater and fish. She waited for Yuri to say something, wondering if she should further prod a response. Something inside, however, admonished her to be quiet. He would speak in due time.

Minutes later, he did just that. "Dalton was always better at everything. He always played by the rules. He made better marks in school. He was smarter." Yuri turned with a sad smile. "He was even able to speak Russian better than me."

He stepped back to the table. "He was better at boat building. My father would show him something once, and Dalton instantly knew what to do. I had to work and work to grasp the concept."

"Maybe you weren't intended for boat building, Yuri."

He looked at her oddly and nodded. "I have long known that, but of course I couldn't tell my father. It was his dream that I would one day take on this business."

"So why did you protest when Dalton wanted to buy into it?"

"Because I didn't want him to show me up. I didn't want him to take my father's admiration and affection as he had taken yours."

"Oh, Yuri. Your father is a good man. He will always love you more than Dalton."

"My father admires craftsmanship and the ability to see a task through to completion. I often fail in those areas. Dalton doesn't."

"But your father put Dalton from this shop when you asked him to. He refused to sell Dalton half of the business because you didn't want to work with him. That should tell you that he cares more about what you desire than what Dalton wants."

"I suppose, but it also makes me feel terrible for the way I acted. Dalton didn't deserve that, but I just couldn't see myself paired alongside him any longer."

"But there are things that Dalton cannot do. Yuri, you needn't compare yourself to him. He cares about you for the friendship you've always shared. I would dare to say his love for you is equal to that of his for me. It's just a completely different kind of love."

"It's too late," he said, shaking his head. "Too much has happened."

"What makes you believe that?"

Yuri picked up a chisel and dropped it again. "I owe money."

"To whom?"

"To some men. I . . . well . . . I gambled." He looked up. "I have a gambling debt."

Phoebe considered this for a moment. "Did you have this debt before Dalton and I married?"

"I had a bit of it. I had started to spend time with the wrong people even before Dalton went south with his sister. They were always enticing me with drink and gaming. I liked the way it made me feel." He came around the table to where she stood. "I don't expect you to understand, but for once, I felt that I had something that didn't involve Dalton. I could drink and play cards with the best of them. I was even pretty good."

"What happened?"

"I started drinking too much. I got careless and too self-confident. Then some new men came to town, and they were much better at cards. Perhaps they were even cheating, but it doesn't matter now. I felt certain I could beat them and continued to play until the amount I owed them was more than I could ever hope to pay back with my meager salary."

"So why didn't you stop?" Phoebe couldn't begin to understand the lure or attraction of gambling. It seemed quite reasonable that if one found they had overextended themselves, they should simply discontinue the activity.

"I couldn't. I needed to find a way to get enough money to pay off my debt. When they heard that I had inherited this place, they demanded I sign it over to them in pay."

Phoebe felt the wind go out from her. "What? Give up your family business?"

He nodded. "It's worth far more than I owe, but it's all I have of value. I convinced them to wait until my father left Sitka. I didn't want him to ever know what had happened. I figured in time, I could tell him I sold it, but for now I have to keep it from him."

"Oh, Yuri. This is terrible. You must talk to Dalton. He can help you."

"But that's just it. I don't want his help. I already feel I've disappointed him too much. He can't possibly want to be my friend after the way I've acted."

"Of course he's your friend. He cares about you, Yuri. His dream had been to work with you, and even if that never happens, you must know he wouldn't want to see you lose this place to strangers." Phoebe reached out and took hold of his arms. "Yuri, don't let your friendship be ruined over your mistakes."

"He could never forgive this."

"Yes, he can." Phoebe squeezed his muscular arms. "And he will. You have to give him a chance. Just talk to him. Tell him what you've told me."

"But if I took his help, I would forever be in his debt. I could never hope to pay him back."

"Then don't do it that way," Phoebe replied. "Sell him the business. Tell him what has happened and how they will steal the place away from you at a fraction of what it's worth. Offer to sell it to him instead. This way at least it won't go to strangers, and you'll get a fair price. Dalton plans to build a shop anyway. He would already have one built, if not for the fact that he's spent all this time working to construct a new house for me and my family."

Yuri pulled away from her hold and shook his head. "He would never listen to me after the way I've been treating him."

"He will listen. Give him a chance," Phoebe assured. She could see that he needed time to think. "I should get home now. Just consider what I've said. It's important to me that you and Dalton work through this. He needs your friendship, and I think you need his, too."

She turned to go, but Yuri stopped her. "Let me walk you home. Maybe I can at least offer him an apology for how I've acted."

Phoebe smiled. "That would be a wonderful place to start. Then maybe you can stay for lunch and discuss the rest of it."

———

Dalton blinked twice and looked away. He turned back to

the sight of his wife walking arm and arm with Yuri Belikov and shook his head. He must be seeing things. Following behind them at a slower pace, Dalton watched as Phoebe laughed at something Yuri said.

How could she? His anger was instantaneous. How long had this been going on? Was she secretly seeing Yuri behind his back? Surely in a town this size, he would have heard about such a thing by now.

When Phoebe and Yuri turned down the alley that would lead to their apartment, Dalton froze. She was taking him to their home?

He was so intent on watching them that he didn't see the cat that skittered across his path. Dalton managed to clip the animal's tail, causing it to let out a yowl that drew everyone's attention. Phoebe noticed him there and seemed shocked to find him nearby.

"Dalton!"

She waited for him to say something, but Dalton had no words. He never liked to speak out in anger, and this time was no exception. If he talked to her now, he might say something he'd regret. He turned to leave.

"Dalton! Come back."

He picked up his pace. He couldn't deal with this just now. No matter what her purpose had been in bringing Yuri to their home, Dalton could see nothing good about it. To his way of thinking, this was a betrayal of the worst kind.

Chapter 25

*P*hoebe had never been so angry. After apologizing to Yuri and promising Dalton would come to see him, she stormed upstairs to their apartment and paced the floor for nearly an hour. She kept thinking that Dalton would return, and when he didn't, she was further enraged.

"Of all the selfish, stupid things," she muttered, marching back down the stairs to the alley. She figured Dalton had returned to work or else had gone to his folks' house. Either way, she would find him.

She marched at a quick pace to the land where the new log structure—her house—was nearly ready. She heard pounding from within and figured that at least someone was there working.

Kjell met her at the door with a smile. "Hello. I thought you might be heading this way."

"I'm here to see your pig-headed son," she announced.

Her father-in-law pointed to one of the interior rooms. "Mr. Pig-headed is in there. Oh, you should also know for future reference that he's a great jumper."

"Jumper?" Phoebe asked, her brows knitting together.

He nodded. "Yes. He jumps to conclusions quite easily."

The meaning was instantly clear. "Well, this is one time he shouldn't have." She brushed past Kjell. "He had no call to act that way."

Ignoring her father-in-law's chuckles, Phoebe followed the sounds of the hammering. Dalton was affixing a wooden mantel in place over the living room fireplace when Phoebe came upon him.

He straightened and turned to face her. "Are you here to explain and apologize?"

"How could you! How could you just storm off in a huff and not even acknowledge me?" She stopped and flailed her arms in the air as she realized what he'd just asked her. "Me? Me apologize? You're the one who jumped to conclusions and ran off."

"I saw you leading my enemy to our apartment," Dalton said matter-of-factly.

"Since when has Yuri become your enemy? You stomp and snort around the house day and night bemoaning the fact that something has gone horribly wrong in your friendship. I was sick and tired of the stiff-necked pride between the two of you, so I went to Yuri myself. And now this. You should be ashamed of yourself."

"Me?" Dalton looked indignant. "Why should I be ashamed? I saw my wife with my former best friend."

Phoebe crossed her arms. "You'd better be careful with what you're implying, Dalton Lindquist. You think you have trouble now, but you haven't seen me with a full head of steam. I invited Yuri to join us for lunch. Remember, I knew you would be coming home for lunch. Why would I have a dalliance with your best friend in our apartment when I knew you would either already be there or come shortly after? If I were you, I'd swallow my stupid pride and get around to apologizing for what you're accusing me of doing."

Clenching her jaw, Phoebe determined not to say another word until he begged her forgiveness. Dalton seemed surprised by her attitude, but for several moments he simply stared at his wife as if trying to figure out what was right and what would serve to get him into more trouble.

Phoebe was already contemplating what she would do if he refused to see reason. She supposed she would just go home to her mother. After all, there was no hope for a marriage where trust didn't exist.

Dalton turned away and walked to the window. The large window had been specially ordered to give them a perfect view of the water and islands. Watching him stand there, Phoebe couldn't help but wonder what was going on in his head. Did he even care that he'd hurt her feelings? Did he understand that he had wronged her? All she had wanted was to see him and Yuri work through their issues.

Finally Dalton let out a heavy sigh. "I am sorry, Phoebe. I let my temper get the best of me. I know you weren't doing anything wrong, and for me to imply such a thing makes me a beast."

"An ignorant beast," she corrected.

He turned and nodded, his eyes piercing her with his sorrow. "An ignorant beast." He came forward and stopped short of taking hold of her. "I'm truly sorry. Please forgive me."

"I do, but please know that we're headed for a lot of problems if you are always inclined to believe the worst of me."

He gently touched her face, and some of the anger left Phoebe's heart. "I know. I promise that I won't let it happen again."

She nodded. "Very well. Now, can we talk about Yuri?"

"All right." Dalton dropped his hold. "What do you want to say?"

"He's in trouble, Dalton. He needs you more than ever. I won't divulge what he told me—it's his to share—but you mustn't wait. Please go to him and let him explain."

"It sounds serious."

"It is. I visited Yuri to make him see that if he had ended his friendship with you because of me, he had no grounds. I have never encouraged anything more than friendship, and he was wrong to believe there was more. He agreed. Then the longer we talked . . . well . . . there are some very dangerous things going on in his life and he needs you."

"If this has to do with his drinking and gambling, I already know about those bad habits. I've tried to encourage him to do otherwise, but he hasn't listened. I can't see that he'll listen now."

"No, especially if you won't talk to him."

Dalton's look was one of reproach. "I hardly see that his sins are my fault."

"No one said they were," Phoebe countered. "But if we see our brother in need and do nothing . . . well . . . isn't that like Jesus saying that what we do to the least of these, we do to Him?"

She could see her statement had hit its mark. Dalton moved away and picked up his hammer before replying. "I don't think Yuri even cares about such things."

"Maybe not," Phoebe fired back, "but you do. Even if Yuri isn't a Christian—even if he doesn't believe the way we believe—we are held to a certain standard. We are called to go after the one that leaves the flock. To seek the lost souls and share the good news. Have you ever talked to Yuri about his eternal soul?"

Dalton grinned. "You sound like a preacher now."

Phoebe put her hands on her hips. "Well, maybe it's time one of us did."

He held up his free hand. "I see your point and concede. You're right. You have adequately shamed me."

She softened and came to where he stood. "That was never my intent. My hope was that you would see the truth. Yuri is dying, in a sense. It's no different from when I was drowning in the harbor and you saved me. He needs you, Dalton. You can't give up on him. You just can't."

———

"So is it true, Aunt Zee, that the Tlingit shamans have special powers?" Britta asked.

Zee smiled at the child and glanced at Lydia. "I suppose they think they do."

"Well, do they or not?"

Kjerstin rolled her eyes. "You are being silly. Nobody but God has powers."

"Your sister is right, Britta. God alone holds the power to do anything," Lydia replied. "However, sometimes when people seek Him and His will, He allows them the ability to do things they might not otherwise have been able to do."

"Like when the disciples healed people?" Britta asked.

Her mother nodded. "If the shamans seek God and put Him first in their life, they might find the same ability, but it's not something they can do by themselves."

"And sometimes there are evil powers," Kjerstin said and looked at her mother. "Isn't that so?"

"Yes. There are evil powers at work in this world," their mother stated. "Satan is always looking for someone to deceive and destroy."

Zee handed Britta the dish towel the girl had been embroidering. "Your work is coming along quite nicely." She sat down across from the child. "Britta, the native people here have lived for generations upon generations with their own stories of creation and how the world has come to be.

"But many of the Tlingit have come to believe in Jesus, as we do. I know I've spoken harshly of the mission school in the past, but I'm starting to see some of the good that has come from it. Many of the children would not have had a chance to get away from superstitious beliefs and practices had they not been forced to live at the school. While I have great sorrow that they should have to give up all of their cultural practices, I suppose I'm better able now to see the benefits they have also enjoyed."

Britta frowned and seemed to consider Zee's words for a moment. "But if they love Jesus then they will be able to do great things—right?" She looked to her mother. "You said that Jesus told the disciples that after He went to heaven they would be able to do even greater things than He did."

Lydia nodded. "That's what the Bible says."

"I think that's really good. That means that the Tlingit will be really strong, then. They have their old ways that gave them powers and now they have Jesus. They can really be strong when they have to do something important."

Zee laughed. "Why do you worry over such things, Miss Britta?"

She shrugged. "I just think it's good to be strong. That's all."

A knock sounded on the front door before Illiyana and her sister Natasha came bounding into the house. "Hello!" they called out in unison.

Lydia smiled. "Hello, girls. How nice to see you."

"Mother said we could come. Can Kjerstin and Britta play with us?"

"Absolutely. Zee and I can spare them, can't we?"

Zee nodded. "I think it would be the perfect afternoon to go outdoors. The sun is shining and the temperature has warmed up nicely."

"Still, I want you to wear your wool sweaters. There's no sense in taking a chill."

The girls jumped up from the table and headed for the peg where their sweaters were hanging. Kjerstin was already telling Natasha about some new kittens that had been born the day before, while Britta was whispering to Illiyana in a most conspiratorial manner.

Once the girls had gone from the house, Zee turned to Lydia and chuckled. "We won't see them for hours now."

"If I know Kjerstin and Natasha, they will spend all their time with the kittens, and Illiyana and Britta will no doubt take up residence in the new playhouse Kjell built."

"That is quite the little house he put together. I like that it's built up off the ground like a cache. The girls aren't so inclined to have a wild animal wander in that way," Zee said as she gathered up the girls' embroidery.

"I'm glad," Lydia began, "that you aren't feeling quite so angry at the mission workers."

Zee tucked the sewing away and straightened. "I don't approve of everything they've done, but I'm starting to see now that there is no perfect way to minister. I suppose my biggest frustration is that we as white people come into a culture and demand that the natives do things our way. I want to see their lives bettered as much as anyone, but who says we have somehow arrived at the perfect way to live? Especially for specific areas of the world?"

"What do you mean, Zee?"

She came into the kitchen, where Lydia was already working to prepare supper. "Well, take this area for instance. The people here had established a way of living—of eating, of farming the land, of dressing. They knew what worked and what didn't because of the generations that had gone before them. Then the whites come in and demand they change their way of living. They demand the children dress like whites and cut their hair. They demand they no longer speak Tlingit, but English. And for what purpose? Jesus certainly doesn't require such things in order to be saved."

"Of course He doesn't," Lydia agreed.

"But the white mission workers act otherwise. They tell the Tlingits that in order for their children to assimilate into the white world, they must cast aside every part of their Tlingit culture. I think that's wrong."

"I agree, but is there a way to seek a balance?"

"I believe so, but apparently Sheldon Jackson doesn't," Zee said, shaking her head. "I truly think the man intends good. He's done great things, and I am not without admiration for him. Still, I think when it comes to the natives, it's wrong to strip them of their heritage. If they are forced to stop speaking their language and hearing their old stories, it won't be long before it will be completely forgotten. I think that would be a tragedy."

"But on the other hand, if the children are caught between superstitions and false spiritual teachings, shouldn't we step in to help them see the truth?" Lydia asked. "I believe that was the desired result by Mr. Jackson and the Presbyterian mission's board."

Zee considered her words for a moment. "I'm just not sure we always go about things in the best manner. Again, it's one thing to try to help another people understand who Jesus is—that He died for their sins and offers them salvation, just as He does the whites. It's another to step in and say you can't be saved if you go barefoot and wear a blanket as your clothing. You can't be saved if you speak a language other than English. You can't be saved if you attend a potlatch feast. It's just wrong, to my way of thinking."

"I can see your point, Zee." Lydia smiled sympathetically. "The Tlingit are fortunate to have you on their side."

"For all the good it will do. I have helped to get plans for the new maternity hospital started, as well as worked with many of the young brides to learn about hygiene and sewing, but the force of our people is a hard one to stand up against."

"Then perhaps we need to figure out ways not to oppose each other, but to blend together," Lydia said. "Take the good from both sides."

"I couldn't agree more, but that's not the attitude I see from our people. We storm into a place and say, 'Our way is the only way!' I cannot abide that. I don't see Jesus doing that in the Bible. He said He was the only way to God, but He didn't say that people had to first change everything else about their lives in order to be saved. He said, 'I am the way, the truth, and the life: no man cometh unto the Father, but by me.'"

"But repentance from evil is necessary," Lydia added.

"Yes, of course that's necessary, as is putting aside idols," Zee replied. "I agree with you. But I don't see that all customs have to change." She picked up a peeler to help Lydia with supper. "I don't see that at all."

"But shouldn't we take some supplies?" Illiyana asked.

Britta shrugged. "The village is just up the mountain. It's not that far. We can walk real fast and get back before it gets dark."

Illiyana considered this for a moment. "And the shaman will be the one with the most powers. He can surely help us. My mother said in the old days he could make special potions to do all sorts of things. He had powers to bring the salmon and to help in hunts."

"Mama and Zee said good powers come from God alone, but that He lets us do great things, too." Britta shook her head. "I don't really understand how it works, but I'll bet the shaman does. Aunt Zee told me a long time ago that most of the old Tlingit people were letting Jesus come into their heart. That means he'd have to have good powers, right?"

The little girl seemed to give this careful consideration. "I just don't see how it could be bad, if he loves Jesus. So you think he could have powers to keep me here so that we could go on being friends forever?"

"I think so," Britta replied. "He will have a special way to keep your parents from moving back to Russia. I'm sure of it."

Illiyana smiled and nodded with great enthusiasm. "That's all I want."

Chapter 26

E vie could hardly contain herself as Lydia opened the door. "I'm so excited about this. Joshua doesn't suspect a thing."

Lydia's eyes widened at the news. "Are you certain?"

"Yes. I think he's actually forgotten his birthday is even coming up," Evie replied. "He definitely doesn't expect us to throw him a surprise party."

"Good. If he did, it wouldn't be a surprise anymore. So did you bring all the ingredients we asked for?"

Following Lydia into the house, Evie glanced around. "Yes. I was able to get everything." She put down the bag of goods. "Where is everyone?"

"Britta and Kjerstin were just enticed outside by the Belikov girls, and Zee went to tend to other chores. We're alone for the moment." Lydia pulled out a chair at the table and motioned Evie to sit. "Would you like some tea?"

"Yes, please. The walk here was refreshing, but I always find a cup of tea is the perfect conclusion." Evie sat down and put aside her shawl.

Lydia was only a moment. She gathered two cups and saucers and brought them to the table. "I had just brewed a pot, so your timing is perfect. When Zee returns, we'll have her join us."

Evie nodded. "I'm so grateful to you for helping me with this. Joshua and I were talking about birthdays once last winter, and he said he had never had a birthday party in all of his life. Then when he arranged for such a nice dinner last month for my birthday, I knew I had to do something special."

Lydia laughed. "It's a great deal of fun to surprise someone with such a festive event. Are you two still going to come over tonight for supper?"

"To be sure." Evie took the offered tea and sipped. "Oh, this is quite delicious. Thank you so much. I figure if we come tonight, and you just casually mention having us over next week, then he won't be any wiser to what's happening."

"It also helps that we aren't actually celebrating on his birthday," Lydia said as she took her seat.

"Exactly." Evie put her cup down. "Phoebe is going to help me get the invitations out to folks. She's been such a great help."

"I think Dalton definitely found a winner in her," Lydia remarked. "She loves to keep busy. I could never accuse her of laziness. She keeps the cleanest house I've ever seen."

"That's true. Oh, by the way, what time should we plan on arriving tonight?" Evie asked.

"Come after work. Joshua and Kjell both usually finish up around five this time of year. So just head out after that."

"All right. What about Dalton and Phoebe? Have you included them?"

"I haven't yet, but you could certainly get word to them on your way home. I'd love for them to join us. I keep thinking surely one of these days they'll be announcing that Phoebe is with child. I don't know why, but I just expect it won't be long."

Evie put her hand over her flat stomach. "I'd like to think it could happen for us, as well, but I don't count on it." She looked up at Lydia. "I would so love to give Joshua children. He says it's not the end of the world if we can't have them, but I think it would make me very sad."

"Don't borrow trouble, Evie. You have no reason to think you can't have children. You aren't that old. Give it time."

Reaching across the table, Evie placed her hand atop Lydia's. "You have always been such a dear friend to me, Lydia. I cherish that. You always encourage me and give me hope. Thank you for welcoming me here. I'm so glad that God put you in my life."

"I feel the same way about you. Not only that, but I'm blessed that Dalton had a chance to be raised with you in his life. Especially now that he knows about the others, and about his father."

"The trip to Kansas City was good for him, Lydia. It made him realize some important things. I know he still struggles with some of it. I remember the deep hole it left in my heart when Mama died. I can't help but imagine Dalton has struggled with a similar hole where our father is concerned."

"But Kjell has always been there for him," Lydia protested. "He was a much better father than Floyd could ever have been."

Evie nodded. "Yes, and Dalton knows that. He loves Kjell as his only father, but you must understand. There will always be those questions—those unanswered questions. Am I like him? How has his blood influenced me? Will the past affect my future? Our father is dead and gone, but in here," she said, tapping her chest, "in here, we can't help but ask those questions."

Lydia considered this for a moment. "I suppose I can understand. I used to ask some of those things myself. I worried that Dalton would turn out to look and sound like Marston or Mitchell. Worse yet, I feared he would be hateful and mean like Floyd."

"And Dalton can't help but harbor those same concerns, Lydia. You have done a wonderful thing in raising him here away from the influence of anything having to do with the Gray side of his heritage. But Dalton will continue to evaluate his life in the light of his father's memory."

"I'm heading home early," Kjell told Dalton. "I plan to get some repairs done on the horse shed before I lose all of the light." He stretched and Dalton could see him try to hide a grimace of pain.

"Sounds good. I have some doors to finish putting on the cabinets in the kitchen. I figured to get those done before I head out." Dalton looked around the large open room. "It's finally coming together. It was hard to see when we first started, but now I'm so amazed at what we've accomplished."

His father leaned back against the doorjamb. "It's the best thing I've done yet. I wish you weren't so passionate about boat building. I think we'd make a great team in building together."

Dalton nodded. He thought of how his father's back had been bothering him more and more of late. "I'll keep that in mind. Could be that no one will want my boats and I'll fail miserably."

"I seriously doubt that," Father replied. "Oh, but speaking of boats, I heard that there would be quite a few Tlingit boys graduating this year who are skilled at boat building. They've been taught by a man at the Industrial School. You might want to go there and see about hiring them on. You could plan to put together some really nice pieces—even bigger boats than you figured on."

"That's a great idea. I'll plan to go talk with them."

"Sitka is changing—growing. I've heard about a lot of the plans and can't help but think that as folks figure out that Alaska isn't just ice and snow, more and more people will come north."

"I hope there aren't too many who come here," Dalton said thoughtfully. "I rather like our small community. After spending time in Kansas City and seeing so many of the States below . . . well, I'm content to live a more isolated existence."

His father nodded. "I agree. Maybe Sitka is a secret best kept."

After his father had gone, Dalton went back to work. He was glad he'd let Kjell make special cabinets for the kitchen. They had ordered beautiful oak wood from the States, and it complemented the room in a wonderful way. Dalton ran his hand over the door he'd just secured. A sense of pride washed over him.

"Hello?"

He turned. "Yuri?" He walked to the front of the house and found his old friend standing hat in hand. He looked hesitant. Dalton couldn't say as he blamed him. "Come in."

"I was hoping we could talk."

Dalton nodded. "I think we need to. I know I owe you an apology."

"And I owe you one, as well." He looked at Dalton rather sheepishly. "I sure haven't been much of a friend to you."

"I guess we're even then." Dalton extended his hand and Yuri took hold. For a moment, they just stood there. Dalton could see the pain in Yuri's expression. He wanted nothing more than to put his friend at ease. "Phoebe told me I was an ignorant beast."

Yuri laughed. "And what did you say?"

Grinning, Dalton shrugged. "I told her she was right. I honestly don't know what got into me." He dropped his hold. "Come on.

We can sit in the kitchen. There's a table and chairs. It's about the only furniture here right now."

Yuri followed him as Dalton led the way. "This house is incredible. It's so big. You've got enough room here to hold a dance. Phoebe should be pleased."

"I think she is. There are four bedrooms upstairs. We plan for her mother and brothers to live with us. There is one larger bedroom downstairs near the back of the house. We figure it will give us a bit of privacy. Have a seat," Dalton said, pointing to the table. "Sorry we drank all the coffee. The stove's gone cold or I'd put on another pot."

"I didn't come for that anyway," Yuri replied. The two men sat and both folded their hands on the table as if by prearrangement.

Dalton smiled. "I guess we're a lot alike, you and me."

Yuri shook his head. "Not nearly enough. You've always been the better man. I think that's what I've allowed to come between us. I've been jealous of you for a long time now. You were always the better boat builder—the better son."

"That's not true, Yuri. You're a good man and a good son." Dalton remembered Phoebe talking about the degree of danger involved with Yuri's problems. "We all make mistakes, Yuri. The biggest, however, is to let a situation go on without seeking the help that might reverse the problem."

"That's what Phoebe helped me to see. She's a good woman, Dalton. She loves you more than you even realize."

Dalton leaned back in his chair. "I'm just coming to see that. I don't know why I got so angry when I saw you two together. I guess it just reminded me of your interest in her."

"I would never try to take her from you, Dalton. You are married. That is sacred. I can't say that I wasn't upset when you came home to Sitka, and up and proposed marriage to her. I was sure

I would have time to woo her, but now I realize you two probably fell in love when she fell into Sitka Sound."

"I think you're right," Dalton agreed. "I didn't realize love could hit a person that way."

For a moment, neither one said anything. Dalton could see that Yuri was uncomfortable with what he'd come to say, however. He clenched and unclenched his jaw, and Dalton noted the little tick around his eye that always flared when Yuri was troubled.

"So why don't you tell me what's happened to cause you this grief."

Yuri looked up. "I've managed to amass a huge gambling debt. The drinking marred my judgment, and I made bad choices. I kept thinking I could win back the money, but I only continued to lose more. The men I fell into company with allowed me credit, and now they are demanding the shop."

Dalton shook his head in disbelief. "The boat shop?"

"Yes. They've agreed to at least wait until Father and Mother leave for Russia. I figure I will just have to tell Father at a later date that I sold the shop. I can't bear to face him with the truth."

"But, Yuri, he would want to know. You can't give up your inheritance."

"But that's part of the problem, Dalton. I don't care about the shop like you do. I don't want to be a boat builder for the rest of my life."

This wasn't the first time Dalton had heard Yuri complain about the business. He knew his friend was far less interested than he in the craft, but so far he'd never heard Yuri say what did appeal to him. "So what do you want to do with your life?"

"I don't know, and that grieves me even more. I don't feel capable of anything. I thought about fishing, but I would have to apprentice with someone. I don't know nearly enough about it to head out to sea and not end up dead. I've thought about other things, as well, but, Dalton, I don't feel like I'm good at anything."

"My father could use some help. I hate to say it, but ever since he took a fall last winter, his back has never been the same. I notice he moves a lot slower. Things are harder on him."

Yuri shrugged. "I don't know that I'd be any better at house building than working with boats. I could give it a try."

"Well, there's time to figure that out, but right now we have to see to this matter of the shop. If you must sell it to pay off the debt, sell it to me. At least I will give you a fair price and then benefit in return with a ready-made business."

"Phoebe suggested as much. I just didn't want to come to you with this. I acted horribly when you went to my father about buying it. I got you fired, and I am deeply ashamed of that. I have no excuse—at least not a valid one. I guess I felt like your coming into money further divided us."

"Yuri, I'm still the same person. I don't care about the money," Dalton said. "I still love Sitka and want to build boats. And our friendship means more to me than just about anything. Yuri, we grew up together. You are like a brother to me. I would never just cast that aside."

"I've been a fool then, is that what you're telling me?" Yuri asked with a smile.

"I'm saying we've both been foolish. We need to resolve our differences and put this to rest once and for all," Dalton replied. "We need to go to your father and explain what has happened, and tell him that I will buy the shop so that it stays with friends."

Yuri looked startled at this. "No. I can't tell him what I've done. He never approved of what I was doing. He forbade me to drink, and I did so anyway. He hated gambling, and I ignored his warnings."

"Yes, but he will understand that you have made mistakes, and he will be impressed that you are man enough to admit that you were wrong. It will put his mind at ease to know we have worked through our difficulties and found resolutions for yours."

"I just don't know."

"Dalton? Are you here?" a voice called out.

"It's Evie," Dalton said, getting to his feet. "We're in the kitchen." He went to the open archway. "What brings you here?"

"An invitation," his sister said, beaming. "I wanted to invite you and Phoebe to join us for supper at your folks' house. Tonight— after work."

Dalton nodded. "Sounds good." Yuri came to stand beside him and Evie smiled.

"It's good to see you two together again."

"Yes, well, we've both decided to put aside our childish ways," Yuri said.

"Why don't you join us, as well, Yuri?" Evie said. "I know it will do Lydia good to see that you're on speaking terms again."

"So what's this all about?" Dalton asked. "Why the special invitation to supper?"

Evie laughed. "We're trying to make it seem quite second nature to have dinner at your folks' house each week so that we can surprise Joshua with the birthday party."

"I'd nearly forgotten. Goodness, but sisters can be sneaky," Dalton teased. "I've come to realize where sisters are involved, you can never tell what they're up to."

"That is so true," Yuri agreed.

Evie raised her brows and tapped her head. "I have all sorts of plans . . . up here."

"I know just how your planning goes, too. Last time you were in this kind of mood, it ended up with me taking a trip to Kansas City."

Evie laughed. "I assure you my plans these days have nothing to do with Kansas City. If I never see that place again it will be just fine by me. Now, will you be there tonight? You never know, I might need you and Yuri to help keep Joshua busy while we ladies make our plans."

Dalton laughed. "Of course we'll be there."

Chapter 27

She's not in the playhouse or in the barn," Kjell announced, stomping his wet boots on the rug at the door.

Lydia couldn't suppress her sense of panic. "Where could she be?"

"Maybe she went home with Illiyana and Natasha," he offered. "She knows she's supposed to ask first, but she could have forgotten."

Turning to Kjerstin, Lydia questioned her again. "You are certain you know nothing about where Britta's gone?"

Kjerstin grew very serious. "I don't know, but I think Illiyana is with her. When Natasha left, she was by herself. She was very mad because she knew their mother wouldn't like that Illiyana had stayed here."

Lydia turned back to Zee and Kjell. "So she didn't go to the Belikovs'."

"You don't know that, Liddie," Kjell countered. "She and Illiyana could have gone there before Natasha was ready to leave. We have to check every possibility."

"But it's getting dark, and it's not safe for them to be out there alone." Lydia went to the window and checked outside once again. "And it's starting to rain again."

"It's just a mist at this point," Kjell said, trying to be encouraging.

"I'll get some lanterns," Zee offered.

Lydia searched her husband's face for some sign that everything would be all right. "I'm not a fool," she told him. "I know this isn't good. Please don't treat me like a child."

"Sorry we're late," Dalton announced, coming into the house. "Phoebe was insistent that I dress for supper. She made Yuri and I both put on a clean shirt."

"Believe me, everyone will be grateful that you stopped to clean up," Phoebe replied.

Lydia went to them. "Have you seen Britta?" She looked to Yuri. "She was playing with Illiyana. Were they at your house?"

Yuri shook his head. "I didn't go home. I borrowed one of Dalton's shirts. What's wrong?"

Dalton reached out to touch his mother's arm. "What is it?"

"Britta is missing. I called her and Kjerstin in to help set the table nearly half an hour ago. She's nowhere to be found."

He turned to his father. "We can help you look. What areas have you already covered?"

"I searched the immediate area—the playhouse and outbuildings. I didn't see any sign of them there," Kjell replied.

"Is Illiyana with her?" Yuri asked.

Lydia was nearly beside herself. "We don't know. Kjerstin said that Natasha went home alone, so I believe it's possible that the girls are together. But where?"

"Knock, knock," Evie announced at the door. She popped her head inside. "Ummm, it smells wonderful in here." She and Joshua joined the others. "Thank you so much for inviting us to supper."

Dalton turned to his sister. "Britta and Illiyana are missing. Did you see them in town or on the road here by any chance?"

Evie looked from Dalton to Lydia. "No. How long have they been gone?"

"I don't know," Lydia admitted. "They had just gone out to play when you came to see me earlier. Did you see them outside then?"

"No, Lydia. I didn't. I'm sorry."

"It's been nearly two and a half hours. There's no telling where they may have gone in that time," Lydia said, wringing her hands together. "Britta knows better than to wander off like that. What if something happened to them?"

"You are getting yourself all upset, and we don't even know what the truth is," Kjell reminded her. "Josh, you come with me and we'll search down by the water. Dalton, you and Yuri head into the forest and up the northeast trail. We'll meet back here in half an hour."

"The lanterns are ready to go," Zee announced. "I left them on the porch."

Dalton and Yuri bounded out the door. Kjell turned to Lydia. "Try not to worry. We'll be back shortly, and hopefully the girls will have returned and nothing more will need to be done."

Lydia nodded. "I'll search the barn again. You know how much they love to play hide-and-seek."

"They aren't in the barn," Kjell said, reaching out to lift her chin. "Stay here with the others, and we'll decide what else to do when I return."

Dalton and Yuri combed the edge of the forest as they made their way to a narrow trail that led up the mountainside. This had long been a favorite area of exploration when Dalton was little, and he knew his sisters had their own fascination with the thick spruce woods.

"Look, isn't that a shoe print?" Yuri said, pointing.

Dalton held the lantern closer. It looked to be the right size. "It belongs to one of the girls. I'm sure of it."

They maneuvered slowly along the trail with the lantern held close to the ground. The damp cold permeated Dalton's body, leaving him with grave concerns for his sister. "There are more prints up here," he announced.

"Looks like two sets. I think the girls were together up here at one point. Do you see any fresh tracks that head back toward the house?"

"No. You?"

Yuri shook his head. "I hate to say it, but I think they've gone up the mountain."

"But why? Why would they go off like that?" Dalton tried to reason through any possible attractions for the girls. "They know it's dangerous. The bears are starting to come out of hibernation. Snow and avalanches are still a threat."

"Yeah, they both know how serious it can be," Yuri agreed. "Look, I think we'd better go back and check in with your father. We can tell him what we've found, and if he hasn't seen any other fresh tracks, then we can all head up the trail."

"We should probably get some supplies in case it takes us a while," Dalton said. "There's no telling how far two little girls could have gotten in almost three hours."

Back at the house, Kjell and Joshua were relieved to hear that Dalton and Yuri had spotted some sign of the girls. "We saw nothing, and I was beginning to despair," Kjell said.

"There's reason enough to despair if they've gone hiking up into the forest," Mother said. "Why would they do this? There's nothing up that trail that should interest them."

Zee seemed to consider this for a moment. "You know that trail eventually forks off and heads down toward one of the summer camps."

"Summer camps?" Phoebe asked.

"For the Tlingits. Especially the old ones," Dalton replied. "They hold meetings and celebrations well away from the whites."

"You don't suppose . . ." Zee fell silent and looked at Lydia. "Remember when Britta was asking us about the Tlingit shamans and their powers?"

Mother blanched. "Oh no, you don't think the girls went searching for the shamans, do you?"

"Why would they?" Dalton asked.

"I don't know. For some reason, Britta was asking us earlier today about the shamans and their powers. We were trying to explain that God is the one who has ultimate power, and that while there are evil powers, as well, people with Jesus are able to do great things through Him."

"Look, we're wasting time," his father declared. "We have no idea of where they've gotten to or what kind of trouble they might be having. We need to load up and go after them." He looked at Dalton. "Get our rifles. Lydia, you and Zee have the shotgun. If the girls come back, fire two shots and hopefully we'll hear it. You and Evie pack us some canteens with water and some jerked meat. Zee, make us some bedrolls."

"I'll help you," Phoebe volunteered and headed off with Zee.

The women went quickly to work while Dalton's father turned to the men. "We'll go out to my shop. I have rope and axes there, as well as a couple of knapsacks. We'll split into two groups once we come to the fork in the trail. Each of us will have a sack of supplies. You each have knives on you, right?"

Dalton felt for his sheath for reassurance. "We also have the camping gear," he reminded them. "There are extra cans of kerosene for the lanterns and matches, as well as some medical supplies."

Father nodded. "We'll divide it up and put it in the knapsacks. Come on."

Within a short time, they all reconvened on the porch just long enough to collect the remaining supplies. Dalton found the darkness daunting. Poor Britta and Illiyana wouldn't have any means of navigating the forest. He hated to think of how scared they might be.

Yuri was quite concerned about his mother and father. "Would someone please take word to my folks?"

"Of course, we will," Dalton's mother assured.

"I can do that," Zee declared. "I'll hitch up the cart and go straightaway."

"Lydia, keep plenty of water heating," Kjell told her. "Maybe get the caldron outside going. The cold is going to be our biggest problem."

She looked to Phoebe. "You can help me with that, can't you?"

"Of course."

Evie put her arm around Lydia's waist. "We'll both help."

"Let's have a prayer, then," Father said, taking off his hat. The other men did likewise and bowed their heads. Dalton felt peace wash over him. He always found great comfort in his father's prayers.

"Father, we ask for your help and direction. Show us where the girls have gone and help us to rescue them before any harm can befall them. Give us wisdom in our search and guard our girls as they face this night in unfamiliar territory."

"Please keep them safe," Mother begged. "Please watch over them." Her voice broke, and she began to cry.

Nothing was worse than hearing his mother cry. Dalton wanted only to ease her fears, but there was nothing he could do, short of bringing his sister home.

"Father," Kjell concluded, "we trust you with our children, as we always have, and thank you even now for the provision you have made on their behalf. Amen."

"Amen," the others murmured.

With that, the men secured their packs and headed back up the mountain. Dalton was eager to show his father the fresh tracks. Once they confirmed the find, the men headed en masse up the trail.

"There are more tracks up here," Yuri declared as they climbed even higher. "We're going the right way."

But the tracks became more obscured as a light mist turned into an earnest rain. By the time they reached the fork in the trail, the tracks were washed out, and none of the men were convinced of the direction the girls might have taken.

"Even if they were headed to the village, I don't think either one of them would know which fork to take," Father announced. He squatted down and held his lantern closer to the trail. Shaking his head, he stood. "We'll have to divide up here. Dalton, you and Yuri head this way, and Joshua and I will keep going toward the village."

"All right."

"If you find them, fire two shots and we'll head back this way. We'll do likewise and you can join us. I don't think the girls would leave the path if they could help it."

Dalton nodded, not bothering to ask what they should do if they didn't find them. He knew he would continue to search until they were recovered. The others knew it, as well. There simply was no other option.

———

"I want to go home," Britta said, shivering. "I'm so cold."

"We need to make camp," Illiyana declared.

"But we don't have supplies." Britta hugged her arms close to her body. "We don't even have our coats."

"My papa said that it's important to keep warm," Illiyana replied. "We can find some branches from the trees around us and make a little house. Then if we huddle together, we can be warmer."

"I don't want to stay here," Britta said, looking at the deep darkness in fear. "I can't see anything." She paced away from where Illiyana stood. "I can't even see you from over here."

"Then don't go over there."

"I want to go home," Britta reiterated.

"So do I, but it's too dark and now the rain is falling too hard. We can't get home yet. If we stay here, we can wait until light and then we'll find our way."

Britta turned and tried hard to make out any sign of the trail. Thick rain clouds overhead blocked out any hope of seeing the moon or stars. She wanted to cry and would have done just that, but it took too much effort and she was so tired.

"All right. I guess we can make camp," she finally said.

"We just need to find some branches."

Britta knelt on the damp ground and reached out to feel around. "I don't like this. What if there are animals hiding here?"

Illiyana said nothing, and that only served to alarm Britta. "Where are you?"

"I'm over here." Illiyana's muted voice made it clear to Britta that she'd moved off the path.

"Don't go deeper in the woods," Britta warned. She struggled to her feet, but caught the hem of her dress against the heel of her boot. Losing her balance, Britta was prepared to slam down against the soggy ground. Instead, the path seemed to give way, and suddenly she was falling.

Chapter 28

So the men are already looking for the girls," Zee told Darya and Aleksei Belikov. "Yuri asked me to let you know what was going on, as well as to see if there was a chance Illiyana and Britta had come here."

Darya shook her head and looked to her husband. "Where would they have gone?"

Aleksei was already gathering his coat and gun. "Maxim and I will look around town. I'll come back here before heading over to the Lindquists. You stay here in case the girls show up."

Zee smiled. "I'll sit with you a spell," she promised Darya. The woman looked notably relieved.

"It's not like either of the girls to do such a thing. You don't suppose they've run away because of the move?" Darya asked Zee.

"I think it's possible. They have both been pretty upset. Today

Britta was asking us about the shamans and whether they had special powers."

Darya perked up at this. "Illiyana asked me yesterday about the same thing. She asked me to tell her stories about the old days when the shamans seemed to perform miracles. I have to admit, I was rather caught up in the telling." She put her hands to her head. "Oh, this is all my fault."

"Nonsense," Zee declared. She turned to Aleksei as he came back into the room. "You and Maxim should check the Tlingits' main village first. The girls may be seeking the shaman. They want to find a way to keep you from moving back to Russia, and this might be what they've decided is best."

Aleksei pulled on his coat. "Most of the Tlingits are still here. Some have left for the herring, but I'll search every house if need be."

Once the men had gone, Natasha peeked out from a corner near the fireplace. Zee noted that she'd remained very quiet throughout the conversation of the adults. She smiled at Natasha's worried face.

"You aren't to blame, either," she told the girl.

Darya looked to her daughter. "Did they say anything at all about the shaman or the Tlingits?"

Natasha shook her head and began to cry. She rushed to her mother's arms. "I'm so sorry, Mama. I didn't watch over her like you told me to. I was playing with Kjerstin and the kittens. It's all my fault."

"No, Zee is right. Illiyana and Britta made the foolish choice to disobey. I wish you had kept a better eye on her, but you had no reason to think they would put themselves in danger." She hugged the child close. "Illiyana knows it was wrong to run off like that."

"I'm scared for them, Mama."

Darya looked over her child to Zee. The worried mother's

expression was more than Zee could bear. "You know," she began, "when I am afraid, I like to talk to God. He always makes me feel better."

———

"Britta! Britta where are you?" Illiyana screamed.

Hearing her friend, Britta wanted to answer, but the wind had been knocked from her lungs. She gasped and fought to draw a breath, and just when she was certain that death was about to take her, Britta felt the tiniest bit of air enter.

"Britta!" Illiyana continued to call out.

When she could finally draw a deeper breath, Britta yelled. "I'm down here!" She wasn't sure where that was exactly, but she knew she had fallen what seemed to be a long ways.

"Are you hurt?"

Assessing the pain in her body, Britta was fairly certain her leg was broken. "I can't walk, it hurts too much."

Illiyana's voice grew louder. "Are you down there?"

Britta nodded but then realized Illiyana couldn't see her. "You sound very close now. I went over the side. It was like the dirt just fell apart and the side caved in."

"Can you climb back up?"

"No." Britta tried her weight again on the left leg. A flash of pain moved up her leg and nearly caused her to cry out.

"Then we need help. I'll have to go back to your house."

"But how will you find it in the rain and dark? We couldn't even see the trail."

Illiyana said nothing for a few minutes. "I guess I could wait until it gets light, but what if you fall again?"

Britta sat down and snugged up against the rock and dirt. "I'm not going to move. I can't see where I am and it would be too dangerous."

"I can walk really slow on the trail. If I feel the ground get rough or the trees get in my way, I'll know I'm getting off on the side. It's a lot easier going down than up, so maybe it will only take a little time."

"But I don't want you to leave me alone," Britta cried. "It's so dark and cold." She began to shiver again. Her teeth chattered wildly.

"You won't be alone," Illiyana declared. "Remember what your mama said about how God is always with us—that He has angels watching over us?"

She did remember. Her mother was always talking about how faithful God was and how He was with you no matter the circumstance in life. Was He really there with her right now? Were there angels beside her, as well?"

"You won't be gone very long?"

Illiyana said nothing for a moment and Britta feared she'd already gone. "Illiyana?"

"I'm here. I was just praying."

Britta hugged her arms close. "I'm gonna pray, too."

———

"There isn't any sign of them," Dalton said, shaking his head.

"Well, at least the rain has let up. Maybe the skies will clear and we'll get a little moonlight to help us."

"This part of the forest is too thick. It won't help that much." Dalton put the lantern down. "I just don't see how they could have gotten this far anyway. We've been searching almost three hours now. We've covered a lot more territory than a couple of little girls could have done in the dark. Maybe we missed a place where they headed into the trees. Maybe they decided to seek shelter."

"Or maybe they went the other way," Yuri said with a shrug. He shouldered his rifle. "They might have remembered hearing that the summer camp was left at the fork. Our sisters are very smart. They have a way of picking up information even when we don't think they're listening."

"Well, they were foolish enough to head out here," Dalton replied. Just then he heard something. It sounded like a muffled mew. "What was that?"

"I didn't hear anything."

Dalton picked up his lantern and held it high. He walked a few feet up the trail and strained to listen again. There was nothing. "I thought I heard . . ." He fell silent. "There, I heard it again."

"I heard it, too," Yuri confirmed. "Illiyana! Britta!"

Dalton shouted their names, as well. The sound was coming from higher up the trail. "Britta!"

"Help me!" a voice cried back. It was barely audible, but it was clearly one of the girls.

Yuri and Dalton bounded up the trail, hardly paying attention to their footing. Several times they slipped and fell in the mud, but somehow both managed to avoid serious injury.

"Illiyana, it's Yuri! Where are you?"

"I'm here," she answered in a weak voice.

The men stopped and listened. "Keep talking to me, Illiyana," Yuri insisted. "I'm coming for you, but I can't see you. Can you see my light?" He held his lantern high and Dalton did likewise.

"I can see some light," she answered. The excitement in her voice was clear.

"Is Britta with you?" Dalton questioned as he and Yuri continued toward the sound of the child's voice.

"No."

His heart sank. "Where is she, Illiyana?"

"She fell off the mountain."

Dalton stopped short. "Where, Illiyana?"

The child's voice was louder now. "I see your light. I see it!"

Just then Yuri spotted her. "There she is!" He rushed up the trail and knelt down before his sister. He handed Dalton the lantern as he drew near. Picking Illiyana up, Yuri cradled her in his arms. "Where is Britta? Can you show us the way?"

"I don't know. We were up there," Illiyana replied. "I'm so tired, Yuri."

"She's freezing," he told Dalton. "She's soaked to the bone. Get the blanket from my back."

Dalton quickly did as he instructed. He put both lanterns on the ground, but all the while he worked to coax more information from the girl. "Illiyana, we have to find my sister. We need your help."

"When she fell, I told her I'd get help. She hurt her leg."

"How long ago was that, sweetheart?" Dalton asked, wrapping the blanket around her.

"Not long."

Yuri secured the wool tight. "We should start a fire."

"We need to let my father and Josh know we've found her." Dalton reached over his shoulder and grabbed his rifle from its scabbard. He took a few steps away and fired twice into the night air.

To his surprise, two more shots sounded. They weren't that far away. Perhaps his father and Josh had found nothing and had turned back to join Yuri and Dalton on their search.

"I'll get some wood. Sounds like they'll be joining us shortly. If we have a big enough blaze going, we can get Illiyana warmed up and then maybe she can help us find Britta."

Dalton didn't like waiting to search for his sister, but he knew that if they weren't careful, hypothermia would set in and Illiyana would die. Of course, Britta would be just as cold and wet, he told himself.

Searching under old fallen logs, Dalton found some fairly dry kindling. He tucked this inside his coat, then walked a little deeper into the woods to see what other fuel he might find. He was just emerging with an armload when he heard Yuri pleading with his sister.

"Wake up, Illiyana. Don't go to sleep. It's too cold to sleep here." He was rocking her and patting her face to get her attention.

"I'll have the fire started in just a minute," Dalton said, dropping the wood on the soggy ground. He knelt, feeling the damp cold permeate the knees of his trousers. With trained skill, he managed to coax the fire to life.

Yuri squatted down with his sister as the logs caught and blazed up. "See, Illiyana, we will get you warm now."

"Dalton! Yuri!" Dalton heard from somewhere down the trail.

Getting to his feet, he called, "We're up here, Father. Keep coming up the trail."

"Did you find them?"

"We have Illiyana, but she says Britta fell over the side. We aren't sure where." His father said nothing more, and Dalton cast a quick glance down at Yuri and purposefully remained silent about Britta injuring her leg. "I'll go meet them. We'll bring more wood."

He headed down the trail, lantern in hand. It wasn't long before he saw the ominous shadows of lamplight glowing and ripping through the branches of dark spruce. "I see your light."

"And we see yours."

In just a few more minutes, Kjell and Josh appeared on the trail just ahead of Dalton. His father was limping rather obviously.

"What happened?" Dalton asked, pointing to his father's right leg.

"I caught my foot in an old root," he replied in disgust. "I twisted my knee. Where's Illiyana?"

"She's with Yuri. She's soaked and freezing. We got a fire going, but we need more wood. She doesn't know where Britta is, except that she is somewhere up the trail farther."

Father nodded. The men quickly grabbed what free branches they could find. Some were wetter than others, but with careful choices, they worked to uncover some pieces that were fairly dry.

They came back to the fire to find Illiyana barely awake in Yuri's arms. "I don't think she's getting any warmer," Yuri told them. "She's still shivering horribly."

"You should get her out of the wet clothes and rewrap her in a dry blanket," Father declared.

"I'm going on up to look for Britta," Dalton told his father.

"Why don't we get Illiyana changed, and then Josh can take her back down to the house." Kjell looked to his friend. "Would you do that?"

"Of course." Joshua looked to Yuri. "If that's okay with you. If you'd rather take her, I can stay and help."

"No, I want to help find Britta," Yuri said, meeting Dalton's gaze. "She's like a sister to me, as well."

With the decision made, the men quickly went to work. Kjell built up the fire while Yuri got Illiyana changed. Yuri took off his coat and then pulled the shirt over his head. "I'll dress her in this."

Once she was cared for, Josh lifted her into his arms. "I'll get her back as quickly as I can, but it won't be easy without light. I doubt I can balance the lantern and her at the same time."

Dalton could see that his father wasn't doing at all well. He was in pain and needed to get out of the damp cold. Reaching out, Dalton touched Kjell's arm. "You go with him. I'll find Britta. I promise you that. You know the way better than anyone."

"I can't just leave," his father protested. "She's my child."

"I know," Dalton replied, "and my sister. Look, Yuri and I are better able to scale down the side if need be. Go ahead with Josh and see Illiyana safe." He made no reference to his father's physical condition. He didn't need to.

Father considered the situation for a moment and finally nodded. "I'll be back as quick as I can."

"Hopefully we'll make it back down before you even start back."

Dalton knew it had been a hard decision to accept. His father wasn't as strong as he used to be. Working with him on the house had proven that. Dalton didn't like to think of Father aging. The man had done heavy labor all of his life, however, and it had taken its toll. He didn't want him risking his life to rescue Britta. If something serious happened to harm his father, they would all be much the worse for it.

When Illiyana was safely on her way back to the house, Dalton and Yuri quickly made their way up the trail. They called out periodically for Britta, but heard no response. Yuri knew time was of the essence. They had to find her soon. If she was injured, she might well be bleeding. Dalton appeared further frustrated when the path split in two different directions.

"Which way did they go?"

Yuri searched the ground with his friend. "There are signs of footprints going both directions. Maybe they got confused here and tried both ways."

"We've got no choice. You go to the left and I'll go right. It can't be that far," Dalton declared.

"All right." Yuri did as Dalton had instructed. He knew this was agonizing to his friend. Only moments ago, when Illiyana had been missing, Yuri felt as though he might go out of his mind. He had such a helpless feeling knowing that the girls were out there somewhere, in danger.

"Britta!" Yuri called out as he moved along the trail. Holding the lantern up, he could see where the path came closer to the edge of a sheer drop. He looked for signs of a disturbance, but saw nothing.

Moving ahead, he continued to scan the sides. "Britta, it's Yuri! Are you here?"

"Yuri?"

The voice was muffled. He stopped. "Britta, where are you?"

"I fell, Yuri. I'm down here."

He looked along the edge of the path and moved closer to the side of the mountain. "Keep talking to me, Britta. I can follow your voice."

"I hurt my leg," she told him. "I think it's broken."

Yuri pinpointed the sound and followed it. He held the lantern toward the side and could see where the ground had been freshly torn away. Getting on his stomach, he edged closer, not knowing how stable the earth might be.

"Britta, can you see my light?" He held the lantern over the side and peered down. There, about eight feet below him on a small ledge of rock and mud, Britta was huddled in pain.

"I see you. Don't move," Yuri commanded. He reached for his rope. "I'm going to make a loop in this rope, Britta. When I throw it down to you, you need to pull it over your head and under your arms. Do you hear me?"

"I hear you, Yuri."

He tied one end of the rope off around the base of a spruce on the opposite side of the path. That way if the ground gave way as he worked to pull Britta up, they would still be secured to something stable.

"Here it comes now, Britta." He positioned the lantern so he could see. It was difficult, but he managed to drop the rope straight down to the child. "Now put it around you. While you do that, I'm going to fire my rifle off to let Dalton know I found you."

Britta maneuvered the rope over her head and under her arms. Yuri quickly took up the rifle and fired two shots. No doubt, Dalton would be there in no time at all.

"I'm ready," Britta called, her voice weak and trembling.

"Now, I know one of your legs is hurt, but you need to stand. When I pull on the rope, you need to try to walk up the side of the mountain. Otherwise, you'll get all cut up as I pull you to the top. Do you understand?"

She struggled to her feet. "I'll try, but it really hurts."

"I know, sweetheart. Look, the pain will only last for a few minutes. As I pull, you can even kind of bounce yourself up on your good leg. Now, get ready. Here we go."

He pulled against the rope and found it surprisingly easy to raise her. She couldn't have weighed more than fifty pounds. He heard her cry out, but she didn't ask him to stop, and Yuri knew she was nearly to the top.

When he saw her head appear, he held the rope fast and moved his hand down. "Grab hold of me."

She did as he told her, and Yuri pulled her the rest of the way up. Rolling to the side on the water-soaked ground, he pulled Britta atop him. "There. You're safe."

Britta wrapped her arms around his neck and began to cry. "I love you, Yuri. You saved me."

"Yuri! Britta!" Dalton called.

"We're here," Yuri said, struggling to sit up with Britta in his arms. He got to his feet just as Dalton came into the light.

"Britta!" He rushed to take her in his arms.

"Yuri saved me," she told him. "He pulled me up the mountain."

Dalton threw Yuri a look of gratitude. "I know. He's a pretty special guy, isn't he?"

Britta nodded and closed her eyes. "I'm going to marry him someday."

———

"It's not broken," Zee said after examining Britta's leg. "It's just a bad twist in the ankle. You are very lucky, Miss Britta. You, too, Kjell. That knee is swollen, but I think if you stay off of it, you'll heal quickly."

"I don't guess I have much of a choice." He glanced up to see Lydia watching him. "Do I?"

"You don't. You'll be a very good patient," she replied, "even if I have to tie you down."

"Yuri saved me," Britta said, ignoring her mother's comment. She smiled at her hero. "He was so brave."

"Indeed, he was," Lydia replied. "Thank you so much for what you did."

"I was glad to help." He looked over to where his mother and father sat with Illiyana. "It certainly made for an exciting evening."

"Having the girls back safe and sound is the best news possible," Darya declared.

"Well, if everyone is hungry," Zee announced, "I believe we have dinner ready."

"I'm starving," Britta said. "Next time I go on a hike, I'm taking food with me."

"There will be no next time, young lady," her father asserted. "Do you understand? You are never again to go off by yourself like that."

Britta bowed her head and nodded. "I understand. We just didn't want Illiyana to go away."

Darya hugged Illiyana close. "You both could have died. I'm sorry that we must leave, but you will always be good friends. Distance won't change that, unless you let it."

Chapter 29

April 1890

While his mother and wife put the finishing touches on the surprise birthday party for Joshua, Dalton went to town to work out his business arrangement with Yuri and his father. Mr. Belikov was listening to his son with such tenderness and compassion that Dalton found himself humbled. Had the man been more loving and less judgmental when Yuri was younger, perhaps things wouldn't have gotten this bad for Yuri.

"Sometimes, I feel I can only face life from behind the shelter of a bottle," Yuri told his dad sadly.

"Liquor can be a great temptation, even for me," his father admitted.

"But it's not so much a temptation," Yuri said, shaking his head, "as a promise of relief. Even if just for a few hours."

"Relief?" Dalton questioned.

Yuri nodded. "Yes. From the pain of remembering how useless I am, how I've failed at so much in life, how I have no direction or purpose. That is why I drink—to forget. Then when I have had enough liquor, I suddenly feel capable of making great decisions. Then I find myself seduced by the cards."

"So this gambling debt is why you didn't want Dalton to buy half of the business?" Yuri's father asked.

Dalton's friend nodded. "I knew if he did, he would find out what I planned to do once you had gone. I hated myself for that. It was also the reason I told you I no longer wanted him to work with us. I knew he would need another place of employment. I didn't realize then that he had as much money as he does." Yuri laughed. "He'll soon own all of Sitka, if we're not careful."

"I have no desire to own all of it," Dalton assured him. "Just my little piece."

Mr. Belikov looked to Dalton. "You are sure you want to buy the business? I would understand if you said no. You've already made me a substantial loan for my trip."

"Yes. I'm certain. I was going to build my own shop anyway, so this gives me a head start. Besides, I have great memories here." He smiled and gazed around the workroom. "I feel as though I became a man in this very place."

"We did great work here," Mr. Belikov said, looking first to Dalton and then to his son. "I have wonderful memories that I will take with me to Russia. I will miss you both."

"It won't be the same without you," Dalton told him.

"What will you do?" Mr. Belikov asked. "You will have no one to work with you."

"I plan to hire some of the Tlingit boys who were trained at the school. With a little bit of hard work and good advertising, I believe I can have one of the finest boat building businesses in all of Alaska."

Dalton looked to Yuri. "I've told Yuri he can stay on, as well, but I think his heart is elsewhere."

"And where would that be?" Mr. Belikov asked his son.

"I wish I could tell you. I know I'm not half the builder Dalton is. He suggested I could work with his father for a time, and I might give it a shot. Otherwise, I don't know—maybe fishing." He grinned. "I could buy one of Dalton's boats."

Dalton appreciated that Yuri was trying hard to keep things light, but Mr. Belikov was obviously concerned about his son. His grim expression gave Dalton little doubt that he feared Yuri might well fall back into the same bad company that had brought him to this place.

"No matter what Yuri chooses, I know we shall remain close friends." Dalton hoped Mr. Belikov would understand his meaning. Yuri might be given to the temptations of liquor and gambling, but Dalton hoped he could influence his friend otherwise.

Mr. Belikov sighed. "If you are agreed to this arrangement, Dalton, I cannot do anything but thank you. It comforts me to know that Yuri will be out of trouble and that the business will remain in friendly hands."

"I am happy, too," Yuri said, turning to Dalton. "I hope you know how much this means to me."

Dalton put his hand on Yuri's shoulder. "I think I do. I know what it is to feel displaced and not know where you belong. I hope you will find your calling soon, but you will always have my friendship, no matter your path."

Yuri grew quite serious. "Will you do me one more favor?"

Dalton nodded. "What is it?"

"Will you go with me to settle my account?" Yuri frowned. "I'm afraid I might . . . well, that is . . . I might be induced to stay."

"Of course," Dalton replied. "I will happily go with you and bear this burden."

———

"We spent our first night here yesterday," Phoebe announced to her mother as she started giving her a tour of the new house. She couldn't contain her excitement. "It was so wonderful. I cannot tell you how quiet it is compared to being in town. Dalton and his father wrapped the porch around the side of the cabin and to the back so that we would be able to spend a great deal of time outside—even if it rains. Wasn't that clever?"

"Phoebe, the house is so beautiful," her mother declared. "I can scarcely believe how big it is."

"I know." Phoebe laughed. "When they were building it, I just couldn't see it. I thought, 'Oh, surely this is too small for all of us. We're going to need more space.' But now it seems massive— especially when I think of cleaning it. Even Theodore and Grady should have enough room to themselves."

Phoebe's mother took hold of her hand. "There is something I need to tell you."

"Is something wrong?"

"I hope you won't think so," Mother replied. "Come sit with me and let me explain."

Apprehension gnawed at Phoebe's stomach. What was this all about? She went with her mother to the front room, where several chairs and a sofa made by Dalton's father welcomed them. Phoebe took a seat beside her mother and reached out for her hand. "Now tell me."

"I've given a great deal of consideration to this matter, and after much prayer, I have made up my mind to return to Vermont."

"No!" Phoebe said, shaking her head. "Don't go. Why would you leave now? We have the house and plenty of money."

Mother patted her hand. "Sweetheart, the house is wonderful, but I have other considerations. Theodore is nearly ready for a higher education. Grady will soon follow. His intelligence is even greater than his brother's. His teacher has informed me that he has very nearly learned as much as she can teach him."

"I had no idea."

Mother continued. "I didn't, either. It seems that Grady has always been a high achiever, but after losing Father, well, he thoroughly applied himself to learning—seeking comfort and solace in his education. His teacher thinks that he will be ready for the university in another year at most."

"That does change things. Obviously, there is no chance of an advanced education here," Phoebe agreed. "But what will I do without you?" She looked at her mother and shook her head. "I hadn't even considered that you might leave. Not after . . . after Father passed on."

"I know. I'm sorry that I've said nothing to you on this matter. I didn't want to grieve you or to say something until I was certain. I've written to my sister. Her husband is even now securing us a home. The boys and I will leave shortly after the governor returns from his inspection of the islands. We will head south on the *City of Topeka* and make our way east from San Francisco."

"Well, I am certain we can help make your journey less arduous," Phoebe told her mother. "Dalton can help you to arrange things. Perhaps he and I can even accompany you south. He has need of more supplies for the business."

"It would be wonderful to have your company, even that much longer," her mother said. "And I must admit, I had hopes that Dalton could help us . . . financially." She lowered her head. "Your father left very little of value. Governor Knapp has kindly given me a stipend, but it has barely been enough to live on."

"Why did you say nothing?" Phoebe asked. "We would have happily helped. Oh, Mother, please tell me you did not go hungry."

"Of course not. And besides, I had the candles to sell. You

will continue to make them, won't you? It will be something that joins us together."

Phoebe nodded. "It hasn't been easy to keep up with supplies, but Dalton recently learned of a way to get beeswax shipped here. I was going to surprise you with the news, but since you are returning to Vermont, it won't be necessary."

"I will be happy to see that you have a ready supply of other ingredients," her mother countered. "You have only to write and let me know what you need. Of course, with your connection to Zee, you have brought us many wonderful new scents from the local flowers and herbs. I shall miss those."

"I will send you some. We will dry them and ship them to you," Phoebe promised.

"I love that you will continue the tradition. I hope you will teach the making of candles to your daughter, as well."

"Of course," Phoebe said, feeling the words choke in her throat.

She got up and walked to the fireplace. "I can't believe you are going away. It's just not at all what I had expected this day. I hoped to talk of your moving in this next week. I thought we would be planning curtains and such." Tears came to her eyes, and she quickly wiped them away.

"I know you're right in going," Phoebe said, trying hard to remain strong. "Theodore and Grady will need their education. They will be happier in Vermont, I think. Their choices are limited here. In the East, they will be able to get a good education and find gainful employment. If Grady is as smart as the teacher believes . . . well, who knows what he might accomplish."

Phoebe looked at her mother as if seeing her for the first time. She looked so tired. Alaska had been a difficult place for her, aging her beyond her years. "You will be happier there, as well."

Phoebe smiled, despite the heaviness in her heart. "And that is most important to me."

"Life there won't be so . . . isolated," her mother replied. "Sometimes I find myself lonely here, and not even so much for other people. It's hard to explain, but I suppose it has to do with having lived most of my life in a place where the culture and community offered so much more. Here, I can't even get used to the weather."

"When we first came here, I didn't think I could ever love anything about Sitka," Phoebe admitted. "I hated the way it smelled, and the people seemed so rough and frightening at times."

"But now, you've had a change of heart," her mother said with a smile.

"So much has changed. I feel as if . . . well . . . I came to some sort of adult understanding here. I learned so much about life—about other people." Phoebe came back to sit beside her mother on the sofa. "I am truly happy. I hope you know that."

"I think you shall always be very happy here, daughter. Dalton is such a good man. I had my concerns—your courtship seemed like such a whirlwind, and I feared there was no solid basis for a marriage. I'm glad to be proven wrong."

Phoebe thought of her husband. "When my friends and I used to talk about the man we wanted to marry, I would often say that I wanted an adventurous man who was handsome and who would love me madly." She smoothed down her sleeves and shrugged. "And that is exactly what I got."

"I expect to have you visit—at least once every other year. Especially when my grandchildren begin to arrive."

The thought of having children without her mother close by only added to Phoebe's sorrow, but she said nothing. Instead, she nodded. "You can count on it, Mother. You can count on it. But you must also visit us here, if the trip is not too hard on you."

Her mother laughed. "I'm not so old as that. Once I have Theodore and Grady settled down, who knows? I might very well want to return to Sitka."

"I hope so. I hope you will at least come for visits. I will miss you so much." She embraced her mother and held her tight.

"We will always be close, child. No matter the miles that separate us. We will always be close."

———

Phoebe lost herself in the haunting strains of the Adagio from Alessandro Marcello's Concerto in D Minor. The piece was designed to feature the oboe, but since Sitka's little orchestra didn't have one, Lydia had managed to adapt it for the flute. Against the delicate harmony of the strings, Phoebe's flute sounded almost magical.

The music brought tears to her eyes as she thought of her mother and brothers going away. It would be hard to see them go. When she'd told Dalton of the news, his gentleness had caused her to fall apart. She'd cried in his arms, and he hadn't even tried to hush her. He seemed to understand that she needed to let out her tears—to mourn the loss even though it had not yet come.

Her mother had once said that finding that special person with whom to share your life—that soul mate who would understand your heart's joys as well as sorrows—was the finest blessing one could hope for. Phoebe had found that in Dalton.

As the final notes faded, those who'd gathered for Joshua Broadstreet's surprise party clapped with great enthusiasm. The cheers left Phoebe little doubt that their audience was well pleased.

Slipping into the sewing room, Phoebe cleaned her flute and put it away with the gentleness of a mother for her babe. She found such fulfillment in her music and thanked God silently for having brought her to this place where she could continue to play and enjoy the talent He had given her.

"That was incredible, Phoebe," Dalton said, joining her. He drew her into his arms and whirled her around. "I've never heard anything quite like it. Mother said it was special, and though I heard you practicing the piece, I was still unprepared."

She smiled up at him. "I found that I was unprepared for most everything about Alaska . . . including you. I thought I was coming to a vast wilderness where I would be set adrift in loneliness and longing. Instead, I have found more fulfillment than I could have imagined."

He kissed her gently. "I feel the same," he whispered against her lips.

Phoebe wrapped her arms around his waist and held him tight. "I love you. You are such a part of me that I feel I have loved you forever."

He pulled back and smiled. "It's as if you look into my heart and speak the words you find there."

Reaching up, she gently touched his face and nodded. "Only because they are my own, as well." She placed her head against his chest. The rhythmic beat of Dalton's heart brought to mind the pulsating strains of the Adagio. Such sweetness.

———

"Come on, lazy bones," Dalton said, giving Phoebe's backside a swat. "You'll miss it."

Yawning, she sat up in bed. Her golden hair tumbled around her shoulders and down her back. By the time they'd returned home from Joshua's party, Phoebe had been too tired to do anything but take out her hairpins.

"Hurry, Phoebe," Dalton urged in a whisper.

She forced her feet to touch the floor and rose from the bed as if being led to her execution. Pulling on her robe and slippers, she padded after her husband to the French doors at the end of their bedroom. Dalton had already gone outside onto the small balcony. He held his finger to his lips and motioned her to follow.

Suppressing another yawn, Phoebe stepped into the chilled morning air. The sun had risen just enough to cast light down on the harbor. Below, a family of seals frolicked and played. Phoebe couldn't help but smile.

"I told you we would get some amazing sights from this balcony," he whispered.

"They're wonderful." She wanted to laugh aloud as one seal seemed to be playing tag with another. It reminded her of puppies at play.

Dalton wrapped his arms around her from behind and pulled her back against his chest. He didn't speak. He didn't have to. Phoebe stood there embraced in his warmth as the barely audible notes of morning's refrain drifted down over the valley as the island awoke to a new day. She had found much to love in Sitka. Here, she had come to realize the passion and heart of God for His people. Here, she had come to know the desire and tenderness of a husband for his wife. And here, the music within her heart took flight. It was all that she could have hoped for. It was home.